PAC
U P

Also available from Titan Books:

# PACIFIC RIM UPRISING: ASCENSION

### THE OFFICIAL MOVIE PREQUEL

# PACIFIC RIM™
## U P R I S I N G

FROM DIRECTOR
**STEVEN S. DEKNIGHT**

NOVELIZATION BY
**ALEX IRVINE**

**TITAN** BOOKS

Pacific Rim Uprising: The Official Movie Novelization
Print edition ISBN: 9781785657689
E-book edition ISBN: 9781785657696

Published by Titan Books
A division of Titan Publishing Group Ltd
144 Southwark Street, London SE1 0UP

First edition: March 2018
1 3 5 7 9 10 8 6 4 2

A CIP catalogue record for this title is available from the British Library.

Printed and bound in the United States.

# PACIFIC RIM
## UPRISING ™

april 2. 2018

65 000572662

# 1

## EDITORIAL: THANKS, PPDC, AND SO LONG

Look, the Breach has been closed for ten years. If the Kaiju were coming back, they would already have done it. You think they're not spoiling for a chance to get back at us after we dropped a nuke straight through the Breach into their... world? Dimension? Whatever. It's not going to happen. We've got a Pan Pacific Defense Corps that stands guard against a threat that doesn't exist. There are how many Shatterdomes? How many Jaegers? How many Rangers and support staff? How much does all that cost?

Shouldn't we be spending that money to rebuild everything that was destroyed during the war? When I fly into Los Angeles now, all I can see from Long Beach all the way up to Santa Monica is ruins. Ten years later! Europe was rebuilt sooner than that after World War II! Why, you ask?

Because everybody knew the war was over. They put their money into rebuilding. They didn't waste it on more armies, more bases. No. They got on with their lives.

continued...

We're not doing that. We're still staring out at the Pacific Ocean thinking it's full of monsters, and it's not.

It's time to move on. It's time to demobilize the Pan Pacific Defense Corps. Mothball the Jaegers, shutter the Shatterdomes, and get on with the twenty-first century.

The Pan Pacific Defense Corps scrapyard in Santa Monica, California spread over hundreds of acres that had once been prime beachfront. During the course of the Kaiju War, much of Santa Monica had been destroyed, and fallen Jaegers from up and down the West Coast now lay behind barbed wire. Around the scrapyard, what had once been one of the Los Angeles area's most beautiful cities was now a ruin. Those who could get out were long since gone, and only the desperate remained.

Jake Pentecost wasn't exactly desperate, but he was in a bit of a bind. He'd gotten on the wrong side of one of the local crime bosses, by the name of Sonny, and now he had to buy his way out of the problem by finding Sonny some high-quality salvage that Sonny could move on the local black market. Ordinarily Jake would have steered clear of burgling a PPDC facility—the penalties were pretty stiff— but he knew the area around this Jaeger graveyard well enough to figure he could skip out before any trouble arose.

Even so, it was risky, and Jake wouldn't have been here if Sonny hadn't made it clear that the alternative involved lots of pain and maybe death. Well, definitely death.

He led Sonny and Sonny's goons up to a part of the electrified fence surrounding the yard and pointed to the spot they should cut through. The goons were quick about it—this clearly wasn't the first time they'd cut a fence— and a minute later Jake stepped through a nice big hole right next to a NO TRESPASSING sign that also bore the logo of the PPDC. Seeing it gave Jake a little spike of regret. He'd been a Jaeger pilot once.

But that was the past. He couldn't do anything about it, just like he couldn't do anything about all the other bullshit that came along with being the son of Stacker Pentecost. When your father died saving the world, there was no way to live up to that. Jake had long since quit trying. He'd turned himself into a pretty good… well, some people would call him a thief. He thought of himself as more of a salvage expert.

It was a good life if it didn't get you killed. In this world you had to hustle. The coastal cities, most of them, were still relief zones, filled with people just trying to get by—rubbing up against Kaiju-worshipping cults that went around bemoaning the closure of the Breach like it was the Crucifixion. Then you had your homegrown gangsters doing what gangsters always did—only now they had another sideline in cobbling together homegrown junk Jaegers from salvaged parts. Anyone with money had moved inland, getting away from the chaos and the possibility that another Breach would open up and the Kaiju War would start all over again. But their fear was his opportunity, because they left behind empty mansions like the one Jake squatted in up in Malibu. He also had a little bit of experience of Jaegers, which meant he had a better nose for where to find Jaeger tech than the average person. That put him in a pretty good spot. Usually. He had gotten a reputation for delivering the goods, and then—okay, being honest here—he'd let it go to his head and he'd started bending the rules a little. Ignoring well-established informal boundaries between different gang lords. Getting your hands on good bits of Jaeger tech was usually worth the risk, since a good score could set you up for a year… but every once in a while it blew up in your face, which was why Jake was in Santa Monica instead of back in Malibu where he belonged.

Once they were inside the yard, Jake got out a beat-up old plasma tracker. It detected the energy signatures of plasma components even through a Jaeger's heavy shielding. Indispensable equipment for the ambitious salvage expert. As he was turning it on, Sonny started to walk ahead. Jake caught him and pulled him back behind the mangled remains of a Mark II Jaeger. When he was a little kid, he'd known them all by sight and talked about them the way kids of a previous generation had known all the details about their favorite Pokémon or baseball players. Just as Jake yanked Sonny back, a searchlight swept over the spot where he'd just been. The PPDC patrolled the yard, but their timing never varied. Jake had done his research.

Sonny glared at him, but he could hardly be mad that Jake had just saved the operation and kept them all out of jail. Jake led them around the first scrapped Jaeger, keeping an eye on the plasma tracker. It emitted a soft ping as they neared another Jaeger. This one wasn't quite as messed up as the first, but it was missing one arm and its head was shattered. Jake recognized it, of course: Romeo Blue, the only tripedal Jaeger ever put into service. Three Kaiju kills, all in partnership with Gipsy Danger. Destroyed by Insidia in Panama City, 2020, with the loss of both pilots. Before that, Jake remembered seeing the parade after Romeo Blue had killed the Kaiju Takubus back in the early years after the opening of the Breach. It was huge, lumbering, slow, but seemingly invincible.

Seemingly. To a little kid whose father was already a hero after Tokyo. But now Jake was all grown up.

"This one," he said.

Sonny and his men followed Jake through a hatch and into the Jaeger's immense interior. Other than Jake, none of them had ever been inside a Jaeger before, and they eyed the surroundings with awed expressions.

"You sure it's here?" Sonny asked.

Jake found the access door he was looking for. On the other side of it would be Romeo Blue's plasma chamber, where the Jaeger's power core and associated hardware would have been collected and shielded. The door was jammed shut, but the control panel next to it would have an override. Jake got his fingers into the seam at the edge of the panel and wrenched it open.

"Power cores are stripped before Jaegers get decommissioned," he said as he felt around inside the panel. "But sometimes they miss the tertiary plasma capacitors. Hell of a score on the black market, if this one's still holding a charge."

"You'd better hope so," Sonny said.

Something about his tone of voice made Jake look back over his shoulder. Sonny was holding a gun. "Okay," Jake said. "Let's not get all excited."

"Just playing the odds," Sonny said. "You cheated Barada in Juarez, skipped out on Azimi in Hong Kong—"

"They had it coming," Jake said. Who wouldn't take the chance to cheat Tony Azimi? That guy was a scumbag.

"And stole from me in my own backyard," Sonny added.

That was a little harder to paper over. Jake had in fact pulled a job in Sonny's territory without telling Sonny about it or cutting him in. From Sonny's perspective, that was a problem. From Jake's perspective, it had been a chance to make a quick score and maybe establish his bona fides as someone who knew where to find the good stuff in the ruins of Southern California. Sonny must have at least partially bought into that, because he was giving Jake a chance to make good by displaying those bona fides. "And now I'm stealing for you," Jake said. "Circle of life. We good?"

"You deliver, and yeah, we're good." Sonny's expression didn't change. Jake tried to gauge whether or not he was telling the truth. It didn't really matter at the moment.

His fingers found the emergency release lever behind the control panel. Jake grinned and pulled the release. A heavy thunk sounded from the door as its bolts disengaged. It opened with a low grinding noise. The Jaeger wasn't powered anymore, but the backup battery systems on the old Mark I models held their power for a long time.

Jake stood and noticed that Sonny hadn't put the gun away. Not a good sign. But he put his best face on it, keeping up his grin and gesturing through the open door. "Let's get rich," he said.

He went into the chamber first. These old Jaegers had big plasma chambers because PPDC techs hadn't been able to optimize the plasma density before they had to get the Jaegers into service. The space was the size of several rooms in his mansion. Cables and conduits ran along the walls, converging on a central spot where the plasma capacitor was located.

Or should have been.

Jake stopped in the middle of the room, unable to believe the bad luck. The capacitor shunt cables were still sparking, which meant that someone had gotten there within the last few minutes. Any longer and the residual energy would have all bled out already. "No, no, it says it's here," Jake said. He glanced down at his tracker, which still said the capacitor was right there in front of him.

He turned toward Sonny. "It should be right here—"

Sonny smashed him across the face with the butt of his gun. Jake went down, landing on hands and knees. Blood dripped off his chin from a cut high on his cheek.

"Somebody please kill this guy for me," Sonny said. His goons drew guns and leveled them at Jake.

"Wait, wait!" Jake gave the tracker a smack. The screen flickered and went dark… then came back on. Now it showed the capacitor on the move.

But not too far away.

"Someone else is in here!" he said, jumping up.

"Someone what?" Sonny seemed to have forgotten about killing him for the moment.

Jake scrambled over cable housings and big emplacements of dead machinery, aiming for an exit door halfway up the far wall. "They have the capacitor!" he said. "Come on! The signal's close!"

Sonny and the goons came after him. "Jake!" Sonny shouted. "Jake, you sonofa—"

His voice was cut off as Jake pulled the release lever on the door and it slammed shut. Now all Jake had to do was keep track of the capacitor signal and get out of the Jaeger before Sonny's goons caught up with him. He ran through the maze of maintenance corridors inside Romeo Blue's torso, ducking into a tunnel lined with heavy power cables. Echoing through the Jaeger's interior, he could hear Sonny shouting. He wasn't sure he'd be able to beat them to one of the exits... but then again, maybe he didn't have to. A plan started to form in his head. Like most of his best plans, it was half-assed and risky.

The cable tunnel split and as Jake shoved some of the cables aside to make the turn, he came face to face with one of Sonny's goons. The goon was pretty fast, getting his gun up... but Jake was that much faster, laying the guy out with a single punch before he could pull the trigger.

Before the goon had hit the ground, bullets tore into the cables around him. Sonny had found him. He scrambled into the side tunnel, which angled down steeply enough that it was easier to slide to the bottom. When his feet hit level ground again, he was in a shunt room. A dead end. He ran to the far end of it, turning to face the mouth of the tunnel as Sonny and his other men caught up.

"Nice try," Sonny said with a cruel grin. This time he apparently didn't want anyone else to shoot Jake, because he raised his own gun.

And that's when Jake's plan paid off. He kicked out and his booted foot hit a lever on the floor. It cranked over and a maintenance door sprang open under Sonny and the goons, dropping them into a hold under the floor. They landed hard and Jake kicked the lever again, slamming the door shut.

"Yeah," Jake said. "We're good." Sometimes it paid to know odd details about old Jaegers.

Then he took off running, following the signal on the tracker.

He came out of Romeo Blue's torso at the shoulder joint, maybe fifty feet off the ground. Below, a figure in a hoodie was sprinting across the open ground toward a motorcycle, a backpack in one hand.

The capacitor was in that backpack. Jake made a jump for a cable hanging down from a crane near Romeo Blue's head. He caught it and started to let himself down, hand over hand—then the mechanism let go and he was hanging on for dear life. It seized up again after he had dropped about twenty feet, and his momentum jerked him loose. He fell the rest of the way to the roof of a shipping container on the ground, landing flat on his back. The impact knocked the wind out of him, but he rolled off the container and started after the thief again. The motorcycle revved up and the hooded figure skidded off in a spray of gravel. Jake started in pursuit, hoping he could maybe get over the fence and out the access road before the motorcycle went around through the open gate... but he heard engines and froze.

PPDC security vehicles tore past, following the motorcycle. *Dammit*, Jake thought. That's what happens when you fire guns in a Jaeger scrapyard. If the thief was caught, he'd never get the capacitor. If the thief got away, though...

He looked down at the tracker. The signal was strong, and it was still moving.

# 2

## FOR IMMEDIATE RELEASE

### SHAO ANNOUNCES DRONE INITIATIVE
### SHANGHAI, 9 JUNE 2034

Shao Liwen, founder and CEO of Shao Industries, announced today that her company had secured funding from the Pan Pacific Defense Corps to build a fleet of Drone Jaegers based on prototypes created by Shao and demonstrated at a PPDC Council closed session earlier this year. The potential impact on worldwide PPDC budget expenditures is significant, since current deployment models require the upkeep of Shatterdomes in every region of the Pacific Rim. Each Shatterdome must be staffed with Rangers and enormous support crews of technicians and engineers.

Shao envisions a new PPDC, with fewer Shatterdomes and smaller crews. Drone Jaegers would be operated remotely from a single central PPDC facility, eliminating the operational expense of Ranger team stations at every Shatterdome. Further, Drones would not require the installation of expensive

continued...

Conn-Pods and Drift cradles, reducing the unit cost of each Jaeger by as much as fifteen percent. Another benefit is reduced risk to the lives of Rangers, who suffer a regrettable number of training accidents and Drift-related maladies even apart from the combat dangers risked when they face Kaiju or other threats.

If approved by the PPDC Council, the Drone fleet will be ready for initial deployments and field testing within the next calendar year.

By the time Jake got going after the capacitor thief, the signal was all the way across town, headed south. He followed, going all night until dawn found him in the southern part of Santa Monica, which was even more of a ruin than the area around the Jaeger graveyard.

Before the Kaiju War, he'd heard it was a nice place. But now it was a half-destroyed slum, full of people picking through the ruins to survive. The old pedestrian mall was now an open-air market, and farther south, the towering bones of the Kaiju Insurrector lay on the beach where it had fallen, after destroying much of the Santa Monica Pier. Scavengers and black-market entrepreneurs had stripped the body of everything from its blood to the parasites wriggling in the gaps under its armor plating. All of it was valuable, and most of it was lethal if the scavenger crews didn't take adequate precautions. You could get dissolved by Kaiju blood, infected by Kaiju germs, suffocated when the decaying tissue trapped you inside their corpses. They decayed incredibly fast once exposed to the foreign atmosphere of Earth. And that was if other scavengers didn't jump you before you could get your goods to market. Jake had steered clear of the trade in Kaiju parts, by and large. The sight of their monumental skeletons dotting the coasts filled him with sadness for what the Kaiju had done to the world, and behind it a more distant sadness about his father. Jake missed the world he'd been born into. He wanted it back.

Well, sometimes, anyway. Then there were the mornings when he got up and there was a sea breeze as the light of dawn crept along the tops of the bluffs falling toward the Pacific, and he'd just pulled off a score that was going to set him up for months... then this world didn't seem so bad. If he was smart and a little bit lucky, he'd have one of those days tomorrow, after he got the capacitor back and moved it. Already he was deciding he wouldn't sell it to Sonny. At this point it wouldn't stop the man from trying to kill him again, so Jake figured he might as well get something out of the capacitor.

As dawn broke, Jake followed the tracker through the decaying ruins of Santa Monica, passing buildings tagged with the symbols of various Kaiju cults. Kaiju worshippers clustered in ruins like this one, to be closer to the bones of their gods. He passed beggars, and people trying to sell worthless junk so they wouldn't be thought of as beggars. Ignoring them all, Jake followed the tracker's signal. The plasma capacitor was somewhere on the other side of the pier.

He had to climb the rubble of buildings destroyed years ago by Insurrector before he got a good look at where the thief had gone. There, on the other side of the pier, the PPDC had built a shipyard for support vessels and barges big enough to transport damaged or incomplete Jaegers. Now the whole thing was decommissioned and abandoned, had been for years. There were dry docks, hangars, huge old warehouses, all of them filled with squatters and lowlifes... including the thief who had his plasma capacitor.

That capacitor had already caused Jake a lot of trouble. So he and the thief would have to reach an understanding.

Actually, it would be better if he and the thief never met. If Jake was lucky, the thief was tired from the trip, and Jake could get into the shipyard, find the capacitor, and get back out without them ever knowing he was there.

He started the long scramble down the bones and rubble, aiming for a warehouse at the water edge of the shipyard. The tracker said the capacitor was somewhere inside.

\* \* \*

He worked his way along the edge of the warehouse until the tracker said he was as close as he was going to get. Then Jake pried open the closest window, wincing at the creaking sound. He swung through and dropped into a room that maybe used to be an office or a break room. Now it was clear someone was squatting there. A dirty mattress in the corner, surrounded by food wrappers and other personal trash, told him that much. The rest of the floor was covered with bits of machinery and tools.

Jake scanned the walls and knew he was in the right place. Whoever was living here had a serious obsession with Kaiju and Jaegers. The walls were plastered with magazine pages, newspapers, printouts from online stories—all of it a chronicle of the Kaiju War from the very beginning, the opening of the Breach. A blurry photo of one of the old Mark II Jaegers was taped up next to it. Someone had written "HOW BIG?!!!" in silver Sharpie. The rest of that part of the wall was a gallery of shots of Jaegers and Kaiju, with other notes.

Then the wall's focus shifted to Shao Liwen, a one-time computer prodigy who now ran a multi-billion-dollar company, Shao Industries. She had been a pioneer in several different aspects of Jaeger design, and the most recent headline suggested she still was. SHAO INDUSTRIES: THE FUTURE OF JAEGER TECH?

Jake wouldn't know. He'd been out of touch with that world for a long time.

Scanning down the wall, he stopped when he saw a faded *Time* magazine cover portrait of Raleigh Becket. The only words were Raleigh's name and his dates: 1998–2026.

Seeing that hit Jake hard. Raleigh had been one of his idols when he was a kid and Raleigh was the young loose cannon. And he had served under Jake's father. Then he had been the hero of the Battle of the Breach, surviving the mission that had taken Stacker Pentecost. Jake had a lot of complicated feelings about then that he'd spent the last ten years ignoring, so he wasn't going to start now. He moved on, toward the door at the far end of the room. So far he hadn't heard a sound other than his own quiet footsteps.

On the other side of the door was the main floor of the warehouse, acres of concrete with a roof maybe fifty feet high. And in the middle of that expanse stood a homemade Jaeger. Not full-sized, but its head was close to the ceiling. For a moment Jake just stood, amazed at the sight. Someone in the midst of all this chaos and misery had built a Jaeger out of spare parts. It was ugly, cobbled together from mismatched junk, including some scavenged armor plating Jake recognized as coming from a Mark II. But others could have started their service life in any machine from a water pump to a blast furnace. The overall effect was strange compared to a full-sized Jaeger. This one was maybe forty feet tall, with no room inside its head for a Conn-Pod, but the designer had given it two lights there, like eyeballs. Jake remembered an old engineer telling him people always wanted to humanize machines, even if it didn't make design sense, because somewhere deep down inside they thought of machines as their children. Jake wasn't sure how seriously to take that idea, but he'd been remembering it for a long time so it must have meant something to him. The Conn-Pod— or what passed for one—in this little Jaeger was set into its torso. Armored window frames gave pilots and passengers a view of the world beyond their wannabe Jaeger creation. One of its hands was a three-fingered pincer, and the other arm ended in a… Jake wasn't sure what it was in the gloom. Some kind of saw blade.

Whoever had put this thing together was a seriously gifted tinker… and now, it occurred to Jake, he was in the presence of a truly great score. The plasma capacitor he'd been after was plugged into a hatch in the mini-Jaeger's ankle, but Jake was already thinking bigger. People were always trying to build Jaegers to make some kind of personal statement, but not too many people could actually do it. This thief had pulled it off, and by the look of it there wasn't a big gang involved. They wouldn't have let something this valuable sit around without security. But whoever had built it, well, they must not have understood how the real world worked, because there it was. Who did Jake know with enough assets and ego to pay for a functioning personal Jaeger…?

He felt movement in the room. Behind him. Instinctively Jake skipped to the side and turned toward the person coming at him. He saw a length of pipe swinging toward his head and caught it. The assailant was wiry but small. Jake wrenched the pipe loose and in the same motion slammed the thief down to the floor. He'd learned a long time ago that when a fight started, you didn't let it end until you were sure the other guy wasn't going to get up again, so he raised the pipe—and then froze in mid-swing.

The figure on the floor was wearing dirty jeans and a hoodie. Impact with the floor had pushed the hoodie back far enough for Jake to see that the thief was a young teenager, and also a girl.

"What—*how old are you?*" he asked, still holding the pipe.

She sat up and pulled the hood the rest of the way off. Dark hair, a face that in other times would have led the homecoming parade—but those eyes, they were all grown up. Tough and smart and angry.

"Old enough to kick your ass," she said, and started to get up. Jake planted the pipe in her shoulder and nudged her back to the floor.

"Let's take a minute," he said. Cocking his head back toward the mini-Jaeger, he asked, "You build this thing yourself?"

"What do you think?" she snapped.

"I think I could sell your little toy for a whole lot of money."

"Scrapper's not a toy," the girl said. "And she's not for sale."

*Scrapper*, Jake thought. *Good name. Evocative of both attitude and origin.* You had to admire the resolve, but this was business. "The man holding the pipe says she is, so—"

Sirens sounded from outside the warehouse. The girl looked toward the main hangar doors at the far end of the room. "You led them here!?"

"What?" Jake was offended at being called out by a little runt squatting in the Santa Monica slum. "Nobody follows me! It must have been you."

He glanced over his shoulder in the direction of the sirens and the girl seized her chance. She kicked the pipe out of his hands and rolled to her feet, scrambling away across the floor toward the mini-Jaeger.

"Hey!" Jake started to go after her, but he was almost certain that would end up with him arrested in the back of a PPDC van. She kicked the capacitor hatch closed and scrambled up Scrapper's leg to the Conn-Pod in its torso. She powered it up as she got settled in a gyroscopic cradle.

"Yes! It works!"

*Wait*, Jake thought. *Is this the first time she's used this thing?*

The sirens were closer, and there were a lot of them. Jake took another look at Scrapper's Conn-Pod. There was room for two, and if it worked, it worked...

He headed for the mini-Jaeger and hauled himself up just as she had, diving in next to her just as she slammed Scrapper's chest plate shut. "Hey!" she shouted. "Get out!"

Jake turned around in the tight compartment. "Where's the other one?"

"The other what?" Busy powering up various

subroutines, the girl wasn't looking at him.

"The other cradle! Jaegers need *two* pilots!"

"Scrapper's small enough to run on a single neural load," she said proudly.

"Then move over and let me pilot!"

"Screw that!" Then she punched a final command, and Scrapper's power gauges surged to max readings. The little Jaeger charged forward, smashing through the warehouse wall. Sheet metal and broken glass scattered over the pavement in a parking lot full of PPDC security vehicles. Scrapper kicked them aside, sending PPDC personnel scattering.

"Woohoo!" she cheered, like she was having the time of her life. "Told you she's not a toy!"

"You're gonna get us killed. Now come on…" Jake started trying to uncouple her from the gyroscope so he could take her place in the cradle. She couldn't have known this, but he knew his way around a Conn-Pod.

"Stop it."

"I can get us out of here."

"I just got us out. Get off! Hey!"

They stopped struggling as a huge bogey appeared on Scrapper's HUD. It wasn't as fancy as a full-scale Jaeger's heads-up display, but it was a pretty slick piece of work for a teenager working with scraps. She skidded Scrapper to a halt, throwing Jake to the floor.

"Oh my God," she said, as they got a visual. Straight in front of them was a huge Mark VI Jaeger, one of the newest in the fleet. Steely gray, with black accents and a blue tinge to its exterior running lights, it looked every bit the part of the law-enforcement Jaeger—which it was. Jake recognized it. So did she. "That's November Ajax!"

A moment before, Jake had been trying to get her away from the controls, but now there wasn't time. November Ajax was the PPDC's designated patrol Jaeger for the whole of the devastated area from Santa Monica down through Long Beach. Occasionally it was called into service to handle social unrest, but the PPDC typically didn't send November Ajax out unless there had been an attack on a PPDC installation… or a theft of PPDC property. This meant the PPDC had tracked the theft of the plasma capacitor just as Jake had, and decided it warranted a full response. If they were caught, there would be serious consequences. They'd use them as examples to other would-be thieves, and put them away for a long time.

"You're gonna get us nicked!" Jake said, his voice tight. "Keep moving!"

*"Pilots of unregistered Jaeger."* The voice boomed from November Ajax's external speakers, shaking the two of them in Scrapper's small Conn-Pod. *"This is the Pan Pacific Defense Corps. Power down and exit your Conn-Pod."*

The girl raised her hands.

"That's it?" Jake was disappointed. "You give up way too easy, kid."

"That's what they think," the girl said.

She clenched her fists and smoke canisters shot out of sockets in Scrapper's arms. Clouds billowed around November Ajax's legs, hiding Scrapper—who shot between the larger Jaeger's legs and barreled down the street.

Jake got a grip on one of the cables connecting the Conn-Pod capsule to the counterweights inside Scrapper's torso. They were there to deaden momentum shifts and prevent the pilot from getting knocked around when Scrapper made sudden movements. A primitive solution, but a workable one—as long as you were in the gyro cradle. Jake wasn't, so just had to take his lumps and hang on for dear life.

"Hang on!" she yelled as November Ajax turned and caught up to them with one long stride.

"I am hanging on!"

"Hang tighter!" She was working her command array, and she punched a final command.

The next thing Jake knew, he was upside down. Then right side up again, then rolling over and over and bouncing hard off the inside wall of the Conn-Pod.

Scrapper had apparently curled into a ball and was rolling in tight figure eights around November Ajax's feet. The girl stayed upright and level the whole time—Jake had to hand it to her, she'd done the cradle design just right—but Jake slammed around until he got himself jammed into one of the counterweight alcoves. It wasn't a dignified solution, but it would keep him from getting knocked out or breaking an arm while they escaped November Ajax.

If they escaped November Ajax.

November Ajax swiped down at Scrapper, but the girl had seen it coming. She ducked her body to one side and Scrapper careened that way, crashing off palm trees and over burned-out cars. She rolled Scrapper fast up a high pile of rubble and it came crashing down through the wall of a partially collapsed building.

For a moment everything was silent except the sound of debris shifting around them. Jake started to get himself back together now that he knew which way was up again.

"*See?*" the girl said triumphantly. "I just out-piloted November Ajax."

Jake shook his head. "You didn't."

"Did," she insisted.

With a huge rumble, November Ajax tore away one wall of the building Scrapper was hiding in.

"Didn't," Jake said.

The girl froze. He could see she wasn't sure what to do next. "Okay. What do you got? And I'm *not* getting out."

This was a point where it paid to have plans go wrong

all the time, Jake thought. It meant you were always ready to come up with a new one on the fly. He glanced around the Conn-Pod, figuring there must be something in there he could use. To do what, he didn't know—but Jake was an optimist, at least when it came to his ability to get out of tight situations. He'd find something.

There.

He pointed at a pair of ion cells set into the Conn-Pod's wall. "One of these ion cells redundant?"

The girl frowned. "No."

Jake figured Scrapper could run for a little while without it. Ion cells usually weren't mission-critical, since they were normally wired to different yields than the plasma capacitors that powered the mainframe and systems. They handled things like reserve power, backup systems.

In other words, things you didn't really worry about when November Ajax was chasing you down.

He primed the subroutine that would eject one of the ion cells. The eject chute was on the outer hull. Cells were typically only ejected when their power reserves were exhausted. There was a reason for that, as November Ajax's pilots were about to find out.

"Is now," he said. "Get us close to Ajax's head. Go!"

She was steamed, but she did it. The girl gunned Scrapper forward and climbed straight up November Ajax's arm, which was maybe three times as long as Scrapper was tall. The minute they got level with the Jaeger's head, Jake hit the eject button. "Go! Go!" he shouted.

Scrapper leaped away from November Ajax. Jake was not looking forward to the two-hundred-foot drop, but the girl piloting Scrapper was ahead of him. She aimed for the roof of a building across the street. It looked like it might once have been a bank.

Behind them, the ion cell clanged off November Ajax's

head and ruptured, releasing a blast of ionized energy that crackled around the Jaeger's head and upper torso like a localized lightning storm. November Ajax staggered as the surge disrupted its systems.

They landed on the roof, with Jake craning to get a glimpse of the drunk-looking swaying of November Ajax. He wanted to gloat over the success of his plan a little. But all he caught was a glimpse before Scrapper's weight caved in the roof and they were falling through the shattered interior floors toward the ground level.

When they hit, the pilot was still smooth and cool. But it took Jake a minute to get his breath and focus his eyes after the jarring impact. She was looking at him. He could see the surprise on her face even though she was trying to play things cool and hide it. She wanted to know how he knew that would work. But she wouldn't ask, and Jake wasn't going to tell her.

She saw that in his eyes, or perhaps he was imagining it. In any case, she charged forward and Scrapper plowed through the rubble around the bottom of the building out into the street. A warning flashed on the Conn-Pod HUD: RESERVE POWER AT 12%.

"Told you we needed that!" she yelled.

"It worked, didn't it?" he yelled back.

"How long before Ajax can reboot his systems?"

Jake thought it was interesting that she thought he would know. Maybe she'd figured out by now that he knew a little about Jaegers. He also admired her cool, for wanting to be sure how much of a head start she could expect before the Jaeger was back in action. Before he could figure out what to say, November Ajax's enormous foot slammed down in front of them, kicking up a huge blast of sand and bits of concrete.

"About that long," Jake said.

*"Power down and exit your Conn-Pod,"* November Ajax's pilot boomed. *"This is your final warning."*

Jake was surprised when the girl spun Scrapper around and ran off. She had more guts than he'd figured, to do that on twelve percent reserve power with no chance of actually getting away.

Their dash for freedom didn't go on for long. November Ajax raised one fist and fired a set of grappling hooks, trailing cables across the empty space. They clamped onto Scrapper's fuselage, and as soon as they had attached, an electric pulse surged through the cables.

Inside Scrapper's Conn-Pod, Jake felt his hair standing up. Circuits were sparking and smoking all over, including the suite of scavenged electronics controlling the gyroscopic cradle. It jammed as the Conn-Pod went dark. The only light was what filtered through Scrapper's visor and down from its head into the torso.

Slowly Scrapper tipped over backward and crashed to the ground, leaving Jake bruised again and the pilot hung up on her back in the cradle. She looked mad. Jake couldn't decide whether that was to cover fear, or whether she was just really feeling more anger than anything else. People fronted all kinds of stuff when they were about to go down for serious crimes.

A series of heavy thumps sounded in the confined space. November Ajax was tapping on Scrapper's hull.

Jake looked at the girl and shrugged. They'd made a good run. Did themselves proud. But they weren't ever going to get anywhere against a full-sized Jaeger.

He levered the hatch open and climbed out, raising his hands. The girl followed him, looked up at November Ajax and screamed, "Look what you did to my Jaeger, you dick!"

# 3

## ILLEGAL JAEGER WORKSHOP BROKEN UP IN SANTA MONICA
### LA WORLD STAFF

Working in coordination with local law enforcement, a Pan Pacific Defense Corps security detail located a black-market Jaeger workshop in the former PPDC cargo facility located on the Santa Monica waterfront. The area, devastated by a Kaiju attack near the end of the Kaiju War, has suffered from high crime and mass out-migration in the years since the closing of the Breach. More recently, according to PPDC staffers, it has become a hotbed of illegal trade in Jaeger parts and other related technological components.

The workshop in question contained one completed Jaeger approximately forty feet in height, as well as hundreds of parts that PPDC and local forensic technicians are still cataloguing. It is believed that the homemade Jaeger and the workshop may have ties to the underground mech racing circuits that have gained popularity within the criminal underworld of the Santa Monica slums. Officials cannot confirm or deny this at this time.

continued...

The suspects attempted to escape in the Jaeger and damaged several PPDC vehicles before being apprehended by November Ajax, the PPDC's designated patrol Jaeger for the Southern California region. PPDC staff would not confirm reports that November Ajax was damaged during the struggle.

The names of those arrested are being withheld pending confirmation of their identities.

Jake held it in as long as he could, through the ride in the back of the van to PPDC to the regional HQ where they were processed into a holding cell. But eventually he couldn't keep it in any longer.

"Should've let me pilot," he said.

"Like this is my fault?" Amara snapped back. He'd just learned her name, when she gave it to the security officer who booked them. "You compromised my command center."

"*Command center—?*" That term was a little more elevated than Scrapper's makeshift Conn-Pod deserved, Jake thought. He shook his head and looked away, trying not to laugh. "I'm not talking to you."

She didn't say anything. Jake sat, trying not to look at her or say anything either, but in the end he couldn't help himself. He had to know. "Why'd you build it?"

"What happened to the not talking?" She glanced over at him long enough to register his displeasure, then looked back at the doors, as if she was planning her risky escape.

"You said you weren't gonna sell it, so what? Rob a bank or something?" Jake had heard of that. It was a good way to have your robbery caper end with a missile strike instead of police sirens, but some people liked to go out that way.

Amara had a faraway look in her eyes as she remembered something, and it took her a moment to speak. "I built her because one day they're gonna come back," she said, all her bravado melting away. "The Kaiju. And when they do, I'm not gonna be stuck waiting for someone else to come save my ass. Not like before."

Jake absorbed that. It wasn't what he'd expected. She was different when she let the tough facade slip for a minute.

He didn't have more time to consider that, though, because PPDC officers were at that moment opening the cell. "You," one of them said to Jake. "Let's go."

* * *

Holo emitters on different sides of the interrogation room flickered to life and a hologram appeared. *Ah*, Jake thought. *The old remote interrogation.* Usually they got started that way, then brought a real cop into the room when they thought you needed to be scared a little.

Not that Jake had spent a lot of time talking to cops over the past few years.

The hologram took a moment to resolve, and then Jake found himself looking at the last person in the world he'd have expected to see at that moment:

Mako Mori.

She looked great, in her PPDC Secretary General's uniform. After she'd survived the closing of the Breach, she'd risen through the ranks fast, eventually surpassing her father—well, their father—to become head of the PPDC.

"There she is!" Jake said brightly. He was happy to see her. He also hoped she might help him get out of this jam. "My sister from another mister! You make some calls, pull some strings, I gotta sign some paperwork?"

She didn't answer him right away, and when she did, the air went right out of his initial exuberance. "I was really hoping to not see you like this again."

"Just a stretch of bad luck," Jake said, feeling a little abashed. "I'll figure it out."

She wasn't buying it. "Father used to say we make our own luck."

That was the wrong approach to take with Jake, bringing up their father. Last thing in the world he wanted to talk about. "Yeah, Dad said a lot of things."

He was being flippant to get a rise out of her, but it didn't work. Maybe she was too grown up for that now. "You were in a rogue Jaeger with stolen PPDC tech."

"Wasn't mine."

"You have priors. This is serious, Jake."

Jake's charming act faded a little. Was he in real trouble here even though his sister ran the PPDC? "Which is why I need my big sister to get me the hell out of here," he prompted.

"They're not going to let you just walk out," she said. "But there might be another way."

"Great. Love it. What do I gotta do?"

"Re-enlist," she answered without missing a beat. "And finish what you started."

This wasn't what Jake had expected. He couldn't help it. He laughed at how ridiculous the idea was. "I'm a little old to be a cadet, Mako."

"I don't want you to be a cadet. I want you to help *train* them."

Train them? Jake had barely gotten past the cadet stage himself. How could he train anyone in anything? "What's behind door number two?" he asked.

She ignored the question, like she always did when she'd made up her mind. "The transport is standing by to bring both of you to Moyulan."

Moyulan. The big Shatterdome. China. She was serious. But… "Both of us?"

"You and your new recruit," she said. "Enjoy your flight, Jake!"

"Mako? Mako!"

She broke the connection and the hologram disappeared. "Sonofa—" Jake was all by himself again.

# 4

## MEMORIAL SERVICE DISRUPTED
## BY KAIJU CULTISTS

### FROM WIRE REPORTS

Agitators from several Kaiju-worshipping sects disrupted
a ceremonial dedication of a memorial to siblings Stacker
and Luna Pentecost in their home city of London. The long-
planned memorial, delayed by conflict over its siting and
design, was approved after years of wrangling for a corner of
Bruce Castle Park, near White Hart Lane in the Tottenham
neighborhood where the Pentecost siblings were born.

Luna Pentecost, a pilot with the Royal Air Force, was killed
in the first battle of the Kaiju War, when the creature later
dubbed Trespasser came ashore in San Francisco Bay. RAF
support elements assisted the American Air Force, and both
suffered heavy losses. She was posthumously awarded the
Victoria Cross.

Stacker Pentecost, also initially a RAF pilot, later became one
of the founding Rangers in the fledgling Jaeger program, and

continued...

piloted the Jaeger Coyote Tango on a number of missions, including the famous encounter with the Kaiju Onibaba in Tokyo, during which Pentecost saved the life of current PPDC Secretary General Mako Mori. Sickened by radiation from Coyote Tango's poorly designed reactor, Stacker moved into PPDC oversight, becoming Marshal. His final mission, to close the Breach in March 2025, was successful, but at the cost of his life and that of his copilot, Chuck Hansen.

Police quickly broke up the demonstration and the memorial dedication proceeded without incident. The Metropolitan Police declined to say how many arrests they had made or characterize the amount of property damage.

By sunset, the PPDC transport carrier had crossed the Pacific Ocean, bringing the Moyulan Shatterdome into view. Jake took it in with what might charitably be called mixed feelings. He'd seen Shatterdomes before, and his memories of them were not all positive. Moyulan was a newer location, built in the round of consolidations and relocations following the end of the Kaiju War. It occupied the largest of a group of mountainous islands in Qingchuan Bay, about four hundred kilometers south of Shanghai. The main Shatterdome, containing the Jaeger bay and mechanical operations, was at the center of the complex. To the left as they approached was the main body of the base, a bunker-style complex eight to ten stories tall and hundreds of yards long, reaching from the Shatterdome out to a large parking area for Jumphawks, V-Dragons, and the transport helicopters that made up the bulk of the PPDC's aerial fleet. The Jumphawks looked much like they had when Jake was around Shatterdomes before: massive helicopters designed to carry Jaegers from Shatterdomes to field deployments more quickly than the Jaegers could get there themselves. The V-Dragons were different, and newer. The V in their designation referred to the rotating engine mounts that gave them vertical takeoff and landing capability, or VTOL for short.

Curving from the fleet parking area across the front of the Shatterdome was a broad tarmac with hydraulic lifts at its waterfront side. Jaegers rode those down into the water for local deployments and training exercises in the relatively shallow waters around the islands. Each elevator platform was a rectangle roughly forty by thirty yards in size, giving a Jaeger plenty of room to stand clear of the deck as the platform descended toward the water level.

Beyond the elevator platforms, on the far side of the installation from the Jumphawk parking, the tarmac narrowed and curved into a long arm, supported over the water by immense steel-reinforced concrete pilings. Here were four external staging gantries, where Jaegers stood while they were linked to Jumphawks for deployment. Elevators ran up the interior of the gantries, which were made of heavy girders. At the side of each gantry stood a control tower, staffed by J-Tech supervisors tasked with making final readiness checks once the Rangers were inside each Jaeger and it was powering up for action.

The exterior tarmac area was bustling with activity. Tech crews ran refueling hoses out to waiting Jumphawk transports, while other crews ran carts of supplies and machinery to various destinations in the complex. Everything was tightly controlled and perfectly synchronized, thanks to the crew's superb training. Jake remembered the scene from his previous life as a cadet. He'd been amazed then at how such a giant facility could run so smoothly, and he felt some of that amazement again now.

The carrier came in low past a stand of old rocket thrusters in a row at the edge of the tarmac. When it landed, Jake and Amara stepped out, duffel bags slung over their shoulders. They'd already been issued gear back in California.

Amara was nervous, and showed it by talking nonstop. She'd commented on the size of the transport, the size of the Shatterdome, the size of the Pacific Ocean, and now that they were on the ground she finally got to what was really on her mind. "Why me? I mean why do they want me for the program?"

Jake didn't know for sure, but he could guess. "Built and piloted your own Jaeger," he said. "Don't see that every day."

As if he'd conjured it, Scrapper came into view right

then, suspended between two Jumphawks. They'd followed the personnel transport across the Pacific, but this was the first time Amara had been able to lay eyes on her creation since November Ajax disabled it back in Santa Monica.

The Jumphawks hovered low over the tarmac and released the cables holding Scrapper. The little Jaeger dropped and landed solidly on its feet... then tottered and fell face down with a loud crash. "Hey!" Amara protested, as crews ran to reattach cables so the Jumphawks could set Scrapper on its feet again. "Be careful with Scrapper!"

Jake was about to tell her it would be all right, since the Shatterdome techs would be doing a complete refit of Scrapper the minute they got the little Jaeger into a hangar gantry—but he didn't have the chance, because an old familiar voice cut through the din of Jumphawk rotors and shouting techs.

"Will you look at this?"

The voice belonged to Ranger Nathan Lambert, the strapping, square-jawed poster boy for the Ranger service... and once upon a time Jake's partner. He was wearing a military tank top, managing to walk with a swagger that made his dog tags jingle even though he carried a heavy gear assembly in both hands. "Didn't believe it when they told me you were inbound," he said, addressing Jake.

"Nate." Jake nodded. "This is Cadet Amara Namani—"

"You'll address me as Ranger Lambert," Nate interrupted.

Jake paused. "You having a laugh?"

"This is a military base," Lambert said, dead serious. "Remember how those work, Ranger Pentecost?" Turning to Amara, he lightened up a little. "Welcome to the Shatterdome. This is where you learn how to save the world."

He strode off toward the open bay doors that led into

the Shatterdome. Jake followed, Amara right next to him.

"Did that haircut just call you Pentecost?" she asked incredulously. "As in badass Stacker Pentecost, pilot of Coyote Tango, hero of—"

"It's just a name," Jake said. He was still stewing over Nate's snub. Clearly Nate was holding a grudge about how Jake had left the Ranger program, but that was Nate's problem. The only way it would be Jake's problem was if Nate couldn't let it go.

"A really *cool* name," Amara said, looking at Jake in a whole new way. Jake didn't like it. He didn't want her to admire him. He didn't want anyone to admire him. "Explains why you got a golden ticket," Amara added.

This got under Jake's skin. He didn't see any golden ticket. He saw a one-way ticket back into a life he'd tried his best to get away from. "You know, moving forward, let's limit the conversation, okay?"

He could feel her eyes on him as they followed Lambert through the thirty-story-tall ocean-facing hangar doors that led into the Shatterdome's Jaeger bay. Amara forgot all about Jake and goggled at the sight. Just inside the door, Valor Omega was docking into her service cradle. Jake took a long look at her, remembering his own training, when most of these Jaegers were either still under construction or completing their pre-deployment final technical screenings. Valor Omega was all about firepower, her whole torso designed around massive arms and shoulders ending in forearm-mounted energy cannons. Orange and yellow against a black layer of ballistic under-armor, she made Jake think of fire.

Looking around the vast bay, he saw the rest of Moyulan's complement of Jaegers. There was heavy, broad-shouldered Titan Redeemer, her left arm ending in the massive Morning Star Hand she could lash out on the end of a charged cable. Nearly sixty feet in diameter, the Morning Star had a superdense liquid-metal core that gave it extra punching power, especially when it was fired from its emplacement on the cable. Testing simulations indicated it would have put a Cat-2 Kaiju down with a single shot. The hundreds of spikes on the Morning Star lay flat when it was inert, but flared out when it was deployed, adding damage to the outer armored layers of any target. Titan blended into the shadows falling near her service cradle, her olive coloring acting as camouflage.

Guardian Bravo, by contrast, was a brilliant red and silver, her graphene Arc Whip retracted while it was at rest. Other than her color scheme, Guardian Bravo was set apart from the rest of the Shatterdome's complement by the tall vent stacks that stood up from the backs of its shoulders. Jake hadn't learned much about Guardian Bravo's design, but he thought he remembered the stacks having something to do with creating a static charge, using internal fans to generate extra power to the Arc Whip. In demonstrations, the whip had proven capable of cutting through a meter of steel, while delivering an electrical charge roughly comparable to an average lightning strike.

Saber Athena, on the other side of the bay, was built much leaner and smaller. She was the PPDC's most up-to-date effort to design a Jaeger that could potentially match a living creature's speed and quickness. All of the Mark VI Jaegers were faster on their feet than the previous generations, just due to improvements in neurotransmitting systems in parallel with more sophisticated hydraulic damping that allowed for better lateral movement. Compared to the Mark II or Mark III Jaegers, the Mark VIs all looked like acrobats—but Saber Athena made the rest of them look slow. Her weaponry, twin plasma swords, was designed to work with her quick-strike capability. She didn't have a ton of firepower, but her pilots were trained to hit a target five times while another one of the Mark VIs was still winding up for a second shot.

Next was Bracer Phoenix, an experimental Mark VI with a three-Ranger Conn-Pod designed so that one of the pilots could drop down into the secondary control room and handle Bracer's devastating railgun. It was mounted on a track encircling Bracer's midsection, with a fire rate of hundreds of rounds per minute. Each shell was the size of a truck. Another of Bracer's innovations was a twin knee joint, segmented to flex both forward and backward. This advance enabled the Jaeger to hold her balance and keep moving even while the railgun was firing, as the extra joint in each leg gave it more recoil absorption, without sacrificing much in the way of strength or stability. Bracer had just been an idea on a drawing board when Jake left the PPDC. A three-Ranger crew was considered extravagant during the Kaiju War, when Rangers were at a premium, but now in the postwar era the PPDC was freer to develop different piloting protocols.

Finally Jake's eye fell on Gipsy Avenger, the Mark VI successor to Gipsy Danger. Jake could see the family resemblance in the shape of the head and the detailing of the exterior armor, not to mention the blue-accented color scheme. He had once been assigned to Gipsy Avenger, and seeing her again churned up a lot of feelings that he would rather have left alone under their layers of time and deliberate forgetting. Gipsy was a good ride, strong and quick. She had a forearm-mounted chain sword on the left side, and her right arm contained the apparatus for the experimental Gravity Sling, a weapon Jake had barely started training on when... well, he didn't want to think about that right now. He might be back in a Shatterdome, but that didn't mean he had to dredge up everything in his past. Seeing Nate Lambert so soon after the uncomfortable reunion with Mako had shaken him. Lambert scorned him and Mako pitied him. Jake felt worse about Mako's pity than Nate's scorn. But where Nate had made it clear he didn't want Jake around, Mako was giving him a second chance. Jake knew how generous that was even though it was a chance he never would have asked for and wasn't sure he even wanted.

Still, he was here, and the alternative was jail, so he was going to see which way the wind was blowing and then get the hell out as soon as the chance presented itself.

They were about halfway across the Jaeger bay, weaving to avoid J-Tech crews crisscrossing the deck in Scramblers or on foot. Amara fell behind, lost in her astonishment. Jake remembered feeling the same way about Jaegers. Now he was more cynical. Sooner or later, he figured she would be too. All signs in the Shatterdome were in both Mandarin and English, and most of the techs spoke Mandarin, too. The PPDC had been an international effort from its inception, since the Kaiju had known no national boundaries. Now it retained its international character because no nation on Earth could handle the costs alone while they tried to rebuild from the widespread devastation of the Kaiju War.

"Simtraining starts at 0600," Lambert said, snapping Amara out of her reverie. "You're late, you miss the day. Fall behind, you're on a transport back to wherever they found you."

Amara finally found her voice. "That's Titan Redeemer! And Bracer Phoenix, she's a three-man rig! And Guardian Bravo! And—and Saber Athena! I love Saber Athena! She's the fastest Jaeger in the fleet!" Now Jake understood the posters plastering the walls of her squat back in Santa Monica. She adored Jaegers the way other kids worshipped musicians or YouTube stars.

Jake, for his part, was curious why the whole Shatterdome seemed to be on alert. "What's all the hustle for?" he asked Nate.

"Been ordered to put on a show. Shao and her team are coming in tomorrow."

"Shao?" Amara echoed. "Like, Shao Liwen?" Again Jake remembered her squat, with its mini-shrine to Shao. This was a perfect place for Amara, he thought. There was nowhere else in the world where she would have a better chance to show her stuff.

"What they tell me," Lambert said, like it was no big deal.

But to Amara, it was a very big deal. "Oh my God. Shao Liwen!" She spun to Jake. "You know who that is?! PhD at seventeen, gazillionaire way before she was as old as you are—"

"Yeah," Jake said. "I've heard of her, thanks."

"Half the tech in Scrapper came from old Shao parts." Amara gazed up at the Jaegers surrounding them. "Can't believe I'm gonna get to meet her."

"You're not," Lambert said, glancing over at her.

"What?" Amara looked stricken. "Why?"

"Why do you think? You're a *cadet*."

"That's not fair."

"Get used to it around here," Jake commented. Ranger training was a lot of things, but fair wasn't one of them.

Amara snorted and turned back to the Jaegers. Jake could see what this meant to her. For a girl who grew up idolizing Rangers and the Jaegers they piloted, being in a Shatterdome was a dream come true. He wished he could still feel that.

"So which one's yours?" she asked Lambert.

"Gipsy," Lambert said. He pointed up.

"You pilot Gipsy Avenger?!" Amara was looking at

Lambert in a whole new way now. Gipsy Danger, the Jaeger Avenger was built from, was a legend. Gipsy had sealed the Breach, surviving the Kaiju's final onslaught even though it was one of the older Jaegers still in the field. It had been Raleigh Becket's ride—and Mako Mori's. It was a name to conjure with.

"He used to," said a woman pulling up in a J-Tech Scrambler, a small vehicle designed for hauling heavy loads. "Until his copilot got a better offer in the private sector." She climbed off the Scrambler and introduced herself. "Hi. Jules Reyes. J-Tech."

"Amara. Cadet."

"Jake. Uh, Ranger, I guess." He looked her over. Dark hair and eyes, no-nonsense attitude to go with looks that would turn heads in the street. Jake was a sucker for the combination of competence and beauty. Jules Reyes radiated both.

She eyed him right back. "Heard a lot about you, Pentecost. You know you still hold the record."

That piqued Amara's interest. "What record?"

"Told you to stop talking to me," Jake said. It was rude, and he knew it. He saw Lambert tighten up at the tone of his voice, but Jake didn't care. The last thing he wanted to do was rehash all the old stories from the last time he'd been in a Shatterdome.

Jules took it all in and then went on like she hadn't seen anything. "How'd they lure you back? Couldn't have been the pay."

"Long story," Jake said. "If you'd like to hear it sometime…"

"She wouldn't," Lambert interrupted. He handed Jules the part he'd been holding. "This what you were looking for?"

"Yeah." She grinned and loaded it onto the Scrambler. "Outstanding."

Lambert was grinning back. Jake could see the spark between them. That explained why Lambert had been so quick to cut him off.

"I'll swing by after I'm done with these two and give you a hand," Lambert said.

Near one of the doors that led into the J-Tech wing of the Shatterdome, a series of clattering bangs echoed through the huge space. Jake turned to see a scientist—lab coat, glasses, awkward demeanor—stumbling away from a bunch of stacked canisters he had just knocked over. They bounced around on the floor near another Scrambler. The driver was shouting at him in Mandarin. Jake recognized the scientist: Hermann Gottlieb, one of the pair who had unlocked the secret of the Kaiju's creators, known as the Precursors. Another legend in the history of the PPDC.

Right now he was stuttering and embarrassed at the mess he'd made, and also struggling to understand what the tech was saying. Gottlieb didn't know much Mandarin, which was a bit of a handicap at the Moyulan Shatterdome. He minimized it by spending most of his time in the lab.

"Yo. Gottlieb. You okay?" Lambert called.

"Oh," Gottlieb said, noticing them. "Yes." To the tech he added a quick apology in the same language. He knew at least that much.

Cheerfully he held up a handful of what appeared to be partially burned papers. Smoke still curled from them. "Almost had it!" He blew the singed bits off the papers and disappeared, reading the notes as he went.

"He's weird," Amara commented.

Jules was also watching him go. "You have no idea," she said. As she climbed back into her Scrambler, she added, "Welcome to the Moyulan Shatterdome, Cadet. Ranger."

Jake watched her drive off. Lambert watched him

watching. "Eyes front, Pentecost," he said. A warning. Then he started walking again, Jake and Amara right behind him.

"What record was she talking about?" Amara asked. Jake ignored her. "Come on," she pressed. "We were in jail together!"

Jake sighed. He wasn't going to get out of telling the story. "Part of the final exam, back when I was a cadet," he said as they went. "You had to hold a Drift in one of the old MarkThrees for over twenty minutes."

"How long did you last?"

"Little over four hours."

He could see that impressed her. It should have. A four-hour Drift was a big deal. "Who was your copilot?" she asked.

Jake glanced over at Lambert. This was the part of the story he didn't want to tell. Apparently Lambert wasn't interested in airing it out either. "Keep up, Cadet!" he called over his shoulder. "Time to meet the rest of the family."

# 5

**GREETINGS, EVERYONE. THIS IS RANIA CHIHOOLY** *with PacAsia Radio. You've no doubt heard that Shao Industries is angling to replace Ranger-piloted Jaegers with a fleet of Drones, and as part of that developing story we got curious what some former Rangers might think about this initiative. Our field correspondent Filip Chen caught up with Herc Hansen, former Ranger and briefly Marshal in the PPDC, who left the service after the closing of the Breach and the death of his son Chuck aboard Striker Eureka. Let's go to the audio.*

*FC: Herc! Filip Chen, PacAsia Radio. Have you heard about the new Drone proposal from Shao Industries?*

*HH: Couldn't avoid it if I wanted to, could I?*

*FC: What's your opinion?*

*HH: On Drones in Jaegers? Dumbest thing I ever heard.*

*FC: Even after your son died in a Jaeger, it doesn't seem like a good idea?*

*HH: My son died in a Jaeger, yeah. And if there hadn't been Rangers in that Jaeger, and in Gipsy Danger, we'd all be dead. You think a Drone pilot could decide to blow a Jaeger's reactor and find the manual override? Get out of here.*

*FC: Still, you have to admit—*
*HH: I said get the BLEEEEEEP out of here. And don't ever talk to me about my son again.*


Deep in the bowels of the Shatterdome was a barracks housing new cadets, a group of eight selected from thousands of eager applicants. They were all in their teens, the men with regulation cropped hair and the women carefully observing PPDC regulations about styles that kept the eyes clear. When they were in a group, it was easy to tell what the PPDC looked for in cadets. Wherever they came from—this group of eight represented six home countries—they were all athletic and lean, alert and intelligent. Most importantly, they were driven. Even in their off-hours, most of them were occupied with some kind of training. Meilin and Viktoriya wore practice Drift helmet rigs, trying to sync themselves together so they would work a holographic Jaeger arm and put it through its combat paces. But they were having trouble making it do anything. It twitched and flailed around. "You're out of sync," Meilin said.

Vik swore in Russian. Switching to English, she said, "Helmet's acting up." She took it off and the holo Jaeger arm disappeared. Both of them started tinkering with the helmet. Blonde and muscular, Vik towered over Meilin, who bent close to a circuit panel, frowning under severe black bangs as she sought the reason the Drift connection was getting interrupted. Ranger training wasn't just about combat. A Ranger had to know every detail of how their equipment worked, because sometimes battlefield repairs and workarounds made the difference between life and death... and not just for the Rangers, either.

They all knew the story of how Raleigh Becket had sealed the Breach. With Gipsy Danger's systems failing, sinking deeper into the hellscape of the Precursor dimension on the other side of the Breach, he had to know how to set the manual reactor override and then get back to his escape pod. That knowledge came from obsessive attention to detail.

The ability to pull it off, though, that came from sheer willpower under circumstances none of the cadets could imagine. But they believed in themselves, and they were going to do everything they could to live up to the example of their idols. Becket, Pentecost, Hansen... they had set the bar, and the cadets wanted to wear the title of Ranger just as they had.

As the Jaeger arm blinked out, two other cadets—Renata and Suresh—were sparring in the space between the bunks just beyond it. Renata caught Suresh square in the mouth with a punch at practice speed, and Suresh skipped backward, covering his mouth. "Come on!" he complained. Suresh was the nervous one of the group, with a soulful face that easily softened into a pout. "Not in the face, Renata!"

"Sorry, my bad," she said, mimicking his expression—and then she popped him in the face again. He came back at her, and they traded blows in a flurry, bumping into a bunk where another pair of cadets, Tahima and Ilya, were playing cards.

"I see your hour of rec time and raise two shower chits," Tahima said. Ilya considered.

On the upper bunk, Jinhai was doing sit-ups off the edge while Ryoichi sat on his legs, reading a comic about Jaegers. "Fold, Ilya," Jinhai said when he was at full extension, with his head upside down near Ilya's. "You need all the showers you can get."

"I have a *musk*," Ilya corrected him. "What you smell is a *musk*."

Amara absorbed these impressions all at once as she entered the room with Jake and Ranger Lambert. Ryoichi was the first cadet to notice them. "Ranger on deck!" he called out, stuffing his comic under the pillow.

All of the cadets scrambled into line and snapped to attention. Lambert took a moment to watch and inspect them. Then he said, "Cadets. This is Amara Namani. She'll be joining you in sim training, bright and early."

They all looked her up and down, displaying a variety of reactions. Naturally they were all competitive. Ranger slots were few and precious. Another cadet meant one more person who wasn't going to make it when the final promotions were announced. Vik in particular didn't make any effort to hide her disdain.

"And this is Ranger Pentecost," Lambert added, nodding at Jake.

That got a much different response. The name Pentecost crackled in the room, and they looked at Jake like he had stepped out of a history book. He tried not to show how much it irritated him. "He'll be helping me instruct you until I find a new copilot to replace Ranger Burke." Lambert turned to Jake. "Anything you want to add?"

Jake looked at all the eager young faces staring at him, waiting for him to say something profound. But he didn't have anything profound to say. "Don't do what I did," perhaps. Or maybe "Do what I did, get out while you have a chance." Or even "Let me tell you the real story about Stacker Pentecost and what it was like to be his son."

But all he said was, "Not really."

Lambert glowered at him. Jake knew why. In a situation like this, you were supposed to be rah-rah, and Jake wasn't doing that. To Lambert, that was something close to sacrilege. But that was Nate's problem, not Jake's.

"Malikova!" Lambert snapped. "Get Namani squared

away and prepped for training."

She didn't look happy. "Yes, sir."

"As you were," Lambert said with a final nod. He turned to go. Jake followed, looking over the cadets one last time. He didn't want to be here, and he didn't care if it showed on his face. He would do the job because it was keeping him out of jail, but Jake would be damned if he was going to join in with all the cheerleading about Rangers saving the world. The Breach was closed. They were all just marking time.

When the door closed and Amara was alone with her new—colleagues? Was that the right word?—the first of them to speak was Ryoichi. "Pentecost! We're gonna be trained by a Pentecost!"

"So?" Vik was apparently determined not to be impressed by anything. "Not like he was the one who died helping close the Breach."

She went back to troubleshooting her practice helmet. Once she had the visor off and the contact points exposed, she started tracing each of them to the bundle where the cranial contacts transmitted brain signals to the Drift cradle. They looked all right on visual inspection, but something was obviously wrong, so she started touching each one with a small circuit tester. Amara walked up to her and stood awkwardly, waiting for Vik to look up. When she didn't, Amara said, "Uh… hey, so where do I…"

Vik still didn't look up. She hadn't found a bad contact, so now she was opening up the housing on the bundle to see if there was a frayed or crossed wire there. "Heard you built your own little Jaeger."

"Yeah," Amara said, brightening. "Uh, Scrapper." She was paying attention to what Vik was doing, and it got her thinking about how she'd figured out how to construct a helmet interface. "I operated her, too. With this solo rig I—"

She was pointing at something in the bundle of wires when Vik stood and interrupted her. "You want to put junk together, be a mechanic. Moyulan is for *pilots*." Without another word, Vik moved off toward the far end of the barracks.

Amara stood there, not knowing what to do. Wasn't this the person Ranger Lambert had told to help her get settled? She had to train tomorrow! She didn't even know what the training would be, where her cadet gear was, where she was going to sleep...

"Come on, I got you," another cadet said. He picked up her duffel bag and led her toward another part of the barracks.

"Thanks," Amara said. "Um...?"

"Jinhai. Ou-Yang Jinhai."

"Ou-Yang? Like the pilots from the war, Ming-hau and Suyin?" Amara was starting to feel like she was the only person in the Moyulan Shatterdome who didn't have a connection to a famous Ranger.

"I just call 'em Mom and Dad," Jinhai said with a grin. "So you and Vik are already buddies, huh?"

"Vik?"

"Short for Viktoriya," another cadet said. He'd been sparring when they walked in. Amara hadn't caught his name. "But you don't want to call her that."

"What's her problem?" Amara asked. She was starting to get her feet under her and see which of the other cadets were going to be cool.

"Took her three shots to pass the entrance test," the other fighter said. "I'm Renata. This is Suresh."

"Don't think she likes how you landed here," Jinhai said, talking about Vik again.

"Not my fault," Amara said. "Recruiters never come around back home."

"Heard you were from the coast," Jinhai said. "Why didn't your folks move inland, like everyone else? They poor or something?"

"They didn't make it," Amara answered quietly. "When Santa Monica got hit."

The other cadets had moved on. It was just her and Jinhai. He saw it hurt her to talk about her parents. "Vik lost hers, too," he said. "In the Tomari attack. Hey, know any Russian?"

Amara shook her head.

"I'll teach you some. Calms her down. Let's stow your gear and get you a uni."

They moved off together, and Amara was already feeling more at home. Maybe this was going to work out after all. She had Scrapper, she had a chance to prove herself... maybe she would even have a friend.

# 6

## FINAL COUNCIL DEBATE ON DRONE PROGRAM

### WIRE SERVICE REPORTS

The Pan Pacific Defense Corps' governing council will take up the question of Shao Industries' Drone proposal at its next meeting, PPDC spokesperson Edwina Oglethorpe announced today.

The meeting, to take place at the main Council headquarters in Sydney, will be a highly symbolic moment in the organization's history. Sydney was the site of a main battle during the Kaiju War, during which Jaegers proved capable of stopping a Kaiju when all other defensive measures—notably the city's much-heralded anti-Kaiju wall—failed.

Council observers seem divided on the question of whether the Council will approve Shao's plan. Some Councilors are said to be concerned that the Drone program puts too much responsibility for PPDC Jaeger readiness in the hands of a

continued...

single company. These security concerns are countered by other perspectives arguing that Shao Industries' security is the equal of the PPDC's, and the needs of the PPDC would be better met by a cheaper, lower-maintenance Drone fleet.

Sydney authorities are bracing for massive demonstrations both for and against the program. Much of downtown Sydney in the area of the Council building will be closed off from ordinary pedestrian and vehicle traffic.
This story will be updated.

Jake went into his quarters and found them just like he remembered. Everything utilitarian; the bunk over the desk, the small bathroom, the even smaller closet.

On the outside of the closet hung a Ranger uniform. The name badge said PENTECOST. Jake reached out and felt the material of it, also feeling the weight of a past he wasn't proud of—a legacy he couldn't escape—and now maybe a second chance, a future he wasn't sure he deserved.

But he couldn't escape it. Not the weight of that name, the example of that sacrifice. Who could?

And who could ever hope to live up to it?

Jake wanted to give Amara a few days to get acclimated to her new surroundings, but Lambert was in charge of training and as he had announced in the cadet barracks, he set her first simulation session for early the next day. The simulation bay was arranged around a fully functional Conn-Pod that could be programmed to emulate the capabilities of any existing Jaeger. Today it was Titan Redeemer, and Amara was partnered with Cadet Suresh.

They got a short introduction to the Drift cradle and then the simulation kicked in. Titan Redeemer was dropped from virtual Jumphawks into the middle of the Tokyo megacity sprawl, as the Category II Kaiju Onibaba raged through the city. Jake remembered the story of Onibaba from when he was a kid. The monster had surged ashore from the Sea of Japan in 2016, laying waste to huge sections of Tokyo before the Jaeger Coyote Tango arrived to defend the city. In the battle, more of the city was destroyed, but Coyote Tango ultimately emerged triumphant, making heroes out of its Ranger pilots, Stacker Pentecost and Tamsin Sevier.

During the battle, Sevier had suffered a seizure, and

Pentecost had had to pilot the Jaeger alone for the rest of the fight. The neurophysiological stress of that, together with exposure to Coyote Tango's poorly shielded reactor, left Jake's father with deteriorating health and forced him to retire from active service.

And that wasn't the only personal angle to the Onibaba story from Jake's point of view. One of the civilians who had witnessed the carnage—and barely escaped with her life—was a very young Mako Mori. After the battle, Stacker adopted her.

Watching the simulation begin, Jake wondered if Lambert had chosen Onibaba on purpose, to force Jake to confront his past. It would be a typical kind of psy-ops maneuver for Ranger training. See how tough the cadets are, see what the returning prodigal Ranger can handle.

Jake put it out of his mind. If it came up, he'd sort things out with Lambert. There was plenty they had to get straight if they were going to work together.

Titan Redeemer rushed to meet Onibaba, deploying her Morning Star Hand. The cadets, still new to Drift simulations, were going with the straightforward approach. The Morning Star smashed against Onibaba's carapace, but didn't do much damage. The Kaiju batted the Morning Star aside with its pincers and then seized the Jaeger, tearing away pieces of its armor.

A video feed from inside the Conn-Pod showed Amara and Suresh being flung around in their Drift cradle. Sparks flew: part of the simulation. "Warning," a computer voice intoned. "Hemispheres out of alignment. Warning…"

"We need to reconnect!" Suresh shouted.

Amara struggled to keep Titan Redeemer on her feet. "I'm trying!"

In the simulation feed, Onibaba raised one of its claws and drove it into Titan Redeemer's head. The Conn-Pod shuddered and the interior lights went out. The simulation ended and for a moment all was silent. In the real world, both cadets would be dead.

The hatch on the front of the Conn-Pod opened with a grinding noise, and the lights came back on. Inside, Suresh looked furious, and Amara embarrassed. The maglev system holding them in place disengaged automatically as the Conn-Pod's floor rose to meet them. Behind him, Jake could hear the other cadets muttering to each other.

Lambert stood at the bank of terminals facing the Conn-Pod, frowning down at Amara. "When I heard you gave November Ajax a run for its money, I thought we might have something here," he said. "Now, not so much."

One of the cadets stifled a snicker. Amara tore her helmet off. "How am I supposed to Drift in this thing?" she said, clearly trying to cover her humiliation. "It smells like feet."

Lambert wasn't having the backtalk. "I ask you to open your mouth, Cadet?"

Jake stepped up into Lambert's field of vision. He wasn't too concerned about protecting Amara's feelings—if she was going to be a Ranger, she would have to develop a thick skin—but he didn't like the way Lambert was handling the situation. A big part of Drifting success was about confidence. You had to make cadets believe in themselves while you were pointing out their mistakes. Lambert was only doing one of those things, and he was also deliberately picking on the cadet who had come in with Jake, which made Jake think Lambert's real problem wasn't with Amara at all. "You're putting her up against a Kaiju that almost killed veteran pilots," Jake said. He didn't have to add that one of those veteran pilots was his father. "She's not ready for that."

Lambert turned to face him. "Maybe she's not the only one who doesn't belong here."

Ah, Jake thought. Just as he'd suspected. "You got a problem with me, I'm right here. She's just a kid."

"So were we," Lambert said. That knocked Jake back a little. He realized maybe he was making things personal too, just as much as Nate was. "That's the *point*," Lambert went on. "You make stronger connections when you're young. That kind of bond makes better pilots that can Drift with anyone in their squad—"

"Yeah," Jake said. "I remember the pitch, thanks."

He wasn't going to get anywhere now. But he'd gotten Lambert off Amara's back, and that was enough for the moment. He went back to his station, where the simulation computers were analyzing the strength of the Drift connection between Suresh and Amara. It could have been better, but it also showed signs of potential.

Lambert glared after him, then got back to the situation at hand. "Ryoichi, Renata, you're up. Show our new recruit how it's done."

Asshole, Jake thought. That was a cheap shot at a kid who was squatting in a warehouse thirty-six hours ago. He looked down at Amara, who was unhooking from the Drift cradle, not meeting anyone else's eyes. If Lambert wasn't careful, he was going to drive her out of the program before they ever found out what her real potential might be.


The rest of the day passed in a series of training exercises and simulations. Jake thought the cadets had potential. They were bright, dedicated, skilled. All they needed was experience— and a trainer who knew when to push which buttons. He wasn't sure that was a skill Nate Lambert possessed. So he was up late thinking about what he should do, and it occurred to him that all this thinking might go better with a beer.

The Shatterdome kitchen was empty at this hour, maybe two thousand square feet of stainless steel and tile floors. Jake found the restricted Rangers-only part of the fridge, and sure enough there were a few beers in there. Probably the number was mandated by PPDC. There would be a report and a document somewhere in a file articulating the reasons why there should be x number of beers in that fridge, no more and no less.

It wasn't until Nate Lambert walked in that Jake considered the fact that he was in flip-flops and his bathrobe. Maybe that was a little casual for the Shatterdome public spaces, but Jake was still adhering to the dress code of his ruined Malibu mansion. You had to bring yourself wherever you went, and this was Jake Pentecost, sipping a beer and rooting around in the freezer for ice cream while he considered whether his job was worth doing.

"Classy," Lambert commented.

Jake stood up from peering into the freezer and saw who it was. "Jules loves it," he said. "Told me it's nice to finally have someone with style around here."

He opened the fridge and tossed one of the beers to Lambert, who nodded his thanks. "Ice cream's in the bottom left drawer, behind the frozen burgers."

*Of course it is*, Jake thought. He found it and pulled it out, a gallon of precious frozen sweetness. "Cheers," he said, and started to gather all the supplies he would need for a sundae.

Lambert sipped the beer for a while, and then said what was on his mind. "So one more time around to prove Daddy wrong?"

Jake was feeling pretty good at the moment, so he didn't take the bait. "Nah, I just came back to see if your chin implant ever settled in."

He saw a muscle jump in Nate's jaw... and then saw his

former partner crack a smile. "Looks good, doesn't it?"

"Very commanding," Jake said with a smile of his own. "The kids must love it."

It felt good to be comfortable around Nate. Jake didn't want the tension. Not with someone who had once been a close friend.

Lambert's smile faded but didn't completely disappear. "They look up to us, man," he said. "We need to set an example. Show 'em how to work together."

Jake loudly sprayed whipped cream. Then he set the can down on the table and said, "The war ended ten years ago."

Lambert shook his head. "You have to understand your enemy's objective to know you've defeated them. We still don't."

Jake pretended to think hard, then said, "I'm guessing it had something to do with sending giant monsters to kick the crap out of us."

"The Precursors wouldn't send Kaiju to flatten a few cities if they were trying to wipe us all out," Lambert said. "That's not a plan, genius."

Like a lot of things Nate said, this sounded right but didn't match Jake's reality. But he wasn't going to argue about it. He was going to try to do what he had to do to get by, and if that meant he had to go along with whatever Nate Lambert said, well, it was better than being in jail or having Sonny shoot him.

"Look, I got no beef with you, Nate," he said. "I'm here because you and your squint was a better deal than some big hairy dude in a tiny little cell."

"I'm touched," Nate said.

Jake wasn't done. "Cadets got what, couple of months before they graduate?"

"Six," Lambert corrected.

"Six?" This was longer than Jake had guessed, or

planned for. "Okay. Six. Tell you what. From now on, whenever you say something soldiery to the kids, I'll nod all like, 'Yeah, what he said,' and before you know it they get to be pilots and I get to go back to my life."

If he'd been trying to get under Lambert's skin, it didn't work. "May happen sooner than you think," Nate said evenly.

"How's that?"

"Big dog and pony show tomorrow. Shao Industries is pushing some kind of new Drone tech. Could make all us pilots obsolete."

Jake considered this. No pilots meant no cadets, which meant no need for trainers, which meant no need for Jake Pentecost to be stuck in a Shatterdome when he could be living it up in California. Was it possible? Amara seemed to think Shao Liwen could do anything. Maybe she could. Either way, the Breach had been sealed for ten years and the world was starting to wonder why it spent so much money keeping the Jaeger program alive. Sooner or later, bureaucrats would win out over soldiers, the way they always did.

"Well," Jake said slowly, "that sounds like my get-out-of-jail-free card."

Nate could tell what was going on. He didn't react to Jake's attempts to provoke him, and just sauntered toward the door. But as he went, he said, "Front all you want, Pentecost, but you know you could've been great if you'd stuck around."

"I didn't bail. I was kicked out."

"And whose fault was that?" Nate didn't wait for Jake to answer. He knocked back the rest of his beer and tossed the can in a recycling bin on his way out.

Then Jake was alone again in the kitchen, staring at his sundae. Nate got to him a little sometimes. They had always taken shots at each other, out of a natural rivalry. Sometimes it spilled over into something a little more intense. Sometimes, Jake had to admit, he overreacted. A little. Maybe. Now…

Well, Jake wasn't sure how to feel about it. But one thing hadn't changed since the last time he was inside a Shatterdome.

He was real, real sick of people telling him what he could have been.

# 7

## BULLETIN OF THE INTERNATIONAL ROBOTICS ENGINEERING AND ARTIFICIAL INTELLIGENCE ASSOCIATION (IREAIA)

### NEW MEMBER PROFILE: DR. NEWTON GEISZLER, SHAO INDUSTRIES

The International Robotics Engineering and Artificial Intelligence Association is proud to welcome Dr. Newton Geiszler as the newest member of its Distinguished Advisory Council.

A native of Berlin with multiple doctorates from the Massachusetts Institute of Technology, Dr. Geiszler is currently Senior Research Scientist and Director of Innovation at Shao Industries of Shanghai, People's Republic of China. There he oversees the development of remote operating systems and integrative approaches to Jaeger technology,

continued...

as well as ongoing research into the physiology of the multiconsciousness integrative protocol known as the Drift.

Prior to accepting his current position with Shao Industries, Dr. Geiszler was a top researcher and experimental roboticist at the Pan Pacific Defense Corp's K-Science division. While there he undertook pioneering experiments in understanding Kaiju physiology and consciousness and co-developed some of the early fundamental technologies that made the Drift possible.

As a member of the DAC, Dr. Geiszler will be a voting member on IREAIA position papers and will participate in the organization's funding and scientific outreach endeavors. The IREAIA is proud to add a scientist of Dr. Geiszler's credentials, reputation, and demonstrated courage to the Council, and looks forward to benefiting from his voice in the future.

Shao Liwen arrived the next day for the Drone Jaeger demonstration. The Shatterdome, so chaotic the day before, was now quiet, as all nonessential activities had been put on hold for the duration of her visit. She was the biggest of big wheels, and the PPDC was pulling out all the stops to impress her. She entered the Shatterdome dressed in white, every detail groomed and perfect. Shao had started life as a tinker and hacker, but now she led one of the world's most important tech manufacturing companies, and she knew how to play the part. She was escorted by a security detail, including Joseph Burke, whom Jake remembered from Ranger training. He saw Lambert staring daggers at Burke, and wondered what it was about—but then he was surprised to see Mako and Newt Geiszler bringing up the rear of Shao's procession, and he forgot about Lambert's personal problems. Jake still hadn't gotten used to his sister wearing the uniform of the PPDC Secretary General. Newt Geiszler looked different, too. The rumpled clothing and tousled hair of the Newt Jake remembered from footage of the Kaiju War had been replaced by a perfectly groomed and manicured corporate model, with the kind of swagger that came from a fat private-sector salary. Marshal Quan, the successor to Herc Hansen as PPDC Marshal, waited with the Rangers as Shao and her security detail approached.

Quan introduced himself in Mandarin and extended a hand. "Ms. Shao. Marshal Quan. It's an honor to meet you."

Shao just looked down at it, clearly uncomfortable. Newt rushed up to explain. "Sorry, sorry! She doesn't do the whole hand thing." He shook Quan's hand instead. "Dr. Newton Geiszler, head of research and devel— whoa, that's a firm grip." Turning to Liwen, he explained in Mandarin what he had said.

She addressed Quan, clearly going through the motions

of greetings and asking where the demonstration was going to happen. Quan indicated Lambert and gestured for them to follow, speaking in Mandarin until he glanced over at Mako. "We'll be in the War Room, Madam Secretary."

She nodded. "Thank you, Marshal."

Jake couldn't help himself. He grinned at Mako. Having her here made him feel more a part of everything. "Good to see you again."

"You too," she said, taking in his dress uniform and Ranger jacket. "That's a much better look on you."

Apparently Liwen agreed. As she passed, Jake saw her give him a long, lingering look. Some kind of interest there, he thought... but he wasn't sure what. Quan and Burke followed her.

Newt Geiszler trailed behind, making a big show of approaching Jake. "Is this him? What am I talking about, of course it's him!" He took Jake's hand and pumped it like he was performing for photographers. "Newton Geiszler, pleased to meet you. Gotta say, huge fan of your old man." His voice dropped into a weird approximation of Stacker Pentecost's cadence. "'*Today, we are cancelling the apocalypse!*' Love that, use it all the time."

Jake couldn't believe this slick phony was the same Newt Geiszler who had Drifted with a Kaiju brain and helped save the world. If that's what corporate money did to you, he'd stay with the PPDC... or go back to hustling on the black market.

Hermann Gottlieb appeared out of nowhere, calling out to his old colleague. "Ah! Newton! I was hoping you'd be tagging along. I could use your help on an experiment—"

Newt cut him off, his tone friendly but patronizing. "I'm on the job here, buddy. I got time after, we'll play with your test tubes."

"The demonstration is not scheduled for some time yet,"

Gottlieb said. "And with your interest in Kaiju physiology, I think you will want to see what I am developing."

Newt glanced over at Shao, who wasn't looking at him. He turned to Jake and Mako with a shrug. "All right! Give me a minute for the show-and-tell, okay? Then you better be ready to see something really cool."


Gottlieb hustled into his lab with Newt in tow. "This will only take a moment," Gottlieb said. "I don't want to impose, but—"

"Hey, come on," Newt said. "We've been in each other's *heads*. Without the intel we yanked from that Kaiju brain, Raleigh never would have been able to close the Breach. That was you and me, pal." They enjoyed that brief moment before Newt glanced at his watch. "But I am running a little tight, so…"

"Yes, umm…" Gottlieb started searching among the notes cluttering the desktop near his computer terminals. When they'd shared a lab, Gottlieb had been the neat freak. Since then, apparently a little of Newt's (mostly) controlled chaos had rubbed off on him. He came up with a set of papers. "Deployment!"

"Deployment?" Newt echoed.

"Of Jaegers. Deploying them into combat via Jumphawks takes too much time. The amount of damage a Kaiju can inflict before…" Gottlieb seized another set of papers. These were blackened and curled around the edges. "Ah! Here! I think I've found a solution."

Newt looked over the notes, starting to chuckle before he'd gotten past the first page. "Rocket thrusters? There's no fuel in the world with that kind of boost-to-mass ratio."

"From *this* world, no," Gottlieb said. When Newt looked up, he saw Gottlieb was holding a vial of blue liquid.

"Kaiju blood?" Newt said. He didn't like seeing it even in a lab setting. The stuff was dangerous...

"Exactly!" Gottlieb cried. "I've discovered it's highly reactive when combined with rare earth elements—cerium, lanthanum, gadolinium—"

"Dude, you can't be fooling around with this stuff," Newt said. "You're going to blow yourself up." He took another look at the notes. "Look at these! You already did, didn't you? You done went and blew yourself up."

"I just need to balance the equation," Gottlieb went on, completely unconcerned. "No one knows more about Kaiju morphology than you. If you could just take a look—"

"Buddy, it doesn't matter. Once my boss's Drones are approved, deployment time'll be a non-issue. Within a year we'll have Drones *everywhere*."

"So you won't help me?" Gottlieb was quietly hurt. Proud but also wounded. Newt wavered. He and Gottlieb had been a great team... but now there were other factors involved.

Newt's watch beeped. He glanced down at it and saw it was time to get to the demonstration of Shao's new Drone Jaegers. "Sorry," he said. "Duty calls. Been nice catching up."

"Newton?" Something in Gottlieb's tone stopped Newt before he got to the door. He turned and saw Gottlieb looking sad and haunted. "I—I still have nightmares. About what we saw. When we Drifted with that disgusting Kaiju brain."

"Yeah," Newt said. He understood. "But sure was a hell of a rush, wasn't it?" He'd been working apart from Gottlieb since right after the close of the Breach, and pursuing some of his own side projects. That made it easy to forget how close they had once been. They were bound in a way by that shared experience, even though judging from Gottlieb's mood they had processed it in very different ways.

"No one knows what it felt like. To be in its mind. Except *us*. You and I. *Together*."

Newt felt Gottlieb's plea for... what? Support of some kind? What appeal was he making? Newt didn't know how to help him, but he did want to. Gottlieb was kind of a hopeless doofus, but they had saved the world together.

He stood there trying to figure out how to resolve his conflicted feelings, and Liwen's Security Chief Kang popped into the lab, saving Newt from the old tug of loyalty he didn't really want to feel anymore. "Dr. Geiszler," he said in Mandarin. "Time to go."

He hustled down the corridor that led out of the K-Science wing toward the War Room, catching up with Shao and the rest of her entourage. "You and Dr. Gottlieb were close, weren't you? During the war." She spoke Mandarin, and Newt tried to tell her they'd shared a lab, but apparently his attempt didn't pass muster.

"English," she snapped, still in Mandarin. "Your Mandarin makes you sound like an idiot."

"Um, yes," Newt said. He didn't think he sounded like an idiot, but she was the boss and he wasn't going to cross her—at least not right now. "We shared a lab."

"He was your friend?"

Newt hesitated over this. He'd never had many friends, had always preferred the company of instruments and diagrams to people... but his past with Hermann... "Yeah," Newt said. "He was."

They were at the edge of the Shatterdome's Jaeger bays, cutting across toward the War Room. Groups of Rangers, cadets, and J-Tech mechanics crisscrossed the floor. Shao seemed to be framing another question about Newt and Hermann, but before she could ask it, one of the teenage cadets saw them and broke away from her group. "Miss Shao?" She was bright-eyed and breathless, starstruck by seeing the great Shao Liwen in person. "I just wanted to say—everything you've—I made my own Jaeger, a—a small one, with a lot of parts from Shao Industries—"

Shao looked at Newt. "They let children in here?"

"I think she's a cadet."

"I'm going to be a Jaeger pilot, ma'am," the girl said. Her name tag said NAMANI.

Shao switched to English, something she almost never did. "Congratulations," she said, and added a smile. She didn't have a lot of practice smiling, and it didn't look natural at all. But the cadet didn't seem to care. She basked in Shao's attention until Shao added, still in English, "Please move out of the way."

Crestfallen, the girl stepped aside, and Shao led the group on. Newt threw the girl an apologetic glance, but she wasn't looking at him. He hustled to keep pace with Shao. "The smile was good, but next time maybe throw in a little chit chat," he suggested. "Or just the chit—"

In Mandarin again, she asked, "What were you and Dr. Gottlieb talking about?" as though the encounter with the cadet had never happened.

"Nothing. Just some nutty idea he has about thruster pods—"

"I can't afford a misstep before Secretary General Mori makes her recommendation at the Council Summit," she said, speaking so fast Newt could barely keep up. "No more contact with Dr. Gottlieb until after the vote."

An hour ago, Newt would have been glad to avoid contact with Hermann, but seeing him had brought back some fond old memories of the time they'd spent crusading together. Also, Newt didn't like being told what to do, and Shao's imperious attitude toward him made him want to defend Hermann all the more. "But he's harmless—"

She stopped, pivoted to face him, and unleashed a torrent of Mandarin that Newt couldn't parse. "Uh... could you say that again?" he asked. "About eighty percent slower?"

In English, enunciating slowly and carefully, Shao said, "I said don't make me question your loyalty."

"No," Newt said, trying to keep his tone light. Shao knew him as agreeable, glib Dr. Geiszler. He didn't want the hassles that would come if she thought he was going to start challenging her. "No question. We barely ever talk anyway."

"Then it won't be a problem," she said. "And work on your Mandarin. I don't like to repeat myself, in any language."

# 8

## JAEGERWATCH—
## AN OPEN LETTER TO MAKO MORI

We are trying to wrap our heads around this Drone thing, Madam Secretary General, and we have to say it's not easy. Would Gipsy Danger still be Gipsy Danger if she didn't have the stories of the Becket brothers tied up in her history? Would Hong Kong Harbor have memorials to Crimson Typhoon if the Wei triplets had not piloted her, or Cherno Alpha if the Kaidanovskys had not died inside? You know the answer. Nobody ever built a monument to a machine. And maybe that's all right. Maybe it's time we stopped building memorials. The Kaiju War is over, isn't it? There are still great things for Jaegers to do—remember when November Ajax stopped a highway overpass from falling on the commuter train in Los Angeles?—but maybe those things could be just as well done by machines.

And maybe not. Rangers were heroes, and we need heroes. People need heroes. And only people can be heroes.

So if you're listening, Mako Mori, remember that. Machines can be spectacular, and they can do great things… but they can't be heroes.

In the War Room, Shao Liwen stood before a massive hologram of a Drone Jaeger. The prototype was designed along the lines of other Jaegers, because it was more efficient to repurpose the existing structural technologies than completely redesign the Drone Jaeger's body. The primary visual difference from human-piloted Jaegers was in the structure of the Drone's head. There was no need to dedicate space for a Drift cradle or human life-support systems, so the Drone's head was smaller and set lower between the shoulders. Where a human-piloted Jaeger typically had a window so the pilots could visually supplement their input from sensors and instruments, the Drone had a single red light that gave it the appearance of a mechanical Cyclops. The "eye" was in fact a multi-spectrum visual and motion sensor, located in the Drone's "face" as a concession to human nature. Shao could have put the sensor anywhere, but she knew the Drones would be less likely to frighten ordinary people if they retained some semblance of a human aspect.

Arrayed around Shao was a mixed group of Rangers and J-Tech personnel. They looked on skeptically, some with outright hostility visible on their faces. Mixed in among them were Secretary General Mako Mori, Hermann Gottlieb, and security staffers.

Shao had chosen Dr. Geiszler and Burke to stand with her for the presentation. They would be able to answer the questions that were sure to arise, and Burke had the added clout of being a former Ranger, not to mention Nate's former copilot, who left the PPDC to take a job in the private sector.

She had already introduced the mechanical specifics of the Drones, and was now moving on to the real paradigm-shifting innovation at the heart of the project. "The system I designed processes commands through a quantum data core," she said, as a holographic diagram of the core appeared. "Thus relieving the neural load. This means that a single pilot can operate the Drone via remote link from anywhere in the world. As soon as the Council approves deployment, the days of struggling to find and train Drift-compatible pilots will be a thing of the past."

Shao had anticipated questions at this point, and planned a pause so Burke and Dr. Geiszler could address or deflect them. Her anticipation proved accurate, as dissatisfied murmurs immediately swept through the room at the suggestion that the PPDC would no longer need Drift-compatible Rangers. The Council in Sydney, composed of delegates from all PPDC member states, would make the final decision on Drone deployment, but Shao knew implementation of the plan would be smoother if she could pre-emptively address concerns coming from individual groups of Rangers.

Ranger Lambert spoke up on behalf of his colleagues, who seemed particularly incensed by the Drone presentation. Again, Shao had expected this, and she had rehearsed answers to a number of different possible questions. "You think a bunch of desk jockeys playing with their joysticks can stop a Kaiju attack?" Lambert asked, scorn clear in his tone.

"Not only can they stop it, they can do so without putting pilots at unnecessary risk, Nate," Burke answered.

"Contrary to what you may have heard," Shao added, "we're not here to shut you down." She made an effort to sound diplomatic and collegial, even though neither of those qualities came naturally to her. She didn't necessarily need the Rangers' support to push the Drone program through PPDC approvals, but the less friction accompanied the process, the better.

"Cooperation between our programs has never been more vital," Burke added. "If there are any questions...?"

The room exploded in an uproar of questions from both Rangers and techs. None of them believed for a single moment that Shao had any intention of working with them. The whole point of the Drone program was to get them out of their Drift cradles and behind desks, and they were not going to go quietly. "We don't want your damn Drones!" shouted a Ranger by the name of Huang. "We're pilots, not a bunch of overpaid office workers!"

Jake felt exactly the same way, but rather than join the shouting, he turned and walked out of the room. He needed to calm himself down before he said something he regretted. This was one of the times when having the surname Pentecost made him self-conscious. Whatever he said would carry more weight with the Rangers because of his father, despite the fact that many Rangers still carried a grudge against Jake for getting kicked out of the Ranger program back when he was barely out of his teens.

He climbed a steel staircase toward a catwalk that ringed one of the outer levels of the Jaeger bay. The magnificent machines stood at attention, waiting for the next time they would be needed to defend humanity... but if Shao Liwen had her way, that moment would never come.

Behind him, he heard other footsteps on the catwalk. Mako came up next to him. "That was pretty slick," he said. "How long before they shut all this down and I can go home?"

"I don't trust the Drone tech," Mako said. "Not yet, at least."

"Looked dialed-in to me," Jake said.

"Remote systems can be hacked or compromised."

Interesting, Jake thought. She had been a Ranger. She understood. "Well, you're the key vote, right? Your decision, so there you go."

"I wish I could just go ahead and approve them. If we'd

had Drones back in the war, maybe Dad would still be alive." She gazed out over the expanse of the Jaeger bay, in the direction of Gipsy Avenger. Jake could see her thinking back to Gipsy's predecessor. "And Raleigh," she added quietly.

Jake wasn't following this. "What did that have to do with the war? News said it was cancer." He saw the sorrow on her face, and realized he couldn't understand what it was like for her to have lost a partner. Someone she'd fought with, Drifted with...

"You all right?" he asked.

She nodded. "Everything about the other side of the Breach is still classified," she said, turning back to Jake's first question regarding Raleigh's death. "There's a kind of radiation, in the Anteverse. We didn't know how bad it was until it was too late." She paused, and Jake realized she might be trying to tell him something. She'd been down there, on the edge of the Anteverse, with Raleigh...

"Are you all right?" he asked again, tensing as his mind ran over all the awful possibilities.

She nodded. "Raleigh ejected me. I got sick and couldn't pilot anymore, but I'm fine. He got the worst of it."

Jake knew that part of the story, about Raleigh ejecting Mako and then priming Gipsy Danger's reactor to detonate before ejecting himself. But he hadn't known about the Anteverse radiation. The Pan Pacific Defense Corps kept a lot of secrets, even from its Rangers.

"I'm sorry," he said. "I didn't know."

"We can't change the past." She was still looking at the Jaegers. "But the future is ours to make. A lot of people want to see the Drones deployed. Nearly half the Council is backing Liwen. They aren't going to like my decision."

"How about I go with you for some moral support?" Jake asked, brother to sister. "Never been to Sydney. Hear it's great."

"I'm glad you offered," she said with a smile. "Because I've already requested Gipsy Avenger for Honor Guard at the Council Summit."

"Whoa, hold up. Honor Guard? That's not what I meant." Jake had been thinking more along the lines of hanging around backstage before Mako headed out onto the summit dais, so he could crack jokes and let her know that no matter what happened someone was on her side. But the Jaeger Honor Guard?

"What about my moral support?" she needled him.

"Gipsy is Lambert's ride." That was the real problem. How was Mako going to justify that to Nate? The shouts of nepotism would echo all the way to Sydney before they ever got there.

"His copilot works for Liwen now. He needs a new one," she said. Then she let him figure out the rest… which didn't take him long.

She hadn't followed him up here to try to make him feel better about the possibility of the Drones kicking all the Rangers out of their jobs. She was focused on the here and now, maximizing the abilities of the Rangers she had… and trying to keep Jake from bolting again now that she had just gotten him back in the program. "One that you already know is Drift-compatible, right," he said. He couldn't help but laugh. "I see what you're trying to do, putting me back in a live rig."

Her smile returned. "I have no idea what you're talking about."

"All right, sis. I got your back." A thought occurred to him. "But I want to be there when you tell him. He's gonna be so pissed, he'll make that dumb face like…" He imitated Lambert's rigid, Ranger tough-guy pissed-off expression. Tight jaw, frown, crease between the eyes. Mako laughed.

On that moment, Jake headed off. If he had to be in

Sydney tomorrow, he had a lot of preparation to do.

Watching him go, Mako's smile faded.

# 9

THIS IS LYLE SCALABRINI, NEW SOUTH WALES
Radio. I'm on the ground in the plaza outside the
Pan Pacific Defense Corps Council Building, and the
atmosphere is pretty intense. Police are four ranks thick
around the long half-circle driveway coming off the street
up to the front of the building, in full riot gear, holding
back a crowd that must be in the tens of thousands.
Everywhere you look there are banners. Over on the far
side of the driveway from where I am, a pocket of Kaiju
cultists have staked out a spot. People who served in
the Kaiju War, and survivors' groups, have surrounded
them and there's some... well, let's just say I can't get too
close or else you'll have to bleep out most of the audio.
The cult group is largely ignoring everyone else. They're
praying, and they've brought with them some Kaiju
bones out of which they've made a sort of shrine, right
on the sidewalk close to the eastern end of the driveway.
I'm a little too far away to hear what they're saying, but it
certainly looks like in the midst of all this chaos, they're
holding a prayer service. I'm going to try to get a little
closer and find out exactly what their reasons are for

*being here, because it doesn't seem like they'd have any*
*reason to care one way or another whether Jaegers are*
*piloted remotely or not. More in a moment, the police are*
*starting to move us out of the—*

Like most of the other great cities ringing the coasts of the
Pacific Ocean, Sydney had been hit hard during the Kaiju
War. But unlike, say, Southern California, Sydney had been
largely rebuilt because it was the home of the Pan Pacific
Defense Corps Council. Individual Marshals and other
high-ranking officers exercised control over what their
Shatterdomes did, and how their resources were deployed
in their specified coastal territories. Here in Sydney, the
entire organization chose its directions and presented
a unified front to the world. The Council headquarters
loomed, gleaming and new, at the center of the city, visible
from anywhere in the harbor. Massive anti-Kaiju cannon
emplacements ringed the harbor and the outer coastline,
from Middle Head all the way into Potts Point, in the
shadow of the rebuilt harbor bridges. A tighter ring of
cannons protected the Council Building complex itself.
Sydney was a symbolic place now, the nerve center of the
PPDC and the Jaeger defense forces—and more broadly,
the symbol of international cooperation that had defeated
the Kaiju invaders and thrown the Precursors back into
their Anteverse.

Around the Council Building, the streets were swarmed
with crowds of demonstrators and curious onlookers.
Every group on Planet Earth, from Jaeger fan clubs to the
Kaiju-worshipping cults, had staked out a spot in the plaza
surrounding the Council Building. A cluster of Kaiju-
worshipping monks, solemn and imposing in their robes,
stood praying in the center of a circle formed by other

Kaiju zealots. They shouted and waved signs, preaching the cult gospel that the Kaiju had been sent by God to purge humanity of its sins.

Jake caught all this on a feed from inside Gipsy Avenger as a pair of Jumphawks ferried them across the harbor toward the Council Building. Scattered fights were breaking out between knots of demonstrators, and PPDC security had its hands full keeping a lid on the situation.

As Gipsy Avenger came into view, many of the hostile demonstrators stopped tangling with each other and turned their attention to the Jaeger. Fans cheered and chanted slogans. Some of them tried to rip signs out of the hands of the Kaiju worshippers, and security forces tried to keep them apart without escalating the situation. It was a powder keg, waiting for someone to really lose his temper and light the fuse.

The Kaiju cults had gotten a lot bigger since the beginning of the Kaiju War. Their doctrine was that any resistance to the Kaiju was an affront to God, and therefore the Pan Pacific Defense Corps was an abomination. Crazy times bred crazy people, was Jake's opinion on the topic. Anyone who thought the Kaiju were divine had a real strange idea about God. He'd heard all the sermons—you couldn't avoid them in any of the coastal ruins. The cults sent preachers out looking for converts among the poor and displaced, and sometimes it seemed like they were on every street corner in California. You could argue with them, reason with them, it didn't matter. The best thing to do was ignore them.

And in any case, Jake had more important things on his mind right now. He was in a Drift cradle for the first time in years, paired with Nate Lambert, who radiated hostility. In the internal feed from the LOCCENT back in the Moyulan Shatterdome, Marshal Quan kept checking with techs to make sure he and Lambert were maintaining a steady neural handshake. It didn't feel all that steady to Jake, but it was holding. They were both trying to be professional about a situation that neither of them liked.

"All you have to do is stand there and look pretty," Quan said over the comm. "Stay focused and try not to fall over."

"Roger that, sir," Lambert said—but Jake could hear him thinking that they would be lucky if Jake didn't screw things up. That made Jake even more nervous than he already was at being dropped into a Jaeger without any prep after years of trying to forget he'd ever been a Ranger.

"Go for drop in three… two… one… drop!" Quan's command echoed in their ears, and the Jumphawks released the cables holding Gipsy Avenger. The Jaeger dropped from an altitude of less than two hundred feet, landing with a thunderous boom on the reinforced drop pad near the Council Building. The shockwave of the impact raised a cloud of dust that billowed over the crowd—and helped obscure the fact that Gipsy nearly lost her balance on landing.

In the Conn-Pod, Lambert shot Jake a look. Jake tried to play it off. "It's all coming back. Relax."

The closer Kaiju worshippers, outraged at the presence of a Jaeger, started throwing bottles and trash at Gipsy's legs. PPDC security waded in and started making arrests as the situation threatened to get out of hand.

"Got some fans, huh?" Jake commented.

"Kaiju nuts are always stirring it up," Lambert said dismissively. "And hey—we're in each other's heads, so I'd appreciate it if you'd stop thinking about Jules. Not gonna happen."

"How about you stop thinking about kicking my ass," Jake shot back. "Not gonna happen either."

Mostly Jake was thinking about handling the Jaeger gear that had changed and updated since his last time in a Conn-Pod. Back then, they had stood on an actual floor, with their drivesuit boots locked into fixtures and physical instrument podiums in front of them.

But now the Conn-Pod and the operating system were largely holographic and virtual. Each Ranger locked boot soles onto a glowing rectangle on the floor. Then, once the Jaeger's operating AI had measured their initial location so it could interpret motions, the floor dropped away, leaving them suspended in a maglev field that also held the Drift cradles. Every motion within the field accompanied by a direct thought from the Ranger caused an immediate response, with less lag and more powerful signal transmissions than previous versions of Jaeger operating systems had allowed. It was a more immersive experience, that much was certain. Once a Ranger's legs were locked into the maglev harness instead of the old-fashioned rigs he'd trained on, it was easy to feel like you were actually moving as the giant machine. That difference was on Jake's mind, and because of the Drift, it was on Lambert's, too.

Jake could feel Nate's anger in the Drift, and behind it Nate's hurt feelings he tried to hide. There weren't any secrets in the Drift, though. Part of the reason Nate gave Jake such a hard time was that he knew what lay behind Jake's actions—which meant he knew that Jake knew he'd let himself down, let all of them down, let his father down...

Both of them refocused their attention when a signal pinged on Gipsy Avenger's HUD. An incoming helicopter. The HUD readout identified it as belonging to the PPDC and displayed the name of the single passenger: MAKO MORI, SECRETARY GENERAL, PPDC SECURITY COUNCIL.

* * *

Inside the helicopter, Mako looked up from the Kaiju sketch on her data pad. She had Kaiju on her mind, for reasons she hadn't been able to share with Jake, but when she looked up to see Gipsy Avenger towering over the gathered crowds, she smiled. It was good to know Jake was there. After his wandering years, he was back where he belonged—in the Conn-Pod of a Jaeger. She was also glad because the Jaeger program faced a threat that few in the organization knew about, and with Jake around, Mako knew she had an ally in what might be a dangerous time.

At the grand front entrance of the Council Building, PPDC security held back the crowd to permit the approach of a limousine. It rolled to a stop and Shao Liwen climbed out, followed by Chief Kang and the rest of her security detail. The crowd got even more frenzied as people caught sight of her. She had fervent fans screaming her name and waving for autographs, jostling for position with angry anti-PPDC protesters and Kaiju-cult zealots who rained abuse on her. She ignored all of them, walking with calm purpose toward the entrance. On this day she had only one focus: operationalizing the Drone program. Years of work had prepared her for this day, and nothing was going to stop her now that she had gotten so close to her goal.

Inside Gipsy Avenger's Conn-Pod, Jake and Lambert perked up as a massive signal pinged on Gipsy's HUD. "Gipsy to Command," Lambert said. "You reading this?"

The signal was the size of a small cargo ship, but moving in a way that no ship could. Jake heard one of the LOCCENT techs say something in Mandarin to Quan, who relayed it to them in English. "Gipsy, this is Command. Be advised we have an unregistered Jaeger, no call sign designation."

An unregistered Jaeger? These were extremely rare, but a moment later, they got a visual contact that confirmed their suspicions. The Jaeger exploded up out of the harbor, landing in a crouch near the waterfront avenue that passed in front of the Council Building. The crowd gawked in amazement, most of them too stunned to flee. Jake and Lambert scanned the unidentified Jaeger. It was sleek, nimble, matte black with vivid orange lights. The HUD picked out several spots on the Jaeger's armor that were likely weapon mounts, but they couldn't tell any specifics about its armaments.

"What is that?" Jake asked. "Is that one of ours?"

Lambert toggled Gipsy Avenger's loudspeakers. "Pilots of unregistered Jaeger, power down and exit your Conn-Pod."

The Jaeger didn't respond. It stood up straighter and looked around, surveying the surrounding area.

Lambert issued a second order, per PPDC procedure. "I repeat: Power down and exit your Conn-Pod immediately—"

The Jaeger's response was a barrage of plasma missiles.

# 10

**From**: Mako
**To**: Jake Pentecost
<no subject>
<attachment: 899h25Gss24.jpg>

TRANSMITTING...

TRANSMISSION INTERRUPTED
RETRY? Y/N

Y

TRANSMITTING...

TRANSMISSION INTERRUPTED
RETRY? Y/N

Y

Marshal Quan's voice cut through the chatter coming from the LOCCENT. "Missiles fired! Multiple ordnance inbound!"

The first salvo of missiles annihilated the anti-Kaiju cannons. Jake just had time to think that the Jaeger had been pausing to target each of them, planning how it was going to engage, when a tight following barrage slammed into Gipsy Avenger. Other missiles streaked past and the facade of the PPDC Council Building disappeared in a cluster of explosions.

Multiple impacts rocked Gipsy Avenger. Alarms wailed, some inside the Conn-Pod and some coming through the comms from the LOCCENT. Jake fought a rising sensation of panic. He was a simulation cowboy, unbeatable in VR exercises... but he had never been in combat. Time seemed to slow around him, and his sense of his surroundings started to fade. There were voices in his head. Lambert was shouting, but the voice that penetrated into Jake's struggling mind was Stacker Pentecost's. *You don't belong in a Jaeger,* he said. Jake felt himself falling back into his memories, the rabbit hole that was an ever-present danger in the Drift.

"Jake! Stay connected! Jake!" Lambert's voice. But Jake was already gone. Gipsy Avenger staggered and started to lose her balance as he fell back into the past, inexorably drawn by the sound of his father's voice.

"Jake!" Lambert was shouting. Alarms wailed as another volley of plasma missiles nearly knocked Gipsy Avenger off her feet. "Pentecost!"

Jake snapped out of the memory, climbing up out of the rabbit hole with the tears of his fifteen-year-old self still hot on his face. Still disoriented, he tried to get a handle on what was going on. "What... what do we do?"

"Stay focused. Follow my lead and—look out!"

A house-sized piece of the Council Building, destabilized by missile impacts, toppled off the front toward the crowd below. Trapped by the crush of people trying to get away from the hostile Jaeger, the people in its path could do nothing but scream.

In the Conn-Pod, Lambert shot out one hand.

Gipsy Avenger caught the chunk scant feet above the heads of the crowd. Just outside the shadow of Gipsy's arm, Chief Kang and the security detail hustled Shao Liwen back into the limousine. It gunned its engine, nosing through the crowd toward the vacant spaces near the street.

More missiles crashed into Gipsy Avenger. They weren't penetrating her armor yet, but external systems were taking damage, and the kinetic impacts kept Gipsy off balance.

"We're losing power!" Jake shouted, as alerts flashed across the system's monitoring screen. The missiles were doing damage even if they weren't getting through Gipsy's armor.

"Rerouting systems," Lambert said. He worked the holo screen on his side of the cradle.

"Jake!" Mako's voice was splintered by static. "That Jaeger's power reading is the same as—!"

In a flare of white noise, her voice cut out. Jake saw readings on the monitors that told him the Jaeger was jamming comms. Someone had planned this attack for this moment, right when Shao was about to announce the end of piloted Jaegers. Right when she and all the PPDC administrators would be in one place.

Jake wondered who. Kaiju nuts? Some terrorist group that had gotten hold of Jaeger tech? How could that have happened?

He looked in the direction of Mako's helicopter, and in his field of view saw the strange Jaeger raising and powering up what looked like a particle cannon... aimed at the helicopter.

"Nate," he said, his voice high and tight with fear.

Thanks to the Drift, Nate understood instantly. "Power's up!" he said—and in the next instant, Jake threw the chunk of the Council Building across the plaza at the hostile Jaeger.

Debris showered down over the crowd as the multi-ton chunk of concrete and steel smashed into the hostile Jaeger, knocking it off balance and ruining its aim at Mako's chopper.

Jake and Lambert sprang forward in the cradle, and Gipsy Avenger charged toward the Jaeger, barreling into it and trying to grapple. But the black Jaeger was quicker than they had expected. It shook Gipsy off and raked her armor with claws.

Gipsy reeled back into a building, shattering its front walls and windows. She planted her feet, narrowly avoiding the crowds of fleeing people in the street below. That moment of inattention to the hostile Jaeger cost them. It caught Gipsy Avenger by one leg and smashed her into another building, driving her down to the street in a pile of collapsing rubble.

Then the black Jaeger sprang onto Gipsy and sank claws into the armor around the Conn-Pod, trying to rip her head off.

Inside the Conn-Pod, Jake wrestled against the Jaeger's grip. Lambert punched commands into the holo pad projected from the forearm of his drivesuit. Gipsy Avenger's chain sword shot out from her forearm, forcing the hostile Jaeger to let go. Pivoting as she got to her feet, Gipsy swung, but the other Jaeger was too fast—much faster than any other Jaeger they'd ever seen. It dodged the sword stroke and kicked Gipsy into another building. The street was treacherous footing now, with collapsed facades and destroyed cars littering the pavement.

Answering Gipsy Avenger's chain sword, the other Jaeger flexed its arms and twin plasma weapons sprang from its forearm mounts. At first Jake thought they were swords, but then he saw the edges start to spin. Chainsaws. It had plasma chainsaws.

They barely got their own chain sword up to block the first strikes, in a shower of sparks and discharged plasma. Arcs of energy shattered nearby windows and scorched buildings. The hostile Jaeger cut loose with a wild swing that nearly split an office tower down the middle from roof to atrium.

Gipsy stepped back, looking for another opening to attack, but both Jake and Lambert knew they were up against an opponent that was faster than they were. If they went in recklessly, they were going to end up in pieces.

The other Jaeger dropped into a fighting posture and came at them again.

Mako's pilot was turning the chopper in wide circles, looking for a safe place to land. "We need to land!" he shouted.

"No!" Mako wasn't going to leave Jake alone to fight this thing. Gipsy Avenger was clearly overmatched—even if she knew Jake and Lambert would never admit that. They would go down fighting. "We have to help them! Target that Jaeger!"

The pilot complied, but she could see on his face he didn't think it was a good idea. "Target locked," he said.

Mako's eyes narrowed. This was her brother's life on the line. "Fire!"

* * *

Jake and Lambert were pushed to the limit of their abilities countering the foreign Jaeger's attacks. It was faster than any Jaeger they had ever seen, and so quick on its feet that they felt like they were in an old Mark I trying to tackle a Mark V. Jake was getting into the rhythm of operating Gipsy Avenger again, after so many years, and he felt his Drift connection with Nate getting more solid as they worked together—but it wasn't enough. The hostile Jaeger scored hits on Gipsy's torso and shoulders. If they couldn't find a way to anticipate its technique, sooner or later it would land a fatal blow with the plasma chainsaws.

Pressed back by a fresh assault, Gipsy sidestepped to avoid a crowd of people trapped by a cascade of rubble from a nearby office building. The other Jaeger took advantage, rearing up for a downward stroke before Jake and Lambert could get Gipsy's chain sword up.

But as the plasma weapon arced down, a barrage of missiles from Mako's helicopter detonated on the hostile Jaeger's arm and head, deflecting its stroke. Missing Gipsy Avenger by scant feet, the plasma saw chewed through several floors of another building. It jammed against something in the building's interior, and the Rangers saw their chance.

Gipsy Avenger pounced, using the time Mako had bought them to power up another of Gipsy Avenger's combat abilities. The Jaeger's right arm had a force-multiplying rocket piston assembly designed to accelerate the velocity of a thrown punch. The rockets fired at the moment before impact, turning an ordinary punch into a supersonic impact that in testing had destroyed older model dummy Jaegers with a single blow.

This opponent was tougher than a practice dummy, though. The punch connected with an echoing boom that blew out nearby windows and sent the hostile Jaeger flying down the broad avenue. It slowed itself down by thrusting the plasma saws out to either side, using them to drag itself to a halt as they gouged through several blocks of office towers. Immediately it had arrested its slide, the other Jaeger unleashed a fresh missile salvo. Some of the missiles hit Gipsy Avenger, but most streaked by and exploded across a large expanse of Sydney's downtown. Civilians who thought they were safely away from the battle fled anew as the missiles collapsed buildings and parking structures.

One of the missiles hit high on a skyscraper near Mako's helicopter. The blast wave jolted the chopper, cracking its fuselage windows and sending it into a crazed spiral. Electrical fires sparked to life in the cockpit.

Jake saw Mako's helicopter dropping, its tail spinning around as it lost control. "She's going down! We need to move!"

Lambert was right with him. "Activating Gravity Sling!" he called back.

Gipsy Avenger's right hand reconfigured itself into a force-projecting assembly that could manipulate gravity in its limited cone. The Gravity Sling swept up a cascade of falling cars from a collapsing parking garage, and whipped them in a single mass at the hostile Jaeger. The force of the impact punched it over backward into an uncontrolled tumble.

Before it had even hit the ground, Jake and Lambert had Gipsy sprinting across the distance between them and Mako's spiraling helicopter. Jake tried to get the gravity sling to redeploy and catch the chopper, but it wasn't responding after its initial use. "Come on!" he shouted, straining in the Drift cradle, pushing Gipsy Avenger to maximum speed.

He and Lambert leaned forward as one, and Gipsy Avenger dove forward, covering hundreds of yards in the air, hand outstretched to catch the falling helicopter.

Through the Conn-Pod window, Jake saw Mako, frantically tapping something into her data pad. She looked up at their approach, putting a hand flat on the inside of her window as the helicopter scraped off Gipsy Avenger's fingertips. Jake was screaming, maybe just in his mind, as the chopper spun down at an angle and smashed into the pavement below. It tumbled, shedding broken rotors and pieces of its fuselage, crashing off parked cars and finally rolling to a halt in a smoking ruin.

A moment later Gipsy Avenger smashed down from her desperate leap, the impact bouncing debris up into the air and shattering nearby windows. Glass was still showering down as Jake disengaged himself from the Drift cradle and threw open the hatch on the side of Gipsy Avenger's head.

"Jake, wait! Jake!" Lambert called after him. But in that moment, Jake didn't care about the hostile Jaeger, or Sydney, or the PPDC. All he cared about was his sister. He ripped off his helmet and sprinted the stretched-out length of Gipsy Avenger toward the wreckage of the helicopter. He knew what he was going to find. He'd seen the impact, and he knew no human being could have survived it. But he wasn't going to believe it until he called for his sister and she did not answer.

Far behind him, the rogue Jaeger started to approach Gipsy Avenger… then it paused. Coming in from the north, a formation of Jumphawks was bringing three Jaeger reinforcements. The Jaeger watched them, seeming to assess its odds. Then it turned around, moving fast and low back toward the harbor. By the time the Jumphawks were close enough to drop the reinforcements, it was gone beneath the waters.

# 1 1

We who have seen the divine truth celebrate this glorious strike against the heretics of the Pan Pacific Defense Corps and their mechanical forces of darkness. The would-be dictators of the PPDC Council have paid the ultimate price for their heresy, and the power of the Anteverse is on the rise. Sydney chose its fate, failing to learn the lesson of Mutavore when it consented to be the site of the Council citadel.

Our forces have struck a decisive blow against the unbelievers. We rejoice in the destruction of those who would hide the true nature of God and rebel against the Kaiju who are its truest evidence.

We will continue our crusade against the forces of blind humanist arrogance. We call on all humanity to repent of its sins, acknowledge the divine nature of the Kaiju messengers of God, and humbly pray that the Breach will open again, showing us the way to Paradise.

In the name of God and His Kaiju messengers,

We Who Have Seen

Jake had been back at Moyulan for less than an hour, after debriefing on the flight and then sitting through a short after-action follow-up session with Marshal Quan. Then they had let him go, sensing that he needed some time to grapple with his personal loss before he would be able to help them figure out where Obsidian Fury, the rogue Jaeger, had come from... and who might have created it.

He had wandered through the halls, not meeting anyone's eyes, until he found himself in the so-called Hall of Heroes. A plaque on the wall read IN HONOR OF THOSE WHO GAVE THEIR LIVES IN THE SERVICE OF THEIR WORLD. Beyond it, lining both sides of the corridor, were digital memorials to fallen Rangers. The Becket brothers, Yancy and Raleigh. Chuck Hansen. The Wei Tang triplets. Sasha and Aleksis Kaidanovsky.

Jake was standing in front of the memorial to his father. On the screen, Stacker Pentecost stood in full Marshal dress uniform, looking sternly out at his prodigal son, at last returned to his Ranger duties.

Just past Stacker Pentecost was a new memorial. Jake hadn't expected there to be one so quickly, but there it was: Mako Mori, Secretary General and former Ranger, in full uniform, beaming out from the screen next to her adoptive father. The floor near Mako's memorial was piled with flowers and candles, little tokens and handwritten testimonial notes. The whole Shatterdome mourned the loss of one of its own.

*I'm the only one left*, Jake thought. *The whole family is gone now except for me.* He stepped up to Mako's memorial screen and addressed her. "I'll hit 'em back for you, Mako."

Then he taped a photograph to the edge of the screen. It showed Stacker, improbably smiling, his arms draped around Jake and Mako when they were... Jake couldn't remember exactly. Young, anyway. Before Jake and his father had really started to butt heads. Before everything had gone wrong.

Now it was too late to ever set any of it right.

# 1 2

## PPDC SECRETARY GENERAL MORI KILLED IN ROGUE JAEGER ATTACK

### WIRE SERVICE REPORTS

Among the dead in today's rogue Jaeger assault on the meeting of the Pan Pacific Defense Corps Council was the PPDC Secretary General Mako Mori. Mori was en route to the meeting when her helicopter was downed by a missile from the rogue Jaeger, which has already acquired the moniker Obsidian Fury.

The PPDC did not immediately confirm Mori's death despite multiple sources corroborating the initial report.

Before becoming Secretary General, Mori was a Ranger who copiloted Gipsy Danger's final mission to close the Breach in 2025. Both she and Raleigh Becket, the other Ranger on that mission, survived, though Becket would later succumb

continued...

to a rare cancer. Mori's adoptive father, PPDC Marshal Stacker Pentecost, died during the mission. Her career as a Ranger was nearly ended before it began, due to Pentecost's opposition, but she persevered and rose to the top of the Corps before moving into her Council role.

She is survived by her brother, Jake Pentecost, formerly a PPDC Cadet who was last seen in the slums of Santa Monica, California. Attempts to locate him have been unsuccessful.

Someone was yelling behind one of the doors just down the hall, the sound muffled but unmistakably angry. Jake walked in that direction, remembering that cadet Drift training used to be located in this wing... and sure enough, the noise was coming from a door labeled DRIFT TRAINING – CADET LEVEL 1. What they used to call "Drifting for Dummies". More yelling came from inside.

Jake walked in and saw Amara sitting at a training rig. A computer voice said, "Neural connection failed." Amara threw a punch at a holo screen representing her Drift pattern, her fist passing through it as she noticed Jake. She dropped her hand and looked embarrassed, which made Jake feel embarrassed. Then after a prolonged pause Amara said, "So I'm not great with feelings, but sorry about your sister. Half-sister...?"

"Her parents died in the Onibaba attack," Jake said. "My dad took her in. She was my sister. My family."

Amara wasn't sure how to handle the emotional weight of what Jake was dropping on her. So she went with her tried-and-true strategy, making a joke out of it. "Better not let Ranger Lambert see you out of uniform. He'll take the stick out of his butt and beat you with it."

He couldn't help but smile. "Think I'm safe. It's wedged in there pretty tight."

Coming closer, Jake checked out the Drift rig Amara had been beating on. He couldn't help but grin when he saw that one side was wired to a tank containing a human brain, suspended in a tank of synthetic cerebrospinal fluid. On the base of the tank was a plaque Jake knew by heart. THIS IS SARAH. SHE DONATED HER MIND SO THAT YOU COULD TRAIN. TELL ME HER FAVORITE CANDY BAR.

"They're still using Sarah, huh?" Jake remembered the

hours he'd spent learning to Drift with her. It almost made him feel sentimental.

"I can't get her to Drift with me," Amara said, her voice part growl and part whine. "The other cadets have been training forever. I hate feeling like the slow kid."

"You gotta relax or you're just grinding gears," Jake said. It was a lesson he'd learned again that day—and that thought started to lift his mood. He could maybe do some good here, on a day that had been so terrible so far.

Leaning in, he punched a series of holo commands. Sarah retracted and a regular Drift rig appeared to take her place.

"Relax," Amara said, back to her normal sardonic self. "Got it, coach."

"Don't call me coach," Jake said.

"Sensei?"

Jake slid the practice helmet on. "Just clear your mind. Can't connect if you're running your mouth. You ready?"

Nervous but trying not to show it, Amara gave him a double thumbs-up.

"Let's see if we're Drift-compatible." Jake tapped in a fresh series of commands. The Drift rigs connected, and Jake felt the psychic rush of entering a Drift with another human mind. Amara felt it too, more powerfully than Jake did because she was so new to the experience. She gasped out loud and the two of them fell into the melding inter-cognitive non-space of the Drift, their memories jumbling and pouring over each other—

—*Amara as a young girl, chasing her brother across their back yard. They're laughing, and as they pass her parents they smile and lean into each other a little, feeling the simple joy of happy children and a life together—*

—*Amara on her bicycle, a birthday gift. She's just been to the store with her mother and as a reward for* good behavior she got noisemakers to put on the spokes. She pedals faster and faster, as the slapping sound of the noisemakers becomes a whir—

—Amara in the garage with her father. A car engine, partially disassembled, hangs from a block and tackle. He is showing her how the pistons work in the cylinders. On a workbench next to the block and tackle, the engine's head sits drying after they've just cleaned it. Once it's dry they'll set the head gasket and put it back on, and after that they're going to drop it into a car—

—Jake, eight years old, in his father's study. Stacker is at the Shatterdome inspecting the Jaegers. Jake picks up different things on his father's desk: a pen, a folder containing cross-section blueprints of machine parts he doesn't understand. Next he finds his father's Marshal hat, hanging on a coat rack behind the desk. He takes it off its peg and puts it on. It's way too big, covering his eyes. He tips it back so he can see, and catches a glimpse of his reflection in the study mirror. His father is an important man, doing important things. Jake knows this. One day he's going to be like his father. He salutes, feeling big and important himself—

—Jake in cadet training, jogging alongside Nate Lambert. They're both teenagers, filled with grand ideas and ambitions. At night after training they talk about saving the world, being the first line of defense if the Kaiju ever return. The run is punishing, mile after mile in the hills outside the Shatterdome, but if it meant getting into a Jaeger Jake would run to the moon and back. He is Stacker Pentecost's son. Nothing is going to stop him from being worthy of his father's example—

—In the combat training room, Mako comes at Jake with a staff. He tries to parry, but she slips his defense and her staff taps him along the ribs. She backs away and *shows him what she did, teaching him what to look for, little shifts in the opponent's weight or the direction of her gaze. They do it again. He comes closer, but she still gets through. They reset. She's telling him he can do this, but he's going to have to focus, block everything else out except this moment, only this moment—*

"Warning. Neural connection unstable."

Jake snapped out of the Drift fugue and saw the Drift connection meter on the training rig's monitor. The strength of their connection was dropping, close to the red zone where it would break apart and they would have to start all over again.

"Stay focused," he said, channeling what Mako had said to him so long ago.

He felt her renewed concentration, the revitalized clarity of her thoughts and her presence in the Drift. "That's it," he encouraged. "The stronger the connection, the better you fight."

She grinned, and Jake felt the flush of her happiness as she felt herself getting the hang of the Drift. "This isn't so hard," she said. "You lived in a mansion!?" Then a memory struck her and Jake felt her shock—

*—She's on the Santa Monica Pier. The sun is shining but a long shadow falls over part of the boardwalk. She holds a Polaroid picture in one hand. All around her people are running and screaming. There's a noise, like nothing she's ever heard, and a smell cuts through the seaside odors of salt and caramel corn and grill smoke—*

Don't let a memory pull you in! Let them pass through you! Amara!

*Jake's voice. She turned to see him, but instead—*

*—Her father, smiling, holding a Polaroid camera. Amara! Get in there! he says, pointing to where her mother and brother are already at the pier railing. They press*

close together and her father raises the camera. Click. The Polaroid photo slides out of the camera. Amara rushes to her father and takes it from the camera, then dashes back to the railing. She shakes the photo, enchanted as always by the way the picture slowly comes into being from the uniform gray of the exposed film. She starts to see the shapes of their bodies, then their faces, against the endless expanse of the Pacific Ocean.

Amara! You need to let it go—

—There is a sound like an earthquake, and a Kaiju, Insurrector, rears up from the water. Waves surge outward from it, battering the pier's piling. The pier shakes and the Kaiju crushes an entire section, which tumbles into the water. The air fills with screams and Amara freezes, Polaroid in her hand. Her mother and father and brother are on the other side of the shattered gap in the boards—

"Warning. Pilot exceeding neural limits."

—Amara!—

—It's Jake's voice but also her father's voice. He stretches a hand out across the gap. The Kaiju looms, its roars loud enough to shake the pier under her feet. You have to jump! Amara hesitates, terrified of the churning water below. Please, baby, jump to me! I'll catch you, I promise! Amara!

She runs and leaps with all the strength she can muster, but just as her feet leave the boards, the Kaiju's foot comes down, obliterating the pier in front of her and everyone on it. Her father is gone in that instant, and her mother and brother and hundreds of other people. Her hands grasp empty space and she plummets into the water. Eyes wide with shock, she registers the shadow of the Kaiju passing overhead, and feels the pull of its gargantuan step. The water churns around her and her chest begins to burn. She can swim a little, but only on the surface and only with a *wacky noodle. She kicks and flails her arms but the surface of the water still seems far away. Light ripples around her again but she's sinking down among the shattered timbers and the dark floating shapes she will not think about. Someone grabs her by the shoulder—*

"Amara! Come on! Hey!"

It's Jake. She's not in Santa Monica, she's not four years old. She's in the Drift training room of the Moyulan Shatterdome and she's fifteen, but it was all just right there, it was real…

"I was back home," she said. "I felt it…"

She was shaking, trying not to panic, and also feeling the first waves of embarrassment and shame at Jake seeing her so vulnerable. She looked up at him and saw the sympathy in his face. "I felt it too," he said. Was the Drift always like that? Did you have to let your partner all the way into your head, to see everything you'd ever been afraid of or sad about, every weakness behind the brave front you put up so the world wouldn't look too closely?

Jake's comm crackled. "Jake, it's Nate. You there?"

Still looking at Amara, Jake found his comm. "Yeah, I'm here."

"Meet me in the lab right away. Marshal wants to see us. And lose the robe."

"Check," Jake said, rolling his eyes for Amara's benefit. "No robe."

Already she was feeling better. She wasn't going to be afraid. She wasn't going to let that stop her. This was her chance.

"I want to try again," she said.

Jake's voice was surprisingly gentle. "That's enough for one night," he said.

"I thought you were going to help me," Amara said. She almost took a shot at him about wearing his dad's hat and saluting like a little boy soldier, but with an effort she stopped herself. As much as she hated to admit it, this wasn't a time to resort to her typical social strategy of acerbic bravado. So instead she went for a flippant remark that she hoped would tell Jake how much this meant to her. "I didn't even figure out what Sarah's favorite candy bar is."

"It's an Almond Joy," he said.

"That's not helping, that's *cheating*, you dick!"

On his way out the door, Jake couldn't help but smile.

When he was gone, Amara sat looking at the Drift rig again. Already she felt wrung out, but she wasn't going to give up now. After all, she'd already relived the worst moment of her life, and with Jake Pentecost right there in her head. What could the Drift do to her now?

She swiped at the holo terminal and Sarah the brain slid back into position. Amara shook her hair back and put the practice helmet back on. "Okay, Sarah," she said. "What else do you like besides candy...?"

She stabbed a final command and initiated the Drift again.

# 13

## EDITORIAL: I HATE IT WHEN I'M RIGHT

The dead are still being counted in Sydney, thanks to a still-unidentified rogue Jaeger attacking the Pan Pacific Defense Corps for reasons nobody seems to be able to figure out. Don't believe the Kaiju nuts who claimed the attack. Even if they could build a Jaeger, why would they attack when another Jaeger was there to fight back? Terrorists don't like an even fight. They would have sent that Jaeger out to massacre innocent people, or maybe gone after the Council at one of its meetings when Gipsy Avenger wasn't there to fight back. Right? It doesn't make any sense.

The real problem here is that the PPDC doesn't know where this Jaeger came from. You saw what happened. That thing kicked Gipsy Avenger's ass, and if it had wanted to, it could have put her down and then done whatever it wanted with the rest of Sydney. So why didn't it? What does that tell you?

I know what it tells me. Someone out there has tech that equals anything the PPDC can put into the field, and we don't know who they are.

That ought to scare you a lot more than a bunch of Kaiju nuts trying to claim something they obviously didn't do.

Jake asked Lambert what was up as they headed for the K-Science wing of the Shatterdome, but Nate didn't want to get into it. "Better you see for yourself," he said. "I'm going to let Gottlieb tell you."

When they got to the lab, Gottlieb was squinting at a holo screen that showed a fragmented swirl of color and numbers. Marshal Quan was there observing. He looked up and nodded as Jake and Lambert came in. Jake looked at the screen, unsure why Gottlieb would have wanted him to see it.

"What is it?" he asked.

"A message," Quan said. "From Mako."

This hit Jake hard, bringing back that last image he had of her, palm pressed against the chopper window as it slid away from Gipsy Avenger... He blinked and tried to keep his attention on the here and now.

"She was trying to send it from her copter right before she—" Gottlieb caught himself. He looked at Jake, unsure how to go on, then cleared his throat and stuck to the facts. "It's a data packet. High density."

"Obsidian Fury was jamming comms," Lambert said. "How'd her signal get through?"

"It didn't," Quan answered. "At least not intact."

"So it's gone," Jake said. What was he doing here then?

Gottlieb was still squinting, but now he was also running another program in parallel with the fractal swirl of data. "'Gone' is relative in the digital realm," he said as he tweaked the program he had up on the parallel screen. "By running a modified fractal algorithm, I might be able to reconstruct a few megabytes..."

Code unspooled on the screen. Gottlieb muttered to himself. Jake got restless, standing there watching a scientist wrestle with data while he wondered if there was going to be a last note from his sister... or not. He wished they'd figured out if they could salvage anything before they brought him here. Now that he knew the message existed, if Gottlieb couldn't unscramble it Jake would spend the rest of his life wondering what it said.

"*There*," Gottlieb said.

The image on the main holo screen coalesced and resolved. There was still static, but... "Is that... is that a Kaiju?" Jake wondered aloud.

It sure looked like one. Sketchy and unfamiliar, but definitely a Kaiju head. Gottlieb worked his terminal, running pattern recognition software on the image, sorting through known Kaiju. "No match against the database."

"Maybe it's a symbol?" Lambert suggested. "Something connected to the Kaiju cults?"

Now Gottlieb ran a search on all symbols, icons, and patterns related to the branch of Kaiju worshippers. "No match," Gottlieb said again.

"Keep looking," Marshal Quan ordered. "Whatever this is, it was important to her. I want to know why."

He left, presumably to brief PPDC intel on the existence of the drawing to see if that could help pin down the origin of the rogue Jaeger they were calling Obsidian Fury. Lambert was still looking at the drawing. "You don't stop fighting till the enemy's down," he said. Then, glancing over at Jake, he added, "If you're really a soldier."

With that, he followed Quan out. Jake couldn't take his eyes off the holo screen. This drawing was the last thing his sister had ever made. She had known what was going to happen to her, and she had wanted him to see it.

Why?

The question preoccupied him long after he'd left the lab. Mako had known she was going to die when the chopper was going down. She wouldn't have expected Gipsy Avenger to save her. Actually, trying to save her had been a stupid idea, Jake thought. It was never going to work, and it took Gipsy away from the main objective: stopping Obsidian Fury. The rogue Jaeger had slunk away into the ocean when it saw reinforcements coming, but Jake couldn't help but think he might have been able to find a hole in its technique if they'd been able to analyze it a little longer. Gipsy had taken a beating, that was for sure. Techs were working her over in the Shatterdome right now. But Jake had learned a long time ago that sometimes you had to take a punch to give one… so you had to make sure your punches counted when you got the chance to throw them.

Now he was spoiling for the chance to meet Obsidian Fury again and land that final punch.

But the truth was, they'd never seen anything like that speed and fluidity in a Jaeger. There had been other rogue Jaegers, sure. People built them once in a while, with discarded tech and cobbled-together armor. Jake could remember one in Serbia, and he thought he'd heard Lambert mention others in Uzbekistan and somewhere in South America, too. It was rare but not unheard of. Oh, and there was also Scrapper. It was a lot smaller than your average Jaeger, but Amara had good instinct. She had built something impressive, considering the obstacles.

Drifting with Amara had helped Jake understand her. A gearhead, into all things with engines as a kid—but was that her, or was that because her dad was into that stuff and she did whatever he did?

That was a question Jake had often asked himself about the Jaeger Corps. Had he gone into it because he believed in it, or because his father was Stacker Pentecost?

He didn't have the answer right then, and maybe it didn't matter. However you got yourself into a place in life, you were there, and had to deal with it as it was. Earlier that day, when he'd watched the Drone presentation, Jake had been ready to walk away from the Jaeger service, put the whole Pan Pacific Defense Corps in his rear-view mirror. Then he'd felt the tug of the Drift, and realized how much it meant to him to be in a Conn-Pod again… and then came the fight against Obsidian Fury, and Mako…

He wasn't going to leave now. He'd come close, but it wasn't going to happen. This was as close as Jake Pentecost would ever get to believing in destiny. He was going to get back into Gipsy Avenger, and he was going to find Obsidian Fury, and put that evil rogue down. The day was coming—soon—when he would see the pilots coming out of Obsidian Fury's Conn-Pod, defeated, and he would know he had begun to answer for Mako's death.

Until then, he would look at the drawing his sister had left for him, and he would try to understand.

# 14

**MEMO**
PRIVATE TO SHAO LIWEN

Pursuant to your orders we have undertaken off-hours surveillance of Dr. Newton Geiszler, and a general program of intelligence collection concerning his personal behaviors. Observations:

Dr. Geiszler frequently drinks to excess at bars near his apartment.

The electricity bills at his apartment are much higher than any others in that building or others similar to it in the same district. None of his other expenses are notable apart from a large amount of money spent on expensive wines.

He has not been observed to keep company with any other scientists or engineers employed by Shao Industries' competitors, or with any Pan Pacific Defense Corps personnel.

He has not been observed to speak about his work with anyone in public, no matter the degree of his intoxication.

He has not been observed in public with a romantic partner despite frequent overheard references to a woman named Alice. Her identity is unknown.

Provisional conclusion: Dr. Geiszler is not a security risk at this time, though continued surveillance is likely warranted and will continue.

—Kang

Newt knew that Shao kept an eye on him when he wasn't at work. He didn't especially like it, but he saw why. She didn't like uncertainty, or surprises, and she didn't understand Newt. He had lived his life skipping from flash of brilliance to flash of brilliance, suffering through the periods of stagnant frustration in between. She was another kind of genius, taking a particular brilliance and ruthlessly applying it, like it was a kind of math she could use to solve the problem of life. She'd gotten rich, and after joining Shao Industries Newt had, too. They sure paid a lot more than the PPDC. Newt didn't mind if she had him followed when he hit the bars or went out on the town. That was fine. She could disapprove, make disparaging comments to Chief Kang or whomever else. Newt didn't care. As long as he was in the lab making the Drones better, Shao would leave him alone.

All this was running through Newt's mind when he walked into his lab at Shao Industries, late at night after the shocking attack of Obsidian Fury on the PPDC Council Building that day. It was too bad about Mako, he thought. He'd always liked her. He'd seen her develop from a shy, jumpy cadet to the Secretary General of the PPDC, keeping the flame of the old Rangers alive after the rest of them were all gone. Newt hadn't thought about it that way until just then, but Mako was the last of them. Only she and Raleigh had survived the Breach, and Raleigh had been gone for... well, Newt wasn't sure, but it was years. He'd been in a lab most of the time, chasing the visions in his head.

Some of those visions came from the time he and Hermann had Drifted with the Kaiju brain. No point in denying it. Newt knew Hermann felt that experience more keenly than he did, but Hermann had never gotten out of the PPDC bubble, and he didn't have Newt's ability to leave things behind. Those had been good times, Newt thought, him and Hermann trying to save the world from the dumpy K-Science labs back when the survival of the human race depended on a couple of misfit Rangers piloting a Jaeger that was already obsolete when it took the field against Otachi, let alone Scunner and Raiju.

Names to conjure with. Newt carried them all in his head. He carried a lot in his head, not all of it good. That was what still tied him to Hermann after they had Drifted with that Kaiju brain back during the war...

Newt was still thinking of this when he walked into his lab and saw Shao Liwen. What was she doing in his lab?

At the moment, digging around in the fiber-optic guts of a Drone Jaeger data core. She hadn't noticed him yet.

Newt sidestepped toward one of the techs working on neural network stability in the Drones. He couldn't remember her name... Dai-something... Daiyu, that was it. He leaned in close, startling her, and asked, "How long has she been here?"

She stared up at him. Newt realized she didn't speak English. Mandarin was the lingua franca of Shao Industries. "Time? When?" he asked in Mandarin, nodding over at Shao.

"Almost an hour," she said.

Newt crossed the lab toward Shao, cursing a blue streak under his breath the whole time. She was tinkering with the data core's interface, with Burke standing near her in a Drone telemetry suit complete with a VR helmet rig that would let him operate the Drone via its data core. It was kind of like Drifting, only without the messy complications of interacting with another human mind.

"Hey, boss," he said, forcing himself to smile. "Sorry, thought you were still in Sydney."

She didn't return his greeting. "The Council has

approved Drone deployment in an emergency session," she said, getting right to the point, as usual.

Obsidian Fury's missile barrage had apparently killed a number of the PPDC Council members, leaving the rest of the group short of a quorum. Instead of naming new members, they had declared a temporary suspension of the quorum rules and approved the Drone initiative before the fires in the Council Building had even been extinguished.

"Wow," Newt said. "That's—that's great."

Burke was giving him a funny look. "Thought you'd be a little more enthusiastic, Doc," he said. Newt knew Burke was one of the members of Shao's inner circle who didn't trust him.

"No, I am," he said. "It's just, you know. Why they're approving now. Because of the attack."

"I was *there*," Shao snapped at him. "I know what happened." She went on in Mandarin. "And it wouldn't have, if our Drones had been in the field. Now *everyone* sees that."

"Yeah," Newt agreed. Something about her tone of voice made him unsure of himself. "I guess they do."

"Which means the attack was positive, all things considered."

Ah, there it was. Shao the business tycoon, the Drone evangelist, looking at the day's destruction and finding it good for business. "If you look at it sideways and squint, then yeah," he said, "I guess."

Shao was still dividing her attention between Newt and the data readouts from the core. She disconnected Burke from it and said, "There's a point five micro delay in the uplink to the data cores."

"I know. I'm working on boosting the connection—"

"Any other irregularities I should know about?"

"No. All systems double thumbs." He gave her two thumbs up.

"Push your data to my server. I want to run a diagnostic. The Council expects full deployment in forty-eight hours." Switching back to English so Burke and the other non-Chinese there could see her ordering Newt around, she added, "Get it done."

Then with Burke at her side, she swept out of the lab. Newt called after her.

"Sure! No problem! I'm on it like a…" For some reason, words failed him. "…like a guy that's really, really on it." Words never failed him! He felt unsettled by this: He was slipping gears once in a while, but also doing some of the best, most amazing work he'd ever done.

Even so, getting the Drones online, tested, and deployed in forty-eight hours was a tall order. The tech crew appeared stunned by Shao's ultimatum. "What?" Daiyu looked aghast. "No way we'll be ready!"

"Way? Way? Yes, *way*," Newt said. He had to make this happen or he would be out of a job, and the consequences of that… "Know what? You're fired," he said, trying to put a little fear of God into the techs to get them moving. Then he immediately reconsidered. He needed Daiyu. She was too smart to fire right then. "No, get this done, then you're fired. Or promoted. We'll see how it goes. But probably fired. Go! Shoo!"

The techs scattered to their workstations. Holo screens blinked into existence all over the lab as they feverishly ran testing simulations and revised code. Newt strolled among them, letting them know he was watching, and then he came to the large observation window that looked out over the factory floor. Row after row of Drone Jaegers stood on the floor, with automated machinery making final adjustments to their external components. Other factory robots were fitting each Drone with data cores. Could they be done in forty-eight hours? Despite his promise to Shao, Newt wasn't sure.

He took another look at the techs, wondering if he'd taken the right tack. He wasn't ordinarily a high-pressure, threatening kind of guy. He preferred to glad-hand, make people feel good, impress them with his savvy and make them feel like he was the kind of boss who deserved their best effort. But he was under a lot of pressure, and desperate times, as the saying went, called for desperate measures.

# 15

## STATUS REPORT ON CADET CLASS, MOYULAN SHATTERDOME

### RANGER NATHAN LAMBERT

The current cadet class has made satisfactory progress toward Drift fluency and Jaeger technical understanding. Interpersonal rivalries and personality clashes are within expected ranges.

**Current provisional backup assignments to Moyulan's Jaeger detail would be:**

Ilya/Bracer Phoenix
Jinhai/Valor Omega
Meilin/Gipsy Avenger
Renata/Saber Athena
Ryoichi/Saber Athena
Suresh/Guardian Bravo
Tahima/Titan Redeemer
Viktoriya/Valor Omega

continued...

**UPDATE**: The late addition of Cadet Amara Namani has destabilized the equilibrium of the class. Her skills are still being assessed but this writer questions her overall fitness for the program due to her background and lack of discipline. Assignment to a Jaeger would be premature.

The cadets were clustered around a stored newsfeed of the Sydney attack, swiping back and forth through Obsidian Fury's battle with Gipsy Avenger. Amara held the data pad, mesmerized by the rogue Jaeger. Had someone really built that? She knew how hard it was to design and make something even the scale of Scrapper. How had someone found the resources to do this without the PPDC noticing? They kept track of the international trade in technologies used in the creation of Jaeger systems. Drift tech was strictly controlled. Had someone invented it independently? Or was there a mole in Shao Industries or one of the other companies that manufactured Jaeger parts?

However it had happened, Obsidian Fury was an impressive piece of work.

Tahima, leaning over her shoulder, snorted. "Obsidian Fury. Doesn't even sound like a real Jaeger name."

"I don't think Tahima sounds like a real name," Renata shot back, "but your mama did."

Amara ignored the sniping. It was all part of the cadet game, the way they established their pecking order. She didn't want to be part of it. "There's never been a rogue like this. How'd the Kaiju nuts build it? Ones where I'm from couldn't change a battery without getting fried."

"Maybe they stole it," Ryoichi suggested.

"*Da*," Ilya agreed. "You can steal anything in my country with overalls and a work order."

"These pilots... they're too fast. I don't understand how they're exceeding the neural load."

"Ballerinas," Jinhai said, for maybe the hundredth time that day. "I'm telling you."

For some reason this idea drove Tahima crazy. "Shut up with that crap, man. You know how many people died in Sydney?" He acted like it was an insult to them that Jaeger pilots might have ballet training, but to Amara it made sense. Learning that kind of balance and grace couldn't help but be an asset in a fight.

"Newsfeed said they're posting a dozen Jaegers at the memorial," Meilin said. A dozen Jaegers. That was a real mark of how much respect Mako Mori had commanded.

"When I die, I want that many to send *me* off," Suresh said.

"Your pop's gonna make you work with boobs when you wash out," Renata said.

"Jaegers do not show up when the boob guy dies," Ilya observed.

"Your dad works with boobs?" Amara had never heard this.

"He's a plastic surgeon," Suresh explained, exasperated. "He doesn't just work with—" He caught himself, realizing he was wasting his breath. "And I'm not washing out. I'm gonna be a pilot."

"Still," Jinhai said. "You die—*meh*. I'd post *one* Jaeger at your funeral. Maybe *half* a Jaeger."

"I heard that's where they found Amara," Vik said. "In half a Jaeger."

Amara dropped the data pad on her bunk and stood up. She wasn't going to stand there and be insulted when she was the only one in the room who had ever done anything like build Scrapper. "It was a *whole* Jaeger. It just wasn't very big, *Viktoriya*."

The other cadets went quiet when they heard Amara use Vik's full name. That was a challenge, and all of them knew it. Vik stepped up to Amara, looming over her. She was used to scaring people with her size and strength. "Bigger is better," she said.

Amara sized her up. She was starting to reconsider her strategy of escalating the confrontation. It was one thing to stand up for yourself, another to get your ass kicked for no reason. "Look, uh..." Amara paused, trying to remember what she'd learned from Jinhai the day before. "*Idi na fig.*"

Ilya's head snapped up. He was the other Russian speaker in the group, and his reaction told Amara she hadn't said exactly what she meant to say.

Vik laughed out loud in disbelief. "What did you say?"

Amara tried again. "*Idi na... fig?*" She looked over at Jinhai. "Am I saying that right?"

Jinhai, clearly trying not to laugh, nodded and said, "Yep."

Amara had just figured out that Jinhai had pranked her when Vik lunged forward and grabbed her in a chokehold. Amara struggled, but Vik was much bigger and much stronger. She couldn't break free.

"Whoa!" Jinhai said.

Ryoichi tried to break them up. "Vik, come on, let her go—"

"I worked every day of my life to be here! You didn't do anything! You were just picked up off the street like garbage," Vik snarled, squeezing harder.

The insult snapped something inside Amara. With strength she hadn't known she possessed, she broke free of the chokehold. But she didn't try to get away from Vik. Instead she used Vik as a pivot point, scissoring her legs up and around Vik's neck. The counterattack knocked Vik off balance and she went down, with Amara now in control.

"Know where I learned that?" Amara hissed. "On the *streets*, you big dumb—"

"Namani! Malikova!"

Every one of the cadets—even Vik, thrashing against Amara's scissor hold—looked over at the barracks door to see Nate Lambert.

"Ranger on deck!" Ryoichi shouted. All of them except Amara and Vik snapped to attention. Amara let Vik go and scrambled to her feet. "She jumped me—"

Now Vik was on her feet too. "She does not belong here—"

"*Enough!*" Lambert snapped. He glared at both of the combatants, daring them to say another word. Neither of them did. Amara could tell he wasn't just angry. The day's events had wounded him, and he was not in the mood to deal with dumb status fights among his cadets.

He let them stand at attention for a long moment before he started speaking. They were expecting an angry dressing-down, but instead Lambert's voice was quiet and level. "When I first joined the Corps, I was just like you," he said. "Worse even. I was nobody. From nowhere. But Mako Mori told me I could make a difference."

Over Lambert's shoulder, Amara saw Jake drifting in from the hall. He'd probably heard the scrap just like Lambert had, and come to see what was going on.

Lambert kept talking, his voice tight with emotion that he was trying hard to control. "She said whoever you are, wherever you come from, the minute you enter this program, you're part of a family. And the people beside you are your brothers, and sisters." He had noticed Jake by now, and Amara thought this part of the speech was directed at Jake as much as at the cadets. "No matter what they do… no matter how stupid they act… you forgive. And you move on. Because that's what family does. Start believing that out here and you'll start believing it in a Jaeger."

Amara was normally immune to inspirational speeches, but this one resonated. Family. She didn't have one anymore. Everyone in the room, cadet or Ranger, had lost someone. That loss bound them together into a new kind of family, even if some of the other members were assholes sometimes. She caught Vik's eye and saw Vik was understanding the same thing. Sheepish at the way they'd goaded each other, they exchanged a nod. And by the doorway, Amara could see Jake Pentecost thinking along the same lines. She didn't know exactly what had happened between them, but she knew Jake had kicked out, and she knew he and Lambert had been partners. Hearing Lambert's speech and seeing Jake's reaction, Amara started to put two and two together. Lambert was forgiving him. He was walking the walk, doing himself what he demanded of the cadets.

Amara had spent her whole life trying not to feel anything, but she'd never been around a group like this. In that moment she would have died for all of them. This was her family now.

Jules, the J-Tech beauty that both Jake and Lambert were after, stuck her head into the room. "Hey." When Jake and Lambert turned toward her, she said, "Marshal's looking for you guys. Says Gottlieb found something."

Back in the K-Science lab, Jake stood with Lambert and Quan as Gottlieb swiped away a number of programs he'd had running and exposed Mako's Kaiju-head drawing. "It isn't some*thing*," he said, "It's some*where*."

He worked a holo screen, moving Mako's drawing over a section of a satellite map. The outline of the head matched the topography perfectly. Jake drew in a breath. She had been sending a message. Staring death in the face, Mako had kept the presence of mind to make sure that this knowledge wouldn't die with her. "Severnaya Zemlya," Gottlieb said. "Off Siberia's Taymyr Peninsula."

Next to the overlay of the drawing and the map, a larger-scale map appeared, showing the whole peninsula and the scattering of islands reaching north from it into the Arctic Ocean.

"What's there?" Quan asked.

"Nothing anymore," Gottlieb said. He zoomed the map in, focusing on the area under the eye of Mako's drawing. "A facility roughly in this location was used to manufacture Jaeger power cores early in the war. But it was decommissioned years ago."

"Why would Mako be trying to tell us about an abandoned factory in the middle of nowhere?" Lambert wondered. He was eyeing Jake as he said it, and Jake could read between the lines easily enough. He was making Jake an offer. Challenging him. If they really wanted to find out what Mako had been trying to tell them…

Jake turned to Marshal Quan. "Sir, permission to take Gipsy Avenger and see what the hell's out there."

Quan considered, but not for long.

# 16

## PPDC FACILITIES DIVISION

### SEVERNAYA MANUFACTURING FACILITY

**CONSTRUCTED**: June 2019

**PRODUCTION**: Power cores and plasma capacitors, Mark II and Mark III Jaegers; cabling and conduit insulation; reactor housings

**STAFFING**: 267

**DECOMMISSIONED**: December 2022

**REASON FOR DECOMMISSIONING**: Remoteness of location offered protection from Kaiju attacks but caused difficulties in shipping. Personnel suffered from low morale and resultant low productivity as a result of isolation. Shipments were vulnerable to theft due to multiple transfer points en route to Shatterdome locations. Errors in siting survey resulted in

continued...

nearby glaciers causing shifts in subterranean areas of the manufacturing floor.

**METHOD OF DISPOSAL**: Attempts to sell or lease the facility to PPDC industrial and manufacturing partners were unsuccessful. Personnel reassigned to Anchorage and Vladivostok, December 2022. Critical machinery removed February 2023, facility abandoned March 2023. No current monitoring or plans for reuse.

From Moyulan to the Taymyr Peninsula was a long trip via Jumphawks. Gipsy Avenger, with Jake and Lambert holding their Drift, arrived thirty-six hours after Gottlieb's revelation, dropping from the Jumphawks down through a blizzard to the frozen ground of Siberia. The PPDC had built a number of factories in places like this, far from the Pacific Ocean and therefore less likely to be lost in Kaiju attacks. But this one had been mothballed during the war, according to the records Gottlieb had retrieved. Newer power core technologies pioneered in China and Washington state had relocated much of the manufacturing to those places, and the Severnaya facility had been completely abandoned for more than a decade.

They got visual contact on the factory from a distance of a few hundred yards, right at the limit of visibility given the weather. It had been built into the side of a mountain, and since its abandonment a glacier had overspread part of the complex. Cascading ice had almost obscured it, and what they could see looked dilapidated and partially collapsed.

Lambert had Gipsy doing full-spectrum tactical scans of the complex, and he wasn't finding anything. "No life signs. Looks like Gottlieb was right. Place is abandoned."

The scanner chirped and Jake saw a signal of some kind on the readout in front of him. It was tuned to different energy signatures than Lambert's, and until that moment it hadn't shown anything either. Jake looked more closely. "Wait a second." The signal was faint, fluctuating. The scanning package couldn't identify it. "I'm picking up some weird readings," Jake said. Lambert leaned over to look at Jake's scanner. Neither of them could make sense of what they were seeing.

Both of them were so focused on interpreting the scanner's readings that they missed an alarm from Gipsy's defensive sensor package. When the first volley of plasma missiles streaked past them, they jumped, instinctively flinching away from the paths of the missiles. But they weren't the target. The missiles exploded across the wall of the factory, destroying it and bringing down the whole face of ice and rock. Whatever evidence the factory might have contained, it was blasted to atoms now, and buried under a million tons of mountain.

Gipsy spun around to see Obsidian Fury looming out of the blizzard.

With a snarl, Jake leaned forward in his Drift cradle, pushing Gipsy Avenger into a charge. The last time he'd seen Obsidian Fury, he'd been scared, uncertain, still wondering if he'd done the right thing getting back into a Jaeger.

Now he was feeling only one thing: the overwhelming vengeful need to beat Obsidian Fury into the ground and find out who was inside. Mako was going to have justice.

Obsidian Fury slowed Gipsy down with a missile barrage, but they kept charging. Alarms sounded in the Conn-Pod, cataloguing damage to Gipsy's systems. "Get him off his feet!" Lambert shouted.

Jake roared a battle cry and sprang up in the Drift cradle. Gipsy Avenger leaped forward, tackling Obsidian Fury and skidding across the ice. Still locked together, the two Jaegers slid over the edge of a crevasse.

In the fall, they separated. Gipsy unleashed her chain sword and Obsidian Fury answered with its twin plasma saws. They struck at each other as they slid and bounced down the steep bed of the crevasse, neither landing a damaging blow in the confined environment.

First Obsidian Fury and then Gipsy Avenger smashed through a wall of ice at the bottom of the crevasse, tumbling through onto a large ice floe in the shallows off the coast. The floe rocked as Obsidian Fury got to its feet first. The deep orange light in its chest emplacement glowed suddenly brighter, and Gipsy Avenger barely got her chain sword up in time to deflect the blast of Obsidian Fury's particle beam. The sword scattered the beam's force in ribbons of energy that flared between them and brought bursts of steam from the ice floe.

"Systems are overloading!" Lambert shouted over the wail of alarms. The chain sword wasn't designed to absorb energy, and soon the feedback would destroy it—probably along with Gipsy's arm. "We gotta get out of here!"

*To where?* Jake wondered. An idea struck.

He reared up and drove one fist down. Gipsy Avenger did the same, smashing a hole through the ice floe at her feet. Gipsy dropped down through the hole, disappearing into the black water. Inside the Conn-Pod, Jake and Lambert reeled, trying to hold Gipsy's balance as she sank. The water was deep enough to cover them, and as they landed on the bottom, Jake could feel Lambert in his head wondering what the hell they were going to do now.

"Wait for it," he said. Above, the hole in the floe was a bright glow against the dimmer background of the heavy ice.

A shadow appeared in the brightness: Obsidian Fury, looking down through the hole. "Now," Jake said.

Gipsy Avenger fired its own missile volley, straight up through the hole. Each missile was programmed before it left its launch tube, to go up through the hole… and then straight back down, to explode on the ice around Obsidian Fury's feet.

As the explosions sounded in the water, Gipsy leaped up from the sea floor, powered by maneuvering jets built into her lower legs. She surged up through the enlarged hole as Obsidian Fury crashed down. Gipsy caught Obsidian Fury before the rogue Jaeger could regain its balance, driving it back up through the ice and pounding it as they rolled.

But Obsidian Fury reacted quickly, absorbing the first blows and wrestling Gipsy down. The plasma saws appeared again, ready to impale Gipsy Avenger.

Jake stayed calm. They were never going to win a straight-up fight with Obsidian Fury. The last encounter had taught them that much. They had to keep surprising it. The drop into the ice had given Gipsy a chance to do some damage. Now Obsidian Fury thought it had Gipsy down, and it was time to spring another surprise. "Plasma cannon now?" he said.

"Hell yeah!" Lambert thrust out his left hand, and Gipsy Avenger's left hand rearranged itself into a plasma cannon. The blast rocked Gipsy Avenger back, and sent Obsidian Fury flying back across the ice floe to land on its back, trailing smoke.

Gipsy Avenger rose, deploying her chain sword again. Obsidian Fury got up, but not as fast as it had before. They were doing some damage. Obsidian Fury charged, brandishing its plasma saws—only when it redeployed them, they multiplied into a storm of whirling blades on each arm.

"Oh shit," Jake and Lambert said in unison. Gipsy Avenger's armor plating wasn't going to stop those saws for long. But Jake was already watching the nuances of Obsidian Fury's stances. He remembered the fight in Sydney. If Obsidian Fury did what it had done last time, there would be an opening.

Obsidian Fury shifted its weight to slash one of its plasma saws at Gipsy Avenger's head, the move triggering an alert from the combat-readiness program built into Gipsy Avenger's sensors. Yes. They had seen this before.

And the answer was… "Follow my lead!" Jake cried out.

Gipsy Avenger was already ducking as they saw Obsidian Fury begin the move. Sidestepping under the incoming plasma saw, they struck out with the chain sword as Gipsy Avenger slid along the ice, tearing open Obsidian Fury's torso. Obsidian Fury staggered past, pieces of its armor shedding onto the ice. Its power core was exposed, leaking energy that started small fires inside it.

"He's hurt!" Jake crowed.

Lambert leaned into a charge. "Go for his power core!"

Obsidian Fury parried the first blows of the chain sword, and Jake got a little too eager. He extended Gipsy Avenger's arm in a thrust meant to destroy the exposed power core, but Obsidian Fury was still fast. It dodged to one side and the chain sword drove into its thigh. Planting its other leg, Obsidian Fury slashed a plasma saw down and amputated their chain sword.

The sudden loss of mass changed Gipsy's center of gravity and sent her tumbling. Jake and Lambert barely got her up and turned around before Obsidian Fury came at them again with the saws. Gipsy Avenger caught Obsidian Fury's wrists, but the plasma saws gouged into the side of Gipsy's head.

The Conn-Pod shook and small electrical fires filled it with smoke. Jake and Lambert stopped the saws' progress, grunting with the effort and slowly... painfully... beginning to push them back.

If they hadn't already damaged Obsidian Fury, it would never have worked. But they had, and Obsidian Fury gave way, inch by inch, until Gipsy Avenger had twisted the saws away from her head. Jake and Lambert felt the rogue Jaeger's balance shift, and they seized the advantage, torquing Obsidian Fury's arms around and jamming its plasma saws straight into its own chest.

The energy discharge flared through Obsidian Fury as Gipsy followed up with a shattering head-butt straight into its face. They beat the rogue Jaeger down, batting aside its weakening defenses. Still dangerous, Obsidian Fury dragged the saws free and almost caught Gipsy with a desperate strike—but as Gipsy ducked the blow, Jake and Lambert reached out and yanked the broken chain sword out of Obsidian Fury's leg. In the same motion, they reared up and drove the blade into Obsidian Fury's neck. With one hand on the sword, Gipsy Avenger drove Obsidian Fury back. Her other hand punched into the Jaeger's torso and tore out the power core.

The surge from the destabilized core burned through Obsidian Fury, frying its systems. Energy arcs flared out from its head and torso as its limbs spasmed out... and then went limp. Obsidian Fury crumpled to the ground. The ice floe rocked gently and stabilized.

Gipsy Avenger stood over the downed Jaeger and tossed away the smoking power core. Steam hissed away from the spot where it landed on the ice. Time to see who had done all this, Jake thought. Time to meet the people who killed his sister.

He reached down, and Gipsy Avenger lifted Obsidian Fury's faceplate off.

Steam rose from the interior of the Conn-Pod as the warm air inside came into contact with the freezing Arctic air outside. As it cleared, Jake was stunned by what he saw. "What the hell is that...?"

There were no red-suited Kaiju cultists inside, no rogue mercenaries in pseudo-military rip-offs of the PPDC drivesuit... in fact no humans at all.

The interior of Obsidian Fury's Conn-Pod was unlike anything Jake had ever seen. Where an ordinary Jaeger had an open, hemispherical space with the Drift cradle and consoles in the center and critical sensor equipment surrounding it, the inside of Obsidian Fury's head was almost entirely filled by a pulsing mass of Kaiju brain tissue. Nerve tendrils webbed out by the hundred, woven into electronics with no human interface to be seen. The Kaiju brain was clearly damaged by the surge of energy from the failure of Obsidian Fury's data core. Parts of it were scorched and inert. Black streaks marked the interior of the Conn-Pod where circuitry had overloaded and loose conduits dangled near nerve endings that hung in blackened curls from the wounded part of the Kaiju's brain. The scene was beyond nightmarish, a perversion of everything the Jaegers stood for. Jake reeled with the implications of it. Someone, somewhere, had kept a Kaiju brain and redesigned a Jaeger from the ground up to use it.

As they watched, astonished and revolted, the brain tissue began to convulse and seep both Kaiju blood and other unidentifiable fluids. A minute later it was dead and cooling, leaving Jake frustrated and at the same time even more determined. He had eliminated the tool used to kill Mako, yet he hadn't really found her killer.

But he would.

# 17

## INVENTORY REPORT: KNOWN SAMPLES OF KAIJU BRAIN TISSUE

**THIS REPORT COMPILES ALL KNOWN KAIJU BRAINS HELD BY PPDC PERSONNEL OR AFFILIATED CIVILIAN RESEARCH PROGRAMS. THE FOLLOWING INSTITUTIONS POSSESS LICENSED SAMPLES:**

[LIST REDACTED]

At the request of Marshal Quan, urgent contact was initiated with all parties on this list to confirm the status of their samples. All parties reported their samples were present and intact. Further, all parties confirmed that they were not currently engaged in any effort to replicate existing tissue samples or grow new tissue. Parties provided evidence in the

continued...

form of mass-spectrometer scans and visual documentation, as well as documentation of all experiments performed on individual Kaiju brains held. Inventory of Kaiju brain tissue was confirmed at one hundred percent, with no losses and no initial evidence of misuse or violation of research regulations.

**Conclusion**: Obsidian Fury brain tissue did not originate with any PPDC facility or affiliated civilian research program. Other possible origins include black-market sellers. PPDC Intelligence Division is pursuing this possibility.

Technician K. McKinney, Moyulan Shatterdome

They debriefed on the move from the Jaeger bay toward K-Science, Jake walking down long maintenance corridors alongside a heavy forklift with Lambert and Quan. The J-Tech driving the forklift looked sick from the smell. Obsidian Fury was at that moment being lowered onto the tarmac outside the Shatterdome—not far from where Jake and Amara had first disembarked from the PPDC transport. Was that only a few days ago? *Life comes at you fast,* Jake thought. He had already brought Quan up to date in broad strokes, talking about the visual on the factory, his realization that they couldn't stand and fight with Obsidian Fury but had to outsmart it... and then their discovery of what was inside the rogue Jaeger's Conn-Pod. Quan had taken one look at the brain and gone stiff, the expression on his face almost religious in its revulsion. And it wasn't just the smell, either, although the Kaiju brain by then was beginning to stink like nothing Jake had ever smelled before. They got it back under the tarp, as much to contain the stench as to hide the brain, and followed the forklift into one of the big testing rooms at the edge of the K-Science wing. Gottlieb had been warned they were coming in hot with something important, and he was there waiting for them. "Whatever was in that facility, Obsidian Fury didn't want us getting a look," Jake said as he saw Gottlieb approach. "Guessing it has something to do with this."

He swept back the tarp covering the forklift's cargo, revealing the decaying remains of the Kaiju brain from inside Obsidian Fury. The brain had suffered in transit, and they hadn't been real delicate when they took it out of Obsidian Fury's head, so in a lot of ways it looked worse than when Jake had first seen it in the blizzard up at Severnaya Zemlya. It was also rotting quickly, as Kaiju flesh and organs did, and the minute Jake lifted the tarp, a wave of odor rolled out from underneath, a miasma that made Jake's eyes water even though he had been smelling it for more or less the last twelve hours.

The first thing Gottlieb did was try to stop himself from vomiting. He gagged visibly, turned away, hunched over... and then just barely held himself together. When he turned back around, the picture of composure again, Lambert said, "No pilots. Just this—whatever it is."

"I want to know everything about it," Quan ordered. "Inside and out."

The look on Gottlieb's face made Jake uneasy. It was part disgust and part relish, or even a weird kind of intellectual lust. Jake knew Gottlieb had Drifted with a Kaiju brain once. That was part of PPDC lore, along with Raleigh Becket bringing Gipsy Danger in on his own after his brother Yancy was killed, and Stacker Pentecost facing down Onibaba solo after his partner went down. But Jake had heard Gottlieb didn't like it, and the experience had hardened him against the Kaiju, given him a visceral hatred of them he hadn't felt before being in direct touch with their minds.

Gottlieb never talked about it, so nobody really knew the truth but him, and maybe Newt Geiszler. Right now, Gottlieb looked like a man who knew he was going to have to suffer, and also knew that the prize would be sufficient reward.

"I'm going to need a chainsaw," Gottlieb said.


And he put it to good use, cutting away parts of the damaged exterior layers of the brain to see the intact tissue beneath. It was messy, stinking work, and by the time Gottlieb was done his industrial rubber coverall and gloves were covered in splatters of toxic goo. He set down the chainsaw he'd used to get at the inner parts of the brain and peered at the organ while Jake, Quan, and Lambert watched. Gottlieb got instruments from a nearby table and took samples before the tissue reacted too much to the ambient atmosphere. Then he stood up and said, "It's definitely Kaiju. A secondary brain. Used to control the hindquarters."

"Like the dinosaurs?" Lambert asked. He'd heard stories that the dinosaurs were engineered by the Kaiju's creators, known as the Precursors. It was rumored that Newt Geiszler and Gottlieb had learned this from Drifting with a Kaiju brain, back in the darkest days of the Kaiju War. No PPDC official had ever confirmed that, or the other rumor that Raleigh Becket had learned the truth during his cataclysmic visit to the Anteverse itself. If the dinosaur story was true, the resemblance made sense, and the comparison was a natural one.

"Actually that's a persistent myth," Gottlieb said, immediately sidetracked by his scientist's instinct to make sure everyone had their facts straight. "Sauropods did have a sacro-lumbar expansion once thought to—"

Jake didn't care about the details of sauropod or Kaiju anatomy. There were more pressing questions. "How'd it get into our world?" he asked.

"Hasn't been a Breach in ten years," Quan added. "Sensors would have picked it up."

"I don't think there *was* a Breach," Gottlieb said. He was back at a lab table, squinting at the tissue sample and passing various instruments over it. The readings appeared on a holo screen, but they didn't match the baseline readings from the PPDC's database of known Kaiju specimens. "Kaiju flesh has a distinct radioactive half-life signature, particular to the Anteverse. This specimen doesn't."

Jake looked from Gottlieb to Lambert, wondering if Lambert was thinking the same thing he was. They'd both had the thought in the Drift, in the first shocked moments after they'd seen the inside of Obsidian Fury's head. "You saying it came from our universe?" Lambert asked.

"The genetic fingerprints indicate distinctly terrestrial modification techniques." Gottlieb watched a screen as a genetic analysis scrolled by. To Jake it looked like a column of random numbers next to a representation of a DNA molecule like any other DNA molecule, but that's why he was in the Rangers instead of K-Science. Gottlieb was fluent in whatever data language was being displayed, and he nodded at the screen. "Probably engineered from Kaiju tissue left over from the war."

Marshal Quan hadn't been there in Siberia, so he was just now getting his head around the idea. "Precursors didn't do this," he said, as if convincing himself. "*Humans* did."

"How'd a bunch of crazy Kaiju worshippers do all that?" Jake wondered. It didn't seem possible.

Gottlieb agreed. "Doubtful they could have. Only a dozen or so biotech companies in the world could even take a run at it."

"We need to narrow that list down," Quan said. "*Fast.*"

Gottlieb didn't need to be told twice. Every bit of Kaiju tissue used for approved research purposes was catalogued and the results of the research published in a central, PPDC-administered database. That database didn't cover all Kaiju tissue out there in the world, because there had been a lively black market in Kaiju parts during the war, but it did cover the vast majority of the biotech research conducted on permitted samples. It was the best place to start because most of the companies working with black-market samples didn't have the facilities to create something like an engineered Kaiju brain. That kind of project took large-scale replication and cultivation laboratories, not to mention large groups of top-notch biologists and genetic engineers. So Gottlieb's instinct was that the source of this brain was probably somewhere in the PPDC database. It made sense.

Once Gottlieb was working, he ignored them. Quan observed him for a while, then turned to Jake and Lambert. "Good work," he said. "Mako would be proud." To Jake he added, "So would your father."

Jake appreciated the sentiment, but he wasn't so sure. Stacker Pentecost had never given any sign that anything Jake did had made him proud.

From one of the human-sized access doors at the side of the Jaeger bay doors, each taller than any building left standing in Los Angeles, Amara looked out across the tarmac at the broken hulk of Obsidian Fury. The rogue Jaeger's remains lay on the tarmac surrounded by Shatterdome security details, with J-Tech crews swarming over it in the first phases of analysis and investigation. The revelation about Obsidian Fury's Kaiju brain had swept through the Shatterdome like wildfire, sparking a thousand rumors about whether or not there were other Kaiju out there. Had a Breach reopened, somehow undetected by PPDC satellites and geological sensors? Or had they missed other Kaiju during the war? Or had someone in a gene lab managed to create a Kaiju? Because Marshal Quan wasn't talking—at least not to cadets—any story seemed possible.

She'd been with a group of other cadets watching as Gipsy Avenger returned. The marks of the battle with Obsidian Fury scarred Gipsy's armor, and Amara was especially chilled to see the damage to Gipsy's head. She couldn't imagine what it would be like to try and keep your cool while those plasma saws were chewing away at the Conn-Pod plating. The more she learned about Jake, the more she—well, not quite admired him. She wouldn't go that far. But she did have some respect for him, at least compared to how she felt when he was holding a broken pipe over her head back in the squat in Santa Monica.

Lambert, too. He made such a point of being a humorless, overbearing tight-ass to the cadets that it was easy to forget how good he was at piloting a Jaeger. He and Jake had taken down Obsidian Fury, after barely escaping with their lives the last time the Jaegers clashed. Put together with the inspiring speech he'd dropped on the cadets a couple of nights ago, and Amara was starting to think Lambert was more of a human being than she'd suspected.

It seemed like Jake had felt the same way after that speech, and now the results of their newfound spirit of cooperation were there for anyone to see. Obsidian Fury's torso was wrenched open, the black armor plating peeled back to expose the structural systems beneath. Its power core, crumpled and streaked with its lenses shattered, lay next to the main body of the Jaeger. The chain-sword wound gaped in its leg. Like its torso, Obsidian Fury's head lay open to the sky. A specialist J-Tech detail was working inside, beginning its analysis of exactly how Obsidian Fury's creator had learned to integrate the biological systems of a Kaiju brain with the complex electronics guiding a Jaeger.

They'd all seen the brain go by, on a pallet held up by a forklift. A crew had covered it on the forklift, but before that, they dug the brain out of Obsidian Fury's head and laid it on a tarp. Several of the J-Tech team puked on the tarmac, and Jules yelled at them to keep it away from the tarp so they didn't contaminate the samples K-Science would be taking. The cadets couldn't believe what they were seeing. "That hunk of Kaiju was part of a Jaeger?" Suresh couldn't believe it.

"Really thought it was going to be ballerinas," Jinhai commented. If Vik had been around, she might have punched him.

They'd been bantering like that ever since, hanging around the perimeter of the investigation area and hoping that someone would ask them to do something. It hadn't happened yet, but Amara at least wasn't giving up. The idea of a Jaeger that fused Kaiju biology and human tech... it horrified her and fascinated her both, but mostly fascinated. Immediately she intuited that the direct brain interface accounted for the speed of Obsidian Fury's reactions. Even the best Drift cradles had a slight delay as the Rangers' brain signals were processed and transmitted to the Jaeger's control systems. Could a human brain be wired directly? Probably. But what would it do to the pilot?

The other question she had was purely technical. Even without considering the quicker responses due to the direct brain–Jaeger interface, Obsidian Fury was nimbler and quicker than any other existing Jaeger. There were tech innovations there in its ruined body, and Amara really wanted to know what they were. She had to know. Staying there looking at it, she felt a physical itch in her fingers, so powerful was her need to get into that Jaeger and see how it worked.

"We gotta get a look inside," she said.

"Inside?" Suresh echoed.

"That thing's part *Kaiju*. Come on, guys." She turned to the group. "When are we ever going to get a chance to see something like this again?"

"Never," Suresh said. "Never would be good."

"Stay here if you want. But I'm going." Amara looked back over the tarmac. She'd spent the last several years figuring out how to liberate bits of machinery from other people who wanted to keep them. She could get past Shatterdome security in her sleep. And she was going to.

# 18

## JAEGERWATCH—BREAKING NEWS

Your friends at JaegerWatch have some interesting tidbits from our eyes inside the Moyulan Shatterdome. You may have heard of the rogue Jaeger attack in Sydney? Where Gipsy Avenger got more than she bargained for from a mysterious assailant since given the code name Obsidian Fury?

Well, we have it on good authority that Gipsy got revenge. The details are sketchy, but our Moyulan source claims that Obsidian Fury was brought in last night, just after Gipsy went out on an emergency deployment. It's not hard to put those pieces together—though from what we understand nobody's going to be putting Obsidian Fury together again. Gipsy took the rogue down hard, and in a highly permanent way.

High five to the Rangers piloting Gipsy Avenger. You might have gone down once, but you answered the bell the second time around and... well... avenged. Mako Mori and all the others dead in Sydney can rest a little easier.

Yours,
The Spirit of Gipsy Danger -

They took some convincing, but eventually the other cadets went along with her plan. Amara pointed out that the Shatterdome security personnel were stationed at specific intervals, and changed shift at specific times. They were like any other on-base security detail, doing their jobs but not really convinced there was an actual threat justifying their presence. So it ended up being pretty easy to point out three or four spots were a determined group of teenagers could slip through the security perimeter and gain entry to Obsidian Fury via one of the several holes Gipsy Avenger had thoughtfully created in Obsidian Fury's armor.

The one they ended up choosing was down in the leg. It was the closest to ground level. The security details were clustered around the ladders and gantries that led up to higher entry points in Obsidian Fury's head and torso. Single file, they climbed in through the comma-shaped gouge made when Gipsy Avenger had stuck the sword in and then dragged it back out. Only when they were well inside the Jaeger, working their way down a corridor inside its thigh, did they turn on flashlights. Amara looked up, played the beam of her flashlight across the ceiling.

In a regular Jaeger, the ceiling of a hall like this would have been lined with heavy conduits and bundles of smaller cables, each tagged and color-coded so technicians could quickly isolate problems and make repairs. But Obsidian Fury was different. There were wires and cables, sure. But wound through all of them were filaments of Kaiju tissue. She looked up and down the hallway, and found a hatch.

She opened it and peered into the larger space beyond. It was like being inside a body instead of a machine. Long striated sinews and nerve bundles mingled with hydraulic piston assemblies and energy conduits. The sight overwhelmed her, just the scale of it and the oppressive sensation that there was something still living here...

Amara dropped back down into the corridor. "It's fused all the way through the system," she said, running the beam of her flashlight as far along the ceiling as they could see. "Like muscle tissue."

"That's how it was able to move like it did," Jinhai observed. "Cool." He wasn't talking about ballerinas anymore, instead admiring this fantastic interweaving of organic tissue and machine. Obsidian Fury was practically a cyborg. A Kaiju cyborg. What a thought.

Suresh did not share their enthusiasm. "Yeah, cool," he said, in a tone of voice that conveyed the opposite. "Working with boobs is sounding better and better."

An odd bundle of cables caught Amara's attention. Had she seen something like them before? "Shine your light over here," she said, and put down her own light so she could get her hands on them.

Jinhai kept his light steady while she tried to wrestle one of the cables loose. "Oh, great, yeah," Suresh said. "Let's go yanking on the guts of the weird-ass Kaiju kill-bot."

"Sack up or shut up," Meilin said. She didn't say much, but when she did she made her words count.

"Is there a third option?" Suresh was still watching Amara, and getting more nervous by the moment. "I'd really like a third option."

Amara had to brace herself against a heavy bracket and pull with all her strength, jerking the cable back and forth, but eventually she got it loose from a juncture and was able to snap the other end free from where it was spliced into the bundle. She started looking more closely at the cross-section of the cable, peeling back its outer insulating layer to expose the winding around the inner core. She'd seen this before, when she was acquiring cables to build Scrapper's power systems...

Jinhai leaned in close, trying to figure out what had Amara so preoccupied. "What is it?"

She was about to tell him when fat drops of blue Kaiju blood suddenly dripped from the ceiling. They missed Amara by sheer luck, but Jinhai wasn't so lucky. Several splattered on his arm, dissolving the sleeve of his coat and searing the flesh underneath. Jinhai bit down on a scream and dropped to the floor, rolling around in agony.

"Jinhai!" Amara dropped the cable and started pulling his jacket off, trying to get him free before more of the blood ate through the insulated fabric.

"I told you not to yank on those!" Suresh shouted.

Amara looked up and saw where the blood was coming from. While she'd been jerking at the cables, a bracket holding several of them together had scraped against a Kaiju blood vessel running among the tissue that lined the ceiling. Eventually the vessel had burst, and now Kaiju blood was dissolving the cables and dripping down from them to the floor. It hissed and smoked on the steel grating.

She felt so bad about what she'd done to Jinhai—accident or no accident—that she completely forgot about how much trouble they were going to be in. "Go get help! Go!"

"Oh, man, we are so screwed," Suresh said. He and Meilin ran back the way they'd come, weaving around droplets of Kaiju blood that spattered down from other parts of the ceiling as the vessel continued to drain. Meilin was shouting for a medic as they ran, and Amara heard confused shouts from the Shatterdome security outside.

She had Jinhai's jacket off, but his arm was badly burned and the Kaiju blood was still bubbling at the edges of the wound. He gripped Amara's arm painfully tight, teeth clenched to keep himself from screaming. She sat with him, taking the pain, trying to comfort him until the medics arrived.

Then, she knew, the real consequences would start to unfold. They were all in deep shit, but Amara had the feeling she was in the deepest of all. But whatever happened to her, she had to make sure Jake and Marshal Quan heard what she'd found.

# 19

## IN AFTERMATH OF ROGUE JAEGER ATTACK, DRONE PROGRAM MOVES AHEAD

### FROM WIRE SERVICE REPORTS

The origin of the rogue Jaeger known as Obsidian Fury is still a mystery, but its attack on the Pan Pacific Defense Corps Council meeting in Sydney two days ago appears to have given extra momentum to Shao Industries' proposed replacement of human-piloted Jaegers with Drones. Meeting in an emergency session, with quorum rules waived due to the number of Councilors killed in the Sydney attack, the Council gave final approval to the Drone deployment. Individual members cited the need to protect Shatterdomes against potential future rogue Jaegers, as well as the need to have a single central control facility so no existing Jaeger could be hijacked and turned against the PPDC or civilians.

continued...

Fiery opposition came from the two retired Rangers on the Council, both of whom argued forcefully that Drone Jaegers would not be able to react in a battlefield situation with the same speed and intuition a human pilot could demonstrate. Their arguments failed to carry the day, however, and the final count found only their two votes in the nay column.

Shao Industries spokesman Joseph Burke, himself a former Ranger, expressed gratitude for the decision. "We think the Council has acted wisely," he said, "and we look forward to getting the Drone Jaegers in the field so they can prevent anything like this terrible attack from ever happening again."

Shatterdome security put Amara straight into a holding cell while the medics were still working on Jinhai. The room's only furniture was a small table and two chairs. She sat down and waited for over an hour, feeling more and more guilty and anxious as she watched people go by. Most of them didn't look at her. Those who did were either disgusted or pitying. News of her offense had traveled fast.

She saw Jake in the hall outside the holding cell, pacing back and forth. A few minutes later, Marshal Quan appeared. He and Jake started talking and the conversation quickly grew animated. Then really heated. Jake was furious about something, and Quan—if Amara was reading this body language right—was demanding that Jake follow orders. Eventually Quan made one last point and then stalked back down the hall the way he'd come. Jake stood watching him go. He rubbed his face and Amara realized it must be pretty late at night by now. She'd lost track of time. For Jake, it must have seemed even later. He probably hadn't slept since before Gipsy Avenger's feet had made contact with the snow outside the old factory on the Taymyr Peninsula.

He opened the door and came inside. "Is Jinhai okay?" she asked. That was the most important thing. She knew she was in for some punishment, and she could take it. She'd earned it. But if Jinhai's injuries made him unfit for Ranger duty, Amara knew she would never forgive herself.

"There's going to be some scarring, but yeah. He'll live." Amara let out a long sigh, feeling at least that worry leave her. "Marshal's put him on probation," Jake went on. "Meilin and Suresh too. They blink wrong, all of 'em are out."

"It wasn't their fault," Amara said. "I talked them into it." Before they got into the part of the conversation where Jake told her how stupid she was, Amara wanted to make sure he heard about what she'd found inside Obsidian Fury. "Jake, there's something—"

He held up a hand. "Amara, I tried to talk to the Marshal." After a brief pause, he added, "I'm sorry. You're dismissed from the program."

This hurt more than Amara had thought it would. In the past few days, she had just started to see the possibility of a life beyond squatting in the ruins of Santa Monica, dodging gang psychopaths and stealing to meet her needs. She'd found a family, just like Lambert had talked about... and now she'd blown it. Because she had to push the boundaries, had to act like the rules didn't apply to her. "Doesn't matter," she said, trying to stay impassive. "I never belonged here anyway."

Jake crossed the room and sat on the other chair. "I said the same thing, long time ago. But I didn't *want* to be here. Not like you."

Amara knew what he was doing. She appreciated it, but at the same time she wished they would just get everything over with. If she was kicked out, she was kicked out. She would go, and try not to ever look back. "Then why'd you sign up?"

"We were at war," he said. "My dad was leading the charge. I thought... I dunno. Maybe I'd see more of him. Get assigned to his squadron. Maybe even Drift with him. But this weird thing happened. Turns out I was damn good at it." He smiled at the memory of this discovery, but the smile didn't last. He went on with his story, and for once, Amara didn't interrupt him with a sarcastic remark. "Then one night Nate—Ranger Lambert—and I get into it. Over something stupid, I don't even remember what. So I climbed into an old Mark IV to show him I didn't need him or anybody else to be a great pilot."

"Wow. That was stupid." Amara had already heard

the story of Jake holding a Drift for hours, but this was something else entirely. This was nuts, almost impossible, something only a few people had ever managed to do. And Jake had done it just to prove a point after an argument? That was... she didn't know what it was. Crazy, ballsy, reckless, maybe even admirable all at once.

Jake shook his head. Again a little smile appeared and disappeared. "Yeah. Took two steps and blacked out from the strain." His voice started to shake with emotion as he kept talking. "First thing I saw when I woke up in the infirmary was my dad. He told me I was out of the program. I begged him to ask them to let me stay. That I'd try harder, be a better soldier. He said there was no one to ask. The decision was his. Said I didn't deserve to be in a Jaeger. He said—he said a lot of other things. And so did I. Soon as I could stand up, I left and never looked back."

Jake wasn't looking at her, and Amara had the feeling that he wasn't entirely talking to her by then, either. They had Drifted together, so she had an intimate sense of how he viewed his father. But this was deep, buried underneath the top layer of memories that was all she and Jake had shared thus far.

"A year later, he was gone," Jake said. "I never got the chance to prove him wrong. More importantly, I never got the chance to prove it to *myself*." Now he was looking at her again, and talking to her directly—but she still had the feeling he was articulating a conversation he was having with himself just as much as he was trying to give her a last bit of guidance before she went back out into the world beyond the Shatterdome. "Because I was angry. And hurt. Don't let what other people think define who you are, Amara. You won't like where that takes you." He stood and moved toward the door, but paused before leaving. "And keep your head up, and you might just be as good-looking as me in this type of situation." She rolled her eyes. "Seriously, this face is set up well," he added with a grin. "Beauty is a burden. You'll be all right."

He had a hand on the door. Amara tried to process it all. What was she supposed to do with all this? Go to Marshal Quan and beg for her cadet position, like Jake had? Or just go forth in the world and realize she'd learned a hard lesson? Or was Jake hinting that there was another way for her to save herself and stay here, with all these new people she had just begun to care about?

She was so preoccupied with sorting through all those conflicting thoughts that she almost forgot about what she'd meant to tell him right at the beginning. But now he was walking toward the door and she would never have another chance.

"Shao Industries," she blurted out. "That's what I was trying to tell you. Obsidian Fury has tech in it made by Shao Industries."

He stopped and turned slowly around. "Jules and her team scanned every centimeter of that Jaeger. Didn't find any serial numbers or identifying markers." The implied question: How had Amara found something on her little jaunt that a trained J-Tech team had missed?

"Insulating metamaterials wound counter-clockwise in the shunt cabling," she said. "Shao's the only company winds them that way."

She was confident, and her confidence cut at least part of the way through Jake's initial skepticism. "Amara, are you sure?"

She had him. "Yeah. Stole a ton of it to make Scrapper," Amara said, a little of her normal bravado returning. Then, almost offhand, she added, "Thought it might be important."

She saw Jake thinking. Saw him working through the logical consequences of this find. There were three potential reasons for Obsidian Fury to have Shao Industries tech. One was simple theft, or reuse of materials originally built into a legitimate Shao product. The other two...

"Don't go anywhere," he told her, and shut the door behind him.

# 20

"SHAO INDUSTRIES?" GOTTLIEB SOUNDED skeptical. "They don't even have a bio research division."

"That we know of," Jake said.

"Cabling could have been stolen, just like in Amara's Jaeger," Lambert pointed out. "We need more than that to link Obsidian Fury to Shao."

"What about Newt? He'd have access to internal records, shipping manifests…"

"Go see him," Jake suggested. "Keep it low profile."

Gottlieb's face lit up. "A mission," he said, delighted. "I have a secret mission!"


At first Quan was just as skeptical as Gottlieb, but he didn't dismiss the idea out of hand. He was too professional a soldier for that. He might have just argued with Jake over Amara's fate in the cadet program, and he might have had just about enough of Jake Pentecost's continual tendency to bend the rules and shoot off his mouth… but if anything about Amara Namani's accusation could be confirmed, that was potential evidence in the investigation of the death of Secretary General Mako Mori. Not to mention hundreds, if not thousands, of other people in downtown Sydney. The final casualty counts were still coming in as rescue teams dug through the rubble of the area between the waterfront and the Council Building.

Before Quan could make any decisions, he had to work through the implications. Most importantly, he had to decide how the cadet's discovery affected the inquiry into Mako's death. "You think Mako was the real target in the Sydney attack?"

That was where Jake had begun his argument. "The data packet she sent led to that facility in Severnaya," he said, expecting Quan to put the rest of the pieces together himself.

Lambert was more direct. "She must have found out what was happening there."

"If the PPDC knew Liwen was experimenting with Kaiju bioweapons…" Jake paused, and Lambert picked up where he'd left off. It was something long-time Ranger partners tended to do, after dozens of Drifts together. The fact that Lambert and Pentecost were already doing it suggested they had a stronger than average Drift connection.

"No Drone program," Lambert said. "No Shao Industries. Nothing but a prison cell."

Quan wasn't so sure about that. People with Shao Liwen's money and clout usually avoided prison. But there was no question Lambert was right about the Drone program and the fate of Shao's company.

"The attack on the Council, the Kaiju cults—all a smokescreen," Jake said. "Misdirection."

It was plausible. Quan had to admit that. But hardly airtight. "And the only proof is from a cadet I just drop-kicked over the moon?"

"Gottlieb's reaching out to Newt to see if he can dig up anything more solid from the inside," Lambert said.

Quan chewed on that for a while. He didn't like the idea of involving Gottlieb, who was a solid and brilliant scientist but perhaps not the best person to involve in a discreet investigation. Particularly not if it meant informing Newton Geiszler of the PPDC's suspicions. Marshal Quan, like most other staff officers who had ever worked with Newt, considered that he might well be a genius but was definitely an unreliable loose cannon when it came to protocols and rules. "All right," he said. "We'll patch through to the Council and see what—"

"I don't think we should trust the comms," Pentecost said. Quan was about to dress him down for interrupting a superior—he had lost the last of his patience for Pentecost's mouth—but before he could, Pentecost added, "Mako didn't, or she would have told someone before Sydney."

This made sense to Quan. He considered it, looked for holes in the logic, found none. "Then we'll take it to them in person. Meet me on the tarmac in fifteen."

"What about Amara?" Pentecost asked. "She found the link to Shao Industries."

"If you're right about this, we have bigger problems, Ranger." Quan left the two Rangers in the hall, entering the War Room to make arrangements for the trip to Sydney.

Out in the hall, Jake fumed, wishing he could do more for Amara. She had screwed up, yeah, there was no doubt about that. But if in the process of screwing up she had pinpointed Mako's killer, and uncovered a dangerous program of illicit Kaiju-related biotech research? To Jake that was more than enough to give her a get-out-of-jail-free card on the injury to Jinhai and the unauthorized snooping inside Obsidian Fury. Rangers weren't supposed to be robots. They were supposed to know when to take the initiative. Amara had done that, and as far as Jake was concerned, the Ranger corps would be better off with her than without.

But that was a conversation for another time. Specifically after they had discovered whether Amara's discovery led where Jake was beginning to think it would.

Shao Industries was on target to hit its deadline of full Drone Jaeger deployment forty-eight hours from her first order. Shao herself had seen to this, berating and terrorizing the staff, from the lowliest tech all the way up to Dr. Geiszler. They might fear her, some might hate her, but they worked hard for her—and all that work was paying off. She strode through the lobby of Shao Industries' research headquarters in Shanghai, watching results on a data pad in her hands. Chief Kang fell into step with her, fresh from a check on the building's security systems. "The building is secure, ma'am."

"No visitors without the proper credentials," she ordered. That would mean closing the public areas of the Shao Industries building, but at this point Shao didn't care. She was too close to the realization of a dream she had pursued since before the end of the Kaiju War, when she had seen dying pilots and each time thought, *What a waste. Why do we send young men and women out in the Jaegers when they might as easily control them from a Shatterdome?*

When the sun rose in the morning, that question would be answered: we don't anymore. "I don't want anyone interfering with deployment," she added, in case Chief Kang hadn't already gotten the point.

Her data pad chirped. She looked down at it and angled it away from Kang, frowning. "I'll be in my office," she said, dismissing him.

Kang nodded. "Ma'am." He walked briskly off, leaving her to grapple with what she was seeing on her screen. It wasn't possible. Was it?

# 21

## CADET DISCHARGE REPORT

**CADET:** AMARA NAMANI

**REASON(S) FOR DISCHARGE:**

RECKLESS CONDUCT RESULTING IN INJURY
TO PPDC PERSONNEL

INTERFERENCE WITH PPDC INTELLIGENCE
INVESTIGATION

FAILURE TO FOLLOW TRAINING
REGULATIONS

**SUMMARY**

Cadet Namani encouraged fellow cadets to accompany her on an unauthorized foray into the remains of the destroyed rogue Jaeger Obsidian Fury. During the course of this activity, she evaded security and damaged the interior of Obsidian Fury. The damage resulted in the release of Kaiju blood and injury to Cadet Jinhai.

continued...

Cadet Namani exhibited contrition and did not attempt to evade responsibility, which speaks well of her character. Ordinarily conduct such as hers would result in a dishonorable discharge but her record will reflect dismissal without the further censure of a dishonorable designation.

Cadet Namani will be returned to her former home in Santa Monica, California. PPDC will suggest to local law enforcement that she not be prosecuted for her offenses there.

[SIGNED] MARSHAL QUAN

Amara did what Jake had told her to do. She stayed in the room until PPDC security came to get her. But whatever faint hope of mercy she'd still held onto evaporated when they led her out the door and then said, "By PPDC regulations you are permitted to observe as we clear your belongings out of your locker. If you have concerns about our handling of your personal items, you may register those concerns verbally. But under no circumstances will you approach security personnel who are performing the locker clear-out. Is that understood?"

She nodded without speaking so they wouldn't hear the tremor she knew would be in her voice.

They led her to the barracks, where the rest of the cadets stood watching as security emptied Amara's locker. They were competent and professional, even folding her clothes as they stowed them in her duffel bag. In a way this made Amara angrier than she otherwise would have been. If they'd been careless or deliberately destructive, at least she could have gotten angry about that, but no, they were treating her exactly by the book. She would miss that. Back in Santa Monica, there was no book. You got away with what you could until someone stronger or smarter than you put an end to it. Amara was only then realizing how much she was going to miss a world governed by rules.

"This isn't fair," Suresh said.

Amara looked up as Jinhai approached her. His arm was heavily bandaged from thumb to above the elbow. It was hard for Amara to look at, but she made herself do it. Actions had consequences. She had caused this and she didn't have any right to look away because it made her uncomfortable.

"I tried to talk to my parents," Jinhai said. "But they wouldn't listen."

"It was my mission," Amara said, trying to let him off the hook. "This is on me."

She appreciated his gesture, but regulations were regulations. She hadn't caught a break because her parents didn't have any influence, but if she had caught a break, that wouldn't have been abiding by the rules, would it? You couldn't have it both ways.

Her locker was empty and the security detail came to lead her out. "Amara," Vik called. "The next Jaeger you build. Make it a *big* one." She grinned, and Amara almost lost it then, at that gesture of support from Vik of all people. She remembered Vik taunting her: *Bigger is better.* God, how was she going to leave all these people and go back to the life she'd been leading before? Were they even going to let her keep Scrapper?

Security held the door for her as she left. Amara didn't look back because she didn't want the rest of the cadets to see the tears in her eyes.

Newt had been in the lab for almost twenty-four hours straight, cracking the whip over his tech crew as they slowly ticked off deployment after deployment. The plan overall was to have demonstrations of Drone Jaeger teams at all the major cities around the Pacific Rim, from Vladivostok all the way around through Los Angeles and back up through Sydney, Shanghai, Tokyo... It was a lot of Drones, and that meant a lot of Drift-trained pilots Shao had hired away from the PPDC. Other Drone pilots weren't veterans of Ranger service, and had gotten their Drift training from new cradles and simulation rigs of Newt's own design—though of course because he was working for Shao, she held all the patents and got all the credit.

Sometimes that bothered him. She couldn't have pulled this off without him, and she knew it, even though she would never have admitted it in front of him. But that was all right.

Newt had a pretty good idea just how smart and capable he was. Sometimes that came across as arrogance, but what the hell, that was the price you paid for being honest.

Right now he didn't have patents or credit on his mind. He was singularly focused—as focused as he'd been able to get in weeks, if not months.

In Santa Monica, there was one last tricky pair of Drones that were having trouble processing the signals from their Drift pilots here in the Remote Conn Lab.

It took up most of a floor in the Shao Industries tower, nearly a full city block of equipment and Drift cradles modified to operate solo without the immediate visual and tactile stimulus that came from working inside a Jaeger. Here everything was done virtually. One hundred pilots, in nice even rows of twenty, worked identical Drift rigs conveying their commands to identical Drones. Glancing over at them, Newt felt a flush of pride. This was so much better than relying on the two-pilot Drift to control a Jaeger. The interaction of two minds always caused unexpected emotional resonance, which complicated the task of handling thousands of tons of heavily armed steel. With a single remote pilot, not only were commands clearer, the pilots were safer. Kaiju—or any other enemy—couldn't get them here in the Remote Conn Lab.

This was the next step in Jaeger evolution. Newt felt good about it, like he was about to change the world.

He worked the deployment screen, making sure the Drift connections were stable and the Drones were coming online according to the specified schedule. They were almost there...

The Drift rigs handling the Santa Monica Drones went from red to green. Stable Drift, good contact, Drones operational. They were flanking November Ajax, conveying a message of unity to the millions of people watching all over the world. At other Shatterdomes, and other cities, Drones marched out in formation with Jaegers. Where there were no Jaegers, Shao had made sure there were video feeds showing the lockstep presentation of Drones and traditional Jaegers. She very much wanted everyone to believe that the Drones weren't replacing the Jaegers, even though Newt didn't see how anyone could believe that for more than a split second after they saw the Drones in action.

The last two Drones were still being flown in to Moyulan Shatterdome, but their board readouts were also green. Even though the Jumphawks hadn't dropped them yet, they were ready for service. Their pilots grumbled about being the last to actually take the field.

Newt decided he was calling it. Every Drone but Moyulan was up and running, and those last two were deploying at that moment. "Delivery at one hundred percent!" he crowed, setting off cheers from the techs in the lab. "That right there, *that's* the way you do it."

Almost as soon as he got the words out of his mouth, warning lights started to flash.

In the Moyulan Shatterdome LOCCENT, a technician noted strange energy signatures coming from the two Drones now approaching the Shatterdome tarmac.

In the Remote Conn Lab at Shao Industries, warning lights blazed across Newt's command screen. The closest remote pilot was Shao's favorite, Burke. He wrestled with his controls as the holo displays around him started to change color and deform. "Losing uplink to Drone 375!"

Other pilots echoed the warning. Newt spun back to

the command readout. All over the Remote Conn Lab, warning lights flashed and the colors of the screens around the pilots coruscated and changed. Something about the sight was familiar to Newt, but he couldn't think what...

# 22

VALOR OMEGA STOOD SENTINEL OUTSIDE THE
Jaeger bay doors of the Moyulan Shatterdome, awaiting
the arrival of the final Drones that threatened to make it
and all the other human-piloted Jaegers obsolete. That
was the feeling among the Rangers and J-Techs, despite
Shao Liwen's assurances to the contrary. The lights of
approaching Jumphawks, together with the running
lights on the Drones they carried, came steadily closer,
approaching the Shatterdome from the south. Amara
looked up at them as PPDC security escorted her to a
helicopter that was going to take her... well, she didn't
know. Home? There was nothing there for her. What *was*
she going to do next?

Jake caught her eye from across the tarmac, where
he had been about to board another Jumphawk. Amara
wondered where he could be going in such a hurry. She
hoped it had something to do with the information she'd
given him about the cables inside Obsidian Fury, but she
couldn't know. Nobody was talking to her about anything
right now, except when they gave her commands to go
somewhere. The sound of the Jumphawks was getting loud

now, as Jake came trotting across the tarmac toward her. Was he going to tell security to let her go? Amara's heart leaped at the possibility, but she knew it was more likely Jake was just coming over to say goodbye one last time.

Before Jake had taken ten steps, an urgent voice broke through the background noise in his commlink. One of the techs up in the LOCCENT was shouting in Mandarin. He stopped and looked back at Marshal Quan, who translated. "There's something wrong with the Drones!"

Jake looked up just as vivid purplish energy crackled out from the Drones' heads. Tendrils of pulsing Kaiju flesh bulged out at the seams in their armor plating, coiling into each other and fusing with the Drones' electronic systems. The system overload made the Drones spasm and thrash their limbs, destabilizing the Jumphawks' flight patterns. The Jumphawks spun into one another and the cables holding the Drones snapped. They fell the last few hundred feet to the tarmac as the Jumphawks spun down and disintegrated in a blast he could feel all the way across the tarmac.

As the Drones hit the ground near the hydraulic lifts providing water access to deploying Jaegers, they were already opening fire. A barrage of plasma missiles raked the tarmac, destroying vehicles and exploding at the edge of the Jaeger bay doors. Then the Drones turned their attention to the rows of parked Jumphawks and V-Dragons, methodically smashing their way through them. Some of the V-Dragons and smaller helicopters got into the air, but the Drones blew them out of the sky, their flaming wreckage falling to the waters of Qingchuan Bay. Those that got close enough to fire on the Drones were swatted down to the tarmac, where they burned amid the wreckage of Scramblers and forklifts.

"Get to Gipsy!" Marshal Quan ordered Jake and Lambert. They took off running as Quan issued more orders into his commlink. "All pilots! Man your Jaegers and engage hostiles!"

Inside the Jaeger bay, Rangers and J-Tech crews sprinted to their stations. Valor Omega was outside the bay, and the Kaiju Drones turned their attention in that direction. A double volley of missiles blasted Valor Omega apart before her crew could even get the Jaeger online. The violence of the explosion killed her crew and both of her Ranger pilots. Pieces of the destroyed Jaeger skidded across the tarmac and rained down for hundreds of yards in every direction, splashing into the bay and pinging off the outside of the Shatterdome. Valor Omega's severed head bounced twice and then rolled, missing Amara by only a few feet as she dove out of the way at the last second. Her security escorts weren't so lucky. The head smashed through them and demolished the chopper waiting to take her away before crashing to a halt against the outer wall of the Shatterdome. Still on the ground, she looked around, overwhelmed by the horror of the attack. Missile after missile blasted parked Jumphawks, J-Tech transports, clusters of fleeing Shatterdome personnel. The Drones were working methodically across the tarmac, from the landing strips to the far side, where the deployment gantries still stood untouched.

Satellite feeds inside the LOCCENT showed the same unfolding catastrophe all over the world. Drones went rogue and attacked in Anchorage, Guam, Lima, Attu... and Santa Monica, where November Ajax burned against the backdrop of the Kaiju bones at the pier. Quan saw the Shatterdome at Fukuoka collapse, sending up a mushrooming ball of smoke. In the shallow waters of

Lake Washington, a Jaeger lay face down, the ripples of its impact still spreading outward as a Drone pumped missiles into its back. In Manila, Drones strode up the Pasig River, the North Harbor waterfront ablaze behind them. The feed from Jakarta showed one Drone down, but the second stood over the inert remains of the defending Jaeger. All over the world, the scene was the same. Only on the Sydney waterfront, defended by the few anti-Kaiju cannons that had survived Obsidian Fury, did the PPDC appear to be winning. The cannon batteries pounded the Drones trying to follow Obsidian Fury's path of destruction, saving what remained of the PPDC Council Building.

This was supposed to be a day of celebration, a new stage in the development of the PPDC and the Jaeger Corps. Instead, thought Marshal Quan, it was entirely possible that by the end of the night there would be no Jaeger Corps left at all.

# 23

## PAN PACIFIC DEFENSE CORPS JOINT SECURITY DIRECTIVE
### NOT FOR PUBLIC CONSUMPTION

TO ALL LOCAL AND REGIONAL AUTHORITIES IN PPDC OVERSIGHT TERRITORIES:

Drone Jaegers in their initial deployments are attacking Ranger-piloted Jaegers, Shatterdomes, and other PPDC installations. All Drone Jaegers should be destroyed on sight using any and all available weapons short of tactical nuclear options.

All civilian populations and non-essential PPDC staff must be evacuated from the areas near the Drone attacks.

Jumphawks, V-Dragons, and other PPDC aircraft currently deployed should not return to their home Shatterdomes. Activate existing protocols for redirecting PPDC aircraft in emergency situations, per landing agreements at other regional facilities.

continued...

Until further notice, no Shao Industries contractors are to be permitted in any Shatterdome facility without personal clearance from that Shatterdome's Marshal or acting Marshal.

No PPDC personnel are to comment publicly on these events under any circumstances. PPDC Council outreach staff in Sydney will coordinate public response and dissemination of information. It is particularly emphasized that PPDC personnel should not answer questions regarding Kaiju tissue or Kaiju components in Drone Jaegers.

Newt hurried through the halls of Shao Industries, on his way to Shao's offices. She needed a personal update on what was happening, and she really needed to hear it from him. That was urgent in a way that Newt felt without really understanding why he felt it so keenly. He was still in shock from what he'd seen in the lab. Every single Drone Jaeger had first gone offline and then surged back to active status under independent control. The feedback through the remote Drift cradles had killed almost all of the pilots in the Remote Conn Lab. It was a horrific sight. The ones who survived had devastating brain injuries. Most of them lay twitching in their cradles, muttering gibberish or just moaning without words. Newt had ordered the tech crew to try to re-establish control over the Drones, broadcasting automatic emergency shutdown codes, but they had all been ignored.

In short, Newt had just overseen the deployment of dozens of hostile Jaegers that were in the process of destroying PPDC installations all over the world. Not to mention the havoc they were causing in the cities where Drone demonstrations had been planned as public-relations events. It was an unthinkable situation. How was it even possible? Who could have done it? There were reports from the field about strange organic protrusions on some of the rogue Drones, but Newt didn't know how that could be possible. It was just nuts. People under battlefield stress saw funny things, that was all. Just like with that rogue Jaeger, the one the PPDC was calling Obsidian Fury. Couldn't be that fast, right? That much faster than all the other Jaegers? Unless someone really different had created it…?

He was having thoughts like that pretty often the more stressed he got, and to keep his thoughts from going in directions he didn't want them to go, Newt had been talking to himself a lot lately. Anyway, it made him feel better and he wasn't self-conscious about it even though he knew some people thought talking to yourself meant you were crazy, but that was their problem. So at the moment he was rushing down the hall and talking a blue streak to himself as he went, convincing himself that everything would be all right once he got the situation figured out and knew what action to take. "Okay, okay, you got this, it's cool. You cool? Yeah, I'm cool. I'm super cool…"

A lab tech, Qingsheng, called to Newt as he passed by. "Dr. Geiszler! Shao's looking for you."

"I know, I know! I'm heading up!" Newt almost started running, but he thought if he did, he might panic. The old unstable feeling in his mind was back, and it was all he could do to keep himself under control. Those were his Drones. He had designed their systems, he had overseen their manufacturing, he had helped write the training protocols for the remote Drift cradles. How had he missed someone sabotaging the whole thing by—

As he came around a corner, he almost ran smack into Hermann Gottlieb, who grabbed Newt by the arm and pulled him aside. "Hermann? How did you get in here?" He'd thought Kang had the building locked down to all outsiders.

"I do have PPDC credentials," Gottlieb said, a little huffy at the perceived slight despite the panicked circumstances. "And besides, everyone here seems a bit preoccupied with the killer Drones your boss just set off."

"It's not her fault!" Newt said instinctively. But how did he know that? Why did he feel so certain about it? A plausible alternative occurred to him and he ran with it. "The Kaiju worshippers! Maybe they found a way to hack—"

"This has nothing to do with Kaiju worshippers!" Gottlieb was almost shouting. When he saw he had Newt's attention, he glanced around them. Seeing no one else nearby, he went on in a lower voice. "We found evidence linking Obsidian Fury to Shao Industries."

Newt couldn't believe it. Shao, mounting a terrorist attack on the PPDC right when she was about to need the organization to approve her Drone program? That was... a little too on the nose as a false-flag conspiracy theory, wasn't it? Although maybe that made it perfect, Newt thought. Nobody would believe how pat it was, so it would be easier to get away with it. Design a rogue Jaeger, threaten other Jaegers, demonstrate how they need some help, blow up part of the Council Building to make sure your point gets across... Was Shao capable of that? Newt really found that hard to believe. There *had* to be some soulless corporate tycoons who weren't also mass murderers.

Didn't there?

And how would she have designed and built a rogue Jaeger without Newt knowing about it? He'd been working with all the Drone program pilots. He saw all of the quarterly manufacturing reports, especially from the fully automated plants that now made up nearly forty percent of Shao Industries' production capacity. Wouldn't he have noticed the diversion of enough resources to make a Jaeger?

Not if the company was also concurrently making a hundred Drones...

Even so, it was a lot to take in all at once. Maybe it was Shao, but he had a little voice in his head telling him there was probably more to it than met the eye.

"*This* Shao Industries?" he asked, just to be sure. China was a big place. Maybe there was another company doing business under the same name. Maybe Hermann hadn't done all of his research yet.

"No, the Shao Industries that makes knickerbocker glories," Gottlieb said. Newt was thrown off by the joke—

Hermann rarely made them—and also confused because he had no idea what a knickerbocker glory was. Gottlieb kept going before he could ask. "Yes, this one. I came to see if you would help corroborate from the inside, but now that Liwen has shown her hand with these Drones—"

No, Newt thought. Shao had spent years building up the Drone army. Her career, her reputation, her company, all of it was wrapped up in this project. It defied logic that she would do it all just to sabotage it. And Newt still couldn't believe Shao had anything to do with the rogue Jaeger. Whatever evidence the PPDC thought they had, there must be another explanation. "Why would she build Drones to go bananas and attack? It doesn't make any sense. And what the hell's a knickerbocker glory?"

"She used you," Gottlieb hissed as they hustled down the corridor toward a bank of elevators. Gottlieb moved fast even with his cane. That all by itself told Newt how pressing he thought the situation was. "Lured you with money and a fancy title. And while you were basking in the glow, she took your research and twisted it."

Newt chewed his lip, a nervous habit he'd acquired in the last year or so. "You really believe that?"

"It's not your fault. She's been playing all of us. Help me stop her, Newton. Help me save the world, like old times."

"Well, you were technically helping *me* last time," Newt pointed out.

Gottlieb rolled his eyes. "Fine. Help me help you save the world. What do you say?"

Newt wanted to say yes. It was obvious he should say yes, if what Gottlieb said was true. But he couldn't quite make himself do it. He felt almost like something inside him was preventing his mouth from forming the words. His mind spun, trying to get around this internal block, see what it was. "I say…" He looked up at a movement behind Gottlieb. "Don't shoot!"

Newt raised his hands and stepped back as Chief Kang and a group of his officers rushed toward them down the hall, guns drawn. Gottlieb was looking at him, the thought plain on his face: *Now do you believe me?*

*I guess I do*, Newt thought. *But it's too late.*

Amara rushed into the Jaeger bay along with Shatterdome techs and field crew who had survived the Drones' initial attack. The rest of the cadets were inside, looking around impotently for something they could do to help. They saw Amara and clustered around her. "What's happening?" Jinhai asked. More explosions boomed from the tarmac. The Drones had worked their way through the landing strips, and were now concentrating on the hydraulic lifts and the huge collections of materiel staged out on the tarmac. The few Jumphawks and V-Dragons that had gotten away made attack runs, but their light weaponry couldn't do much against the Drones' armor. The braver pilots swung close enough to try to get a shot at the Drones' heads or the power cores set deep inside their torsos, but so far none of them had managed to score a damaging hit and many of them had died in the attempt.

Ryoichi could see outside. "Are those Jaegers?"

"Drones, from Shao Industries!" Amara said. They hustled along the deck, keeping to the side so they were out of the way of Jaegers coming out of their storage docks.

"What are they doing?" Tahima looked out onto the tarmac. Like Ryoichi, he seemed utterly unable to process what he was seeing.

"I don't know!" Amara said. "They just went crazy!" She couldn't get the carnage out of her head. Amara had seen people die before—you couldn't go long in the Santa

Monica slums without seeing death—but on this scale, and so violent…

Jake and Lambert jogged past, in full drivesuits, weaving around some of the debris from Valor Omega on their way to Gipsy Avenger. "Clear the deck!" Lambert ordered the cadets.

At the same time Jake shouted, "Get to your quarters!"

The Drone Jaegers loomed in the Jaeger bay doors. They weren't inside the bay, but they were close enough to see the deploying Jaegers. Plasma missiles screamed over Amara's head as Titan Redeemer stepped out of her dock. The missile volley blew the dock and gantry apart, also taking out the catwalks on that part of the bay's upper levels. At first Amara thought that was all the damage they had done, but as Titan Redeemer leaned into her second step, Amara realized that some of the swirling smoke was coming from her leg. One of the missiles had hit the knee joint, crippling it. As the Jaeger put her immense weight on that leg, the joint gave out. Before Titan Redeemer could compensate, she overbalanced and began to fall. "Go, go!" Lambert shouted. He and Jake shoved the cadets away, seeing that Titan was falling straight in their direction— but Lambert couldn't both push them and get himself out of the way. As Titan loomed closer, halfway through her long fall, Lambert set his feet. Amara saw he wasn't going to get clear in time. There was no way.

But none of them had seen Jules, running at full speed from under a nearby catwalk. She barreled into Lambert and tackled him out from under Titan Redeemer just as the toppled Jaeger slammed into the bay floor. A moment later, the Morning Star Hand smashed down, embedding itself into the steel plate of the Jaeger bay dock. The shock of the impact knocked the cadets off balance, and Jules landed on top of Lambert in an accidental embrace.

"Hey," she said after a beat.

"Hey," he said back.

Jake was incredulous. "Seriously? Now?"

Lambert disentangled himself, still feeling the electricity between him and Jules. He held the look as long as he could, but their comms lit up with warnings. The Drones were taking out unprepared Jaegers all over the world.

It was time to fight back.

# 24

## JaegerWatch:
## Thoughts on Kaiju

Everybody's got theories about these Kaiju rumors, and they're all wrong. Know how I know? Because by definition you can't know anything about aliens unless you happen to believe they think and feel as we do.

The thing you have to remember about the Kaiju, and I know this sounds stupid, but it's simple: They're aliens. That means you don't know how they think, what they want, what they feel or what makes them sad or even if they can be sad or if they can see the color blue or what philosophy they might have about the relative abundance of elements in the universe.

They're alien. ALIEN. Then we have to consider the Precursors, whatever they are. They live in another dimension, or a distant planet, and it's so different there that the particles that came back clinging to Raleigh Becket's drivesuit don't even have names. There are PPDC scientists who will spend the rest of their careers just figuring out what they are.

continued...

So don't tell me—this goes for both the Kaiju zealots and K-Science—don't tell me you know what the Kaiju want. Because you don't.

Because you can't.

Because you're human.

Unless you aren't, and that would be a whole other problem.

Newt and Gottlieb stood together in the elevator, boxed in by Kang's officers. Kang himself stood close to Newt. The elevator was headed down, presumably to the street level where Newt and Gottlieb would be handed over to the police on some charge Shao would trump up to make them look responsible for the Drones going haywire. Newt could see it all now. What a story Shao would tell, a tragic tale of two scientists who had once saved the world, but were corrupted and driven insane by the fact that they'd Drifted together with a Kaiju brain. Shao would pledge to make amends, putting the entire weight of her company behind the effort to counter the Drones and rebuild in the wake of their destruction. And as a result, Newt and Gottlieb would rot in jail forever while Shao's schemes went on...

They had to do something. Newt had an idea. He caught Gottlieb's eye and then looked down at Gottlieb's cane. Hermann didn't understand what Newt was suggesting. Newt tried again, adding a little dip of the chin this time to make sure Gottlieb knew he was indicating the cane. Then all he could do was hope Hermann put the rest of it together. It was time for desperate measures.

He saw understanding dawn in Hermann's eyes, and also fear... but then determination. Hermann coughed loudly, bending over with the simulated spasm—and then came up violently swinging his cane. It smashed across the face of the nearest security officer, breaking his nose with a splatter of blood.

Newt was already moving, too, grabbing Chief Kang's arm as Kang went for his gun.

Hermann flailed like a man possessed, his cane doing serious damage in the confined space of the elevator. Newt wrestled with Kang for possession of the gun. In the fight, the gun went off, the bullets punching holes in the floor but missing all the combatants. Kang had combat training, but Newt had the primitive advantages of surprise and desperation. He wrenched the gun out of Kang's hand and hit him in the face with the butt. Kang staggered, and Newt hit him again. This time Kang went down. Newt looked up and saw that while he had been subduing Kang, Hermann had taken care of the other officers. *Amazing*, he thought. *Who would have believed prim, brainy Hermann Gottlieb capable of that?*

He stabbed at the elevator's control panel and it stopped at the next floor. He and Hermann stepped out, leaving the elevator full of unconscious security guards. Newt dabbed at his lip, split in the scrap. Gottlieb had a bloody nose. But both of them were exhilarated by what they'd done. It was like something out of an action movie, but they'd pulled it off. "Thank you, Newton! I'd hug you if I didn't have a rule about public displays of affection—oh to hell with it!"

Gottlieb hugged Newt, surprising him. He was also surprised that it didn't bother him. He had a lot of affection for Hermann, and despite the awful circumstances, he was glad that they'd been brought back together.

"You're welcome, Hermann," Newt said. "Now if you're done groping me, we need to take care of those Drones."

They burst back into Newt's lab, where Daiyu and the rest of the techs were still trying to get control over the Drones. That wasn't going to be possible for them, but Newt had an idea. "Out!" he shouted, brandishing Kang's gun. Then he added in Mandarin, "Go! Now! Or shoot! Shoot!"

The lab erupted in pandemonium as the techs ran for the door, past Newt and Gottlieb. Daiyu was one of the last to exit. As she passed, she said, "I always knew you'd go nuts."

"You're fired," Newt snapped back.

Then he and Hermann had the lab to themselves. "What do we do?" Hermann asked. "How do we stop this?"

"Back door!" Newt proclaimed. He set the gun down and rushed to a terminal, tapping commands in faster than Gottlieb could follow.

"To what?" Gottlieb asked. "The lab?"

A holo screen appeared above the terminal console, showing the entirety of the Pacific Rim. The location of each Drone was a bright red dot. Many of them were grouped together, and those that weren't moved closer to each other, forming other groups. "To the Drone subroutine," Newt said. "I slipped one in just in case I wanted to get in there and poke around down the road."

"Sneaky bastard," Gottlieb said, but in an admiring way.

"I know, right?" Newt cracked a smile, but then he had to concentrate.

The subroutine's initiation command field opened up and Newt carefully entered the code. He'd written in a failsafe so the subroutine would lock itself down if someone tried to enter the wrong code, and there was no time to wait for the lock to expire. So after he'd typed the command, he reread it several times to make sure it was correct:

LV426

It was right. He punched ENTER.

Gottlieb was watching the screen, expecting the Drones to deactivate or return to the remote Drift protocol. Instead a command-line message appeared.

COMMAND LIMA VICTOR 426 CONFIRMED
INITIATING BREACH PROTOCOL

Gottlieb read the message over twice, eyes widening in horror. "What did you just do?"

"What I've been planning for the last ten years," Newt said. "Ending the world."

He looked up from the terminal to Gottlieb, who saw something dark and malicious behind Newt's eyes. The enormity of what he was realizing in that moment stopped Gottlieb dead in his tracks. He looked at Newt with horror, Newt's words replaying themselves in his mind—*what I've been planning for the last ten years*—and all at once Gottlieb realized that yes, Obsidian Fury had used Shao Industries parts, but not because Shao Liwen had created it. And yes, the Drones had gone rogue, but not because Shao Liwen had done it.

Newt had. It was Newt all along.

A satellite camera view appeared on the holo screen, superimposed over the lower corner. On it, a Drone emerged from the shallows in Honolulu Harbor, joining a group to form a circle. The torso lenses covering their power cores lit up and particle beams flared out, intersecting at the center of the circle. Where they met, a brilliant sphere of energy formed, with a thunderclap that rippled the water across the harbor. Below the sphere, the water churned, and something on the seafloor began to glow.

Gottlieb understood. They were opening a Breach.

"Why?" he moaned. "Why would you do this?"

"He wouldn't," Newt said, his tone mocking and hateful. "Or maybe he would. Maybe he hates all of you. For laughing at him. For treating him like an insignificant little joke of a man."

At first Gottlieb didn't understand why Newt was talking about himself in the third person, but by the time Newt had finished talking, the conclusion was inescapable. "You..." He saw in Newt's gaze another intelligence, alien and malevolent, and everything fell into place. *"Precursors."*

Abruptly Newt's demeanor changed. The sick smile fell away and Gottlieb saw terror in Newt's eyes. "Help me, Hermann," he begged. "They're in my head…"

"Fight them, Newton!" Gottlieb stepped up and grabbed Newt by the lapels of his coat. "Fight them—"

Newt spasmed in his grip as the Precursor in his mind reasserted control. He backhanded Gottlieb, sending him sprawling back against a lab table. "He isn't strong enough," Newt snarled. "None of you are."

The unmistakable metallic double click of a bullet being chambered cut through the air in the lab. Newt and Gottlieb both spun to see Shao Liwen, holding Chief Kang's gun leveled at Newt's head.

Unfazed, Newt chuckled. "Hey, boss. Finally figured it out, huh? What was it? The diagnostic?"

"My numbers weren't aligning with yours," she said, referring back to the Drift delays they had argued about only forty-eight hours before. "How did you do it? Without me knowing?"

"Thirty-eight percent of your manufacturing capacity is fully automated," Newt said. "Wasn't that difficult to reallocate a little here and there over the years without being detected." He switched to perfect Mandarin and added, "Especially since you always thought you were the smartest one in the room."

Gottlieb saw her make a decision. She might not have understood everything that was going on, but from her perspective, she knew everything she needed to know. One of her employees had betrayed her, outsmarted her, and destroyed everything she had worked her entire life to create.

Her eyes narrowed. "In about half a second, I'm going to be."

No, Gottlieb thought. *He may be under the sway of the Precursors, but Newton is still in there. My friend is still alive.* He lunged forward as Shao squeezed the trigger, sweeping his cane upward and knocking her hand up as the gun went off.

Newt shoved him from behind, sending him tumbling into Shao. Both of them hit the floor, but she came up aiming the gun at Newt again. Gottlieb grabbed her arm. "Stop! It isn't him! It's the Precursors! They must have infected his mind when we Drifted with a Kaiju brain during the—"

"Shut up," she snapped as she lowered the gun. Still holding her arm, Gottlieb looked around to see that Newt was gone. Shao shook him off and stepped over to Newt's holo terminal. "And don't ever touch me again."

She stabbed a finger into the intercom control on the terminal and spoke in rapid Mandarin. Gottlieb didn't speak enough of the language to understand everything she said, but he heard Newt's name... and he heard the word for *shoot*.

# 25

1. Whatever you are doing, you can always do it better. This is not a bad thing. If you were already doing the best you could ever do, and you knew it, that would be the time to start doing something else.

2. Also: Whatever you are doing, you can always do it worse. The funny thing is that often you start to get worse when you stop believing that you can be better.

3. The last thing you built might be the best thing you will ever build… but you have to build the next thing to find out.

4. Humans can both ask questions and answer them… but sometimes the answer is a machine. It is a terrible mistake to see machines as something apart from humans, because we envision them. We create them. We improve them and make them obsolete and envision new ones. Creating machines is one of the most human things a human can do.

5. If I had not become an engineer and programmer, I would have been… I don't know. I don't feel like I have done my best work yet, so it isn't yet time to think about doing something else.

Marshal Quan knew that he had lost Valor Omega in the first attack, and then Titan Redeemer moments ago. But as he burst into the LOCCENT overlooking the Jaeger bay, he didn't know the status of Guardian Bravo, Bracer Phoenix, Saber Athena, or Gipsy Avenger—although Gipsy was still undergoing repairs from her battle with Obsidian Fury. "Sit-rep!" he called. "Where the hell are my pilots—?"

Instead of answering that question, Xiang reacted as red circles suddenly blinked into existence all across the LOCCENT holo map of the Pacific Rim.

"Breaches detected!" Xiang cried out. "Multiple locations! It's the Drones, sir!" Quan registered the scale of the problem as he saw the number of Breaches. If even one Kaiju came through each, there weren't enough Jaegers in the world to stop them. "All pilots!" he said, leaning into the commlink. "Breaches detected!"

Down in the Shatterdome Jake heard Quan's alert. *"Drones in the field are opening multiple Breaches across the Pacific Rim—"*

The communication cut off as plasma missiles shrieked through the Jaeger bay and obliterated everyone inside the LOCCENT. The entire structure, undermined by the force of the explosions, came crashing down onto the deck as everyone below scrambled for cover. Jake dove behind the prone hulk of Titan Redeemer, with Jules and Lambert right behind him. Explosions rocked the interior of the bay and burning wreckage scattered across the deck between them and the docks holding the remaining Jaegers. The cadets, staying low, ran to join them in the relative safety behind Titan Redeemer. "We told you to get to quarters!" Jake shouted.

Amara pointed. "The corridor's blocked!"

Lambert was doing a head count. "Where are Tahima and Meilin?"

"I don't know!" Amara looked around but didn't see them.

Next to her, Renata tried to stay focused, but her question came out sounding panicked. "What do we do?"

"Stay here," Jake said. "We're going to try to get to Gipsy."

More missiles strafed the bay deck between them and the Jaeger docks. It didn't seem too likely that Jake and Lambert would survive a sprint across to Gipsy Avenger, but they had to try. If there were Breaches opening, Kaiju would be coming through. The only people on Earth who could stop them were Rangers... and only if they could get to their Jaegers.

Jake looked over at Lambert. "You ready for this?"

"No," Nate said right away. "You?"

"Nope." They were both crouched, tensing to go. "On three," Jake said. "One, two—"

A voice crackled through the static on the commlink. "—ello? Anyone there?"

Jake recognized the accent. "Gottlieb?"


In Newt's lab, Shao worked furiously to hack the subroutine Newt had installed in the Drones' operating code. The code's security scrambled it into an undifferentiated mass of data blocks, but if there was one programmer on Earth as good as Newton Geiszler, that person was Shao Liwen. She would cut through the security sooner or later. The only question was whether she could do it soon enough.

"Jake, thank God!" Hermann said. "I've been trying to raise the LOCCENT—"

"*It's gone! We're under attack! You have to force Liwen to shut down the Drones!*"

"It isn't her. It was Newt. Precursors infected him, got into his head."

There was a brief pause as the Rangers digested this. Gottlieb understood it was a hard thing to believe, but he hoped they would realize he wouldn't say something so outlandish without proof. When Ranger Lambert came back, his response gave Gottlieb at least some comfort. *"Gottlieb, it's Lambert. Can you make him disable the Drones?"*

At least they believed him. But now Hermann had to admit a shameful truth. "No. He—he got away. It was my fault. I—"

On the holo screen, the scramble of data formed into comprehensible lines of code. "I've penetrated the subroutine," Shao said. "Initiating shutdown protocol."

In the Shatterdome, the Drone Jaegers had destroyed everything they could see from the bay doors. They stomped into the bay, training their weapons on the vehicles—and more importantly, the Jaegers—now within range. "Shut 'em down!" Jake yelled.

"Stand by," Gottlieb answered. In the background they heard Shao say something angry in Mandarin. "It's trying to lock you out!" Gottlieb said.

Shao paused as an idea occurred to her. If she couldn't open the subroutine before the security protocols re-formed and shut her out, maybe she had time to rewrite just a few crucial lines of its code… "Feedback loop," she said in English.

"Brilliant!" The data blocks were re-forming, but some of the code was still accessible. "If you modify that algorithm—"

Shao's fingers flew over the keyboard, changing critical values. The screen was almost covered again in data blocks. Gottlieb couldn't tell if she had managed to alter the correct lines in time.

Jake's voice over the comm was tight with tension. "Gottlieb, shut 'em down now or we're all gonna die."

As Jake spoke, he was looking up at a Drone. It towered over the fallen Titan Redeemer, locking in on the group huddled on the other side. They were near Titan's partially crushed head. The violent impact with the floor had smashed open the Jaeger's face shield, exposing the still bodies of the Rangers inside. The Drone raised one hand and the muzzle of a cannon started to glow.

*So this is how we die*, Jake thought. *We're never even going to get to Gipsy Avenger. I'm never going to get to fight back*. If there was an afterlife, Stacker Pentecost was watching the scene and nodding. *Jake doesn't have what it takes,* he would be thinking. *I knew that all along.*

The Drone jerked and an ear-splitting screech echoed through the Shatterdome. Its arms twitched up and its weapon discharged, blasting a hole deeper into the halls behind the collapsed LOCCENT. It staggered, smashing a burning forklift. Kaiju blood spurted out through the seams in its head, burning on the alloy exterior and wreathing its head in smoke. Jake looked across the bay and saw the same thing happening to the other Drone. The screeching noise faded as both of the Drones overbalanced and crashed down.

On the holo screen in Newt's lab, the satellite view of Honolulu Harbor showed the circle of Drones reeling and toppling over as one. Their particle beams flickered and went out. From the churning water inside the circle, a Kaiju had begun to emerge from the Breach, clawing its way out of the Anteverse. When the energy sphere failed, the Breach disappeared, slicing the Kaiju in half. Its blood boiled in the water and its death throes sent up waves that surged over the piers of Honolulu's waterfront.

"Yes!" Gottlieb cheered. "Jake! Liwen disabled the Drones! The Breaches are closed—"

He stopped when he saw that the holo screen now displayed three blinking circles, and an ominous message:

KAIJU DETECTED

"Oh, no," he said.

"What?" Jake called back. Gottlieb didn't answer right away. Jake called his name.

Slowly, Gottlieb gave him the news. "Three Kaiju have gotten through. South Korea, Russian coast, East China Sea. Two Cat-Fours and a Cat-Five."

There was silence on the line as Jake registered the enormity of this. Kaiju of that size were often more than a single Jaeger could handle, as they had learned during the war. Three of them made for a threat that would require all the PPDC's resources... if there were any left after the Drone assaults.

"Copy that," Jake said. "Get back to the 'dome. We're going to need all the help we can get."

# 26

# TOP NEWS

## PACIFIC RIM SHUDDERS UNDER DRONE JAEGER ATTACKS

Terrorist Feared to Hack Drone Jaegers

Disaster For Shao Industries

Drone Jaegers Attack Shatterdomes, Civilians; Thousands Feared Dead

Will Shao Industries Survive the Drone Attacks?

Analysis: What did Shao Liwen Really Know?

Drone Jaeger Attacks Raise Questions about Obsidian Fury

Who Are the Kaiju Cultists and Why Are They Attacking Now?

12 Reasons Why the Kaiju Cults Have Nothing to Do with Obsidian Fury

PPDC on Verge of Collapse After Attacks on Council, Shatterdomes

In Dark Corners of the Internet, Dark Rumors: Did Shao Industries Use Kaiju Parts in the Rogue Drone Jaegers?

Kaiju Cult Claims Kaiju Have Returned: 'God Sends His Messengers Again'

A Look Inside the Black Market Trade in Kaiju Parts

Shao Liwen Destroys Own Drone Force… But Not Before Drones Cripple PPDC Jaeger Corps

Did Shao Liwen Stage the Drone Attacks?

A Defense of Shao Liwen

Markets Plunge in Aftermath of Drone Attack; Tech Stocks Hit Hardest

A few of the J-Tech medics were veterans of the Kaiju War, and had hard-won experience with mass casualty events. Many of the younger medics had lived through Kaiju attacks as children, but this was different. Then, all they had thought about was surviving, and later mourning. Now they had to tend to dozens, maybe hundreds of casualties, triaging and rendering aid in the middle of the devastation in the Shatterdome. The older generation tried to keep them focused and on task, as all of them grappled internally with memories of a time they had thought was past. Everyone was pitching in, trying to evacuate the wounded and get people out from under fallen debris. Jake and Lambert strained against a concrete slab pinning Tahima, as Amara and other cadets tried to work him free from underneath it. "Medic!" Jules called, waving one over. Tahima was alive but seriously injured.

Jinhai tried to joke with him to keep him together—and hide Jinhai's own concern. "Always lying around," he said. Tahima tried to smile. Nearby another team of medics was working on Meilin, who had also suffered wounds from the falling debris after the destruction of the LOCCENT.

Lambert saw Jules and called for a status report. With the LOCCENT out of commission, he'd asked her to get a sense of what the Shatterdome's operational situation was. "What do you got?"

"Reports are still coming in, but Drones took out Jaegers and Shatterdomes across the Rim," she said.

"How many Jaegers do we have here?"

"Operational? Gipsy Avenger. Barely."

"That's it?"

"Have to get more up and running or it's gonna be a short fight."

"Even if we can, all our other pilots are dead or—"

Lambert cut her off before she could demoralize all of

them. "One disaster at a time. Let's focus on those Jaegers."

"Think you can help with the repairs?" Jake asked Amara.

"Me? Thought I was kicked out."

Jake could have pointed out that she no longer had a ride off the Shatterdome because the Drones had destroyed every helicopter and Jumphawk on the tarmac, but right now they needed all the positivity they could get, so he took another approach. "I'm kicking you back in. Nobody has more experience turning junk into Jaegers." He glanced over at Lambert. "You good with that?"

"Outstanding," Lambert said with a grin. They were going to need all the help they could get.

Amara was touched by their belief in her. Could she live up to it? She looked around the Jaeger bay, realizing that she was about to take a big step. Building Scrapper was one thing; getting Bracer Phoenix and Saber Athena ready to go was another.

But she could do it. She knew she could.

"We got incoming!" Jinhai said, looking out through the bay doors to the tarmac. Jake and Lambert, along with a crowd of curious techs, rushed to the doors. None of the Kaiju should have been close already. Was it more Drones? If so, the lights were going to go out at the Moyulan Shatterdome real soon.

Once Jake got a look at the fleet of aircraft cruising toward the Shatterdome, he breathed a huge sigh of relief. They were V-Dragons, but not from the PPDC. Shao Industries had its own private fleet, each with the distinctive Shao logo stenciled on its fuselage.

Jake strode out to meet the V-Dragon that was landing closest to the bay doors. As it touched down and powered its engines off, Hermann Gottlieb popped out... and right behind him Shao Liwen. "I brought some help!" Gottlieb said.

From the other V-Dragons, a small army of Shao techs and engineers headed toward the Shatterdome, bearing tools and pushing cartloads of equipment.

*All right*, Jake thought. *Maybe we can pull this off after all.*

Gottlieb and Shao set up a temporary war room in a former lab space near the site of the destroyed LOCCENT. With Jake and Lambert, they gathered around a holo screen tracking the path of the three Kaiju that had managed to get through the Breaches before Shao's quick thinking— and quick fingers—had destroyed the Drone army.

The idea that Newt Geiszler was behind it all... Jake couldn't quite fathom that. He'd always like Newt, and to think that Newt had secretly engineered Kaiju tissue into Obsidian Fury and the Drones... that was a betrayal Jake couldn't wrap his mind around. But facts were facts, and had to be faced. Just like the fact of the three Kaiju. "Hakuja. Shrikethorn. And the big fellow, Raijin. I took the liberty of assigning the designations," Gottlieb said. That duty traditionally fell to LOCCENT staff.

"Yeah, great names," Jake said. "Sound like real a-holes."

Lambert was frowning at the patterns of the Kaiju's motion. "Shrikethorn and Raijin are moving away from the cities, towards the ocean."

"Maybe they're trying to link up with Hakuja in the East China Sea," Liwen suggested.

This was possible, Jake thought. Kaiju hadn't been known to look for each other like that before. During the war, they had sometimes emerged in pairs, but only once had PPDC forces fought three Kaiju. That was the Battle of the Breach, when Stacker Pentecost had blown his own

Jaeger's reactor to buy Gipsy Danger the time and space to get into the Breach.

Now Jake was about to take on three Kaiju, just like his father had. At least it looked that way, because the three trajectories of the Kaiju were loosely converging. They weren't headed directly for each other, though, which made Jake wonder. "Newt would know what they're up to, if we could get it out of him," he said.

"Have to find him first," Lambert commented.

"He escaped in a Shao V-Dragon," Shao said. "My men are trying to track him, but he disabled the transponder."

"Then that's off the table," Jake said. There wasn't any time to worry about things they couldn't control. Nodding at the screen, he asked, "Any Jaegers closer to those Kaiju than us?"

"What was left from the Chin-do and Sakhalinsk 'domes tried to intercept," Gottlieb said. "Emphasis on 'tried'."

Lambert stared harder at the map. "There's gotta be something there. Something in the East China Sea…"

Jake looked too, sure there was something they were missing. If you looked at all of the trajectories, maybe—

That was it. All of the trajectories. "Maybe that's not where they're headed," he said. "Pull up a map of Kaiju movement from the war."

Surprised, Lambert looked over at Jake. "You know something we don't?"

"You said you have to understand your enemy's objective to know you've beaten them," Jake responded, needling Lambert a little but also letting him know that speech had stayed with him.

A map displaying Kaiju incursions from the war appeared on the screen as Gottlieb brought it over from the PPDC strategic records server. Jake started working the screen, drawing lines that extended the Kaiju's paths if

Jaegers hadn't stopped them. "What if the Kaiju weren't blindly attacking our cities during the war? What if we were just *in their way*?"

Jake was no artist, but the more of the lines he traced, the clearer it became that they intersected at a single point.

"Mount Fuji, Japan," Lambert said.

Gottlieb started performing the same course extrapolations for Hakuja, Shrikethorn, and Raijin. There it was, just as Jake had intuited. Their courses were also set to intersect at Mount Fuji. That left the million-dollar question, given voice by Shao Liwen. "But why?"

Hermann Gottlieb gave a quick gasp of understanding. "Rare earth elements," he said slowly. "Mount Fuji is a volcano, rich in *rare earth elements*."

"Why are you looking like you're gonna pee your pants?" Jake asked. If Gottlieb was this scared, Jake felt like he should probably be scared as well, but he wanted to have a good reason.

"Because Kaiju blood reacts violently with them. It's the basis of my thruster fuel experiments."

"That sounds bad," Lambert said. "That's bad, right?"

"Very," Shao said. "Mount Fuji is *active*. A geological pressure point."

Gottlieb worked the holo screen, doing rapid math that the screen translated into visuals. A cross section of Mount Fuji, showing the lava reservoir below it, appeared, with a simulated Kaiju crawling into the caldera at the top of the mountain. "Based on the blood to mass ratio of the Kaiju…" He was running back-of-the-envelope calculations of Kaiju blood volatility versus the ratios of different rare earth elements in a volcanic interior. *Astonishing stuff to do just off the top of your head*, Jake thought. There weren't many people in the world as smart as Hermann Gottlieb.

The screen now showed a map of the entire Pacific Rim,

with active volcanoes marked. The region was known as the Ring of Fire, because of the intense volcanic activity in the areas where the Pacific tectonic plate ground against its neighbors in Asia and North America. On the screen, volcano after volcano began to erupt. When Gottlieb spoke, his tone was low and somber. "The reaction would cause a cascade event, igniting the Ring of Fire around the Pacific Rim." The simulation continued, wreathing the globe in a gray blanket. "Billions of tons of toxic gas and ash will spew into the atmosphere, wiping out all life."

Shao understood. "That would finish terraforming Earth for the Precursors."

"This doesn't make any sense," Lambert objected. "Why not just open a Breach right over Fuji and drop the Kaiju in?"

Lambert had a sharp tactical mind, and Jake chimed in with another angle on the same problem. "Or send one so big nothing could stop it?"

"From the data we recovered from Dr. Geiszler's files, the Precursors can only penetrate dimensional 'soft spots,' as he called them, between universes," Shao explained. "Every location the Drones chose corresponded to one of these."

"And a Category Five is theoretically the largest Kaiju they could send through, since the energy it takes to widen a Breach exponentially quadruples as the—"

"Yeah, science is our friend," Jake said. This was the downside of being a genius like Gottlieb. You started talking a language normal people couldn't understand. "We get it."

"We can't let them reach Mount Fuji," Lambert stated flatly. That was their mission objective, the only one that mattered.

"I'll check with Jules, see where we are with the Jaeger repairs," Jake said.

"Even if you had a hundred, there's no way to intercept in time," Shao said, looking at the distances on the map. "The Drones destroyed your Jumphawks and my V-Dragons aren't built to carry that kind of load."

There was a long silence. Jaegers couldn't outrun Kaiju without getting into the air. If they couldn't figure that part of the battle plan out, they would just have to sit here in the war room and enjoy satellite images of the Kaiju crawling into Mount Fuji and ending the human race.

Then Lambert looked away from the screen to Gottlieb. "What about your thruster pods?"

Jake remembered Gottlieb talking about those right when Jake was arriving at Moyulan. He'd been puzzled at the time, seeing Newt dismiss the idea and warn Gottlieb away from working with Kaiju blood. After all, coming up with new ideas about how to fight the Kaiju—understand them better—was the whole reason for K-Science's existence. Now that they knew the truth about Newt, that conversation took on a more sinister meaning. Had Newt done it on purpose? How much control did he have? It didn't seem possible that Newt could have carried around a Precursor in his head for ten years without either going crazy or letting something slip. Maybe he didn't always know it was there? Jake figured that if a Precursor could use the Drift to get into Newt's head across a dimensional barrier, it could probably also hide its existence from him. But that was all speculation. Right now they needed concrete solutions to concrete problems. Like the problem of whether they could use Gottlieb's thruster pods to catch the Kaiju before they got to Mount Fuji.

"They're not ready," Gottlieb said.

Shao got right to the point. "Can they be?"

Gottlieb considered the question. "In theory, maybe, with your help."

"What does that mean, 'in theory'?" Jake asked. They didn't have time to deal in theories. They needed results. Immediately if not sooner.

Gottlieb heard the challenge and lifted his chin a little, understanding the task ahead. "Today it means yes," he said.

# 27

THEY HAD A CREW OF HUNDREDS, THANKS TO
the reinforcements from Shao Industries—but not much
time. A quick assessment of Valor Omega determined
that she would have to be scrapped, and Titan Redeemer
was also too badly damaged to take any part in the
current fight. It might have been possible to repair her
damaged leg, with parts scavenged from Valor Omega's
remains, but Titan had also suffered catastrophic damage
in the uncontrolled fall. Her guidance systems needed a
complete overhaul and the interior of her Conn-Pod had
been almost destroyed by missile strikes after she fell.
That left four Jaegers to be the focus of the tech team's
work. Gipsy Avenger needed repairs to her armor plating
and Conn-Pod housing to get her fully combat-ready after
her engagement with Obsidian Fury in Siberia. Bracer
Phoenix, Saber Athena, and Guardian Bravo had all
suffered damage in the Drone attack. They couldn't go
into the field at all without at least some repair. And then
there was the question of the thruster pods. They had
to get the idea from Gottlieb's notes to the Shatterdome

tarmac in less than twenty-four hours or none of the repairs to the Jaegers would matter anyway.

Added to that was the widespread damage to support vehicles and the docking mechanisms. The first thing Shao's crews did was get four of the cradles welded back together so they could hold the Jaegers that needed repair. Then the Jaegers were towed into place and the real work could begin. The Jaeger bay was controlled chaos, with J-Tech and Shao teams crisscrossing it on repeated trips from parts and electronics warehouse storage to the docking cradles.

Outside, Hermann Gottlieb oversaw a caravan of tankers carrying Kaiju blood. Large reserves of it were kept in anaerobic storage in tanks deep below the Shatterdome, along with other Kaiju tissue and genetic material used in K-Science research. Now Gottlieb followed those tankers out onto the arm of the tarmac where the Jumphawk gantries stood. He thought the gantries would be strong enough to hold the Jaegers upright and true at the ignition of the thruster pods, if he could get the thruster pods built and integrated into the Jaegers' command systems soon enough.

Near the gantries he had set up an outdoor assembly line. Crews of welders and engineers took repurposed fuel tanks and thruster cones adapted from V-Dragon engines. They had to build the rest on the fly: fuel lines and valves, electronic control systems that could be quickly mated to the Jaegers' operating software, ignition chambers designed around catalyzing ingots of rare earth metals, brackets and housings to attach the thruster pods to the Jaegers at the correct angle so firing the thrusters wouldn't knock the Jaegers into an uncontrollable spin. There was also the problem of waste heat from the thrusters, which according to Gottlieb's calculations was a danger to the electronics in the Jaegers' midsections and legs. He ran back and forth from the tarmac to the Jaeger bay, making sure crews were adding heat shielding to the backs of the Jaegers and also installing thruster shunts below the exhaust nozzles to direct as much of the heat away from the Jaegers as possible. Then that meant he had to go back and recalculate the impulse angles to keep the Jaegers from spinning or tumbling... There were, as the saying went, a lot of moving parts. Gottlieb had no doubt that his math was correct, and the Kaiju blood would yield enough thrust to get the Jaegers airborne. The rest of the design would just have to go into the field untested.

Inside the bay, medical teams had removed most of the wounded and were working on recovering the dead. The base infirmary was more than two hundred percent over capacity, and wounded filled the barracks closest to the infirmary level. The dead, numbering in the hundreds, were zipped into body bags and held in the base morgue, which was also filled far beyond its design capacity. The traumatic aftershocks of the event would set in soon, but at that moment every member of the Shatterdome's crew was working toward one overriding goal: stopping the three Kaiju from reaching the top of Mount Fuji.

Triage of the damage to the four Jaegers they needed to achieve that goal yielded a long list of necessary repairs. Bracer Phoenix had suffered some of the worst damage. Her right arm was completely burned out, and they had no way to repair it in time. Jules had puzzled over this problem until she had an idea that she took to Lambert and Jake. She found them elbow-deep in Gipsy Avenger's Conn-Pod, retuning the maglev field generators. "Bracer Phoenix is down an arm. No time to get her combat-ready," she said.

"Bracer's railgun doesn't need her arm, right?" Lambert asked. "It's not ideal, but that team might just have to go out with one arm."

"Or…" Jules looked out over the dock floor. Crews had moved parts of Titan Redeemer out of the way toward the collapsed rubble of the LOCCENT. The torso was still in place, but the limbs and head were already pushed aside— except for Titan Redeemer's left arm, which hung in a cable sling between two mobile cranes. "Titan Redeemer's not going to be using that one anymore."

Both Jake and Lambert looked down at the detached arm. Then they looked at each other, and then back at Jules. "That's Titan Redeemer's left arm," Jake pointed out.

"Yeah," Jules nodded. "But we don't have to use the whole thing. Most of the damage to Bracer is elbow down. We can take the Morning Star Hand emplacement, flip it over, and mate it to Bracer's right arm. From there we can run new conduits to the main combat integration system that feeds the HUD in the Conn-Pod, and the crew shouldn't notice any difference."

"I like it," Jake said.

"I do too," Lambert said. "Except Bracer's crew won't have trained with it. Will they know what to do? It's going to change the balance of how Bracer moves. That thing is heavy."

"Better than nothing, right?" Jules waited for one of them to contradict her. When they didn't, she said, "All right. I'm going to get to it."


Amara and Jinhai paused in their work at the side of Bracer Phoenix's head to watch as the twin cranes carrying the Morning Star Hand lifted it into position. They were a hundred feet above it all, but the scale of the Jaeger parts made it all seem closer—until you realized how tiny the people looked, swarming around the monumental limb. Jules' crew had disassembled most of Titan Redeemer's arm, leaving only the Morning Star Hand and the internal spool holding the cable. From the spool housing, cables as thick as a human thigh dangled, waiting to be spliced into Bracer Phoenix's guidance systems. While Jules had been working on Titan Redeemer's arm, a crew from Shao Industries had pulled off Bracer Phoenix's arm below the elbow, and stripped away the external plating up to Bracer's shoulder. They had the new cable junctions ready. Other crews were standing by with the interlocking plates of Bracer's armor, waiting to refit it over the Morning Star Hand assembly.

Bracer rocked in the holding cradle as the crew banged the assembly into place against her elbow. Amara and Jinhai got back to work. One of the Drone missiles had hit the Jaeger square in the side of the head. Bracer's cranial armor had mostly held together, but the blast wave had destroyed the complicated gyroscopic mechanism that served Jaegers the way the inner ear served a human being. Without it, the Jaeger wouldn't be able to keep its balance. Heading back in through Bracer's Conn-Pod hatch, they worked their way past Vik, who was tack-welding brackets back into place after she had repaired the damaged electronics servicing the gyroscope.

Amara and Jinhai got their hands under the gyroscope. They locked eyes. "One," Jinhai said. Two and three were silent, but they lifted at exactly the same time, grunting and staggering with the gyroscope over to its housing. They got the edge of it resting on the flanged edge of the housing, but it started to overbalance as Jinhai shifted to get a grip on the side and ease it in. Before it could tumble out, Vik rushed over and braced it. The three of them, working together, got it in place. They exchanged exhausted fist bumps and Vik got back to her welding. Jinhai fired up a compressor powering an impact wrench to bolt the gyroscope into place, and Amara went back out onto the catwalk.

Suresh and Ilya were there, waiting for her to tell them what to do with a cart full of parts she'd sent them to get from a locker below the docking cradles. "Next thing we need is that shock absorber," she said, tapping her hand on a six-foot-long hydraulic absorber. It was one of eight that spoked out from the gyroscope housing, keeping the Jaeger's balance modulator from being bounced around too much in combat or deployment. Suresh and Ilya maneuvered it past her and in through Bracer Phoenix's Conn-Pod hatch.

Amara went down the catwalk toward Saber Athena, in the next bay, to see how things were going there. She was exhausted from work and lack of sleep, but she was also riding a wave unlike any she had ever felt before. Jake had put her in charge of what he called "Scrapperizing" some of the repairs. The way he explained it, that meant Amara had to figure out how to rig up on-the-fly solutions for repairs that they didn't have time to do according to the procedures in the Jaegers' technical spec. Amara had almost refused, since she was the new kid at Moyulan and didn't want to be put in the position of making the other cadets treat her like the teacher's pet. Jake had cut her refusal off. "Look," he'd said. "You've built a Jaeger. They haven't. So we need what you know and there's no time to worry about how anyone feels about it. If they're giving you trouble, save it for later."

*After we ride Gottlieb's experimental thrusters over hundreds of miles of ocean into combat against three powerful Kaiju, with all of our Jaegers held together essentially by duct tape and baling wire.* The more Amara thought about it, the more she realized Jake was right not to worry about how anyone would feel about it tomorrow... because the odds of there being a tomorrow didn't look all that good.

But if they were going to go down, they were going to go down fighting.

Renata and Ryoichi hung in rappelling harnesses from the catwalk ringing Saber Athena's berth. They were welding a plate closed on Saber's chest, covering a crack left by a plasma missile. Saber was in decent shape overall. Her weapons systems were housed on her back, so the missiles hadn't affected any of them directly. But her front side had taken a lot of impact damage. A small army of J-Tech and Shao personnel hung in other harnesses, welding repair plates into place. It wasn't going to be pretty, but Amara thought they had figured out a way to get the repairs done without compromising Saber Athena's superior speed and agility. At least she hoped they had.

And she hoped they hadn't missed anything when they did the repair analyses on Gipsy Avenger or Guardian Bravo. Of all the Jaegers, Guardian Bravo seemed to be in the best shape. That was why Suresh and Ilya were free to help with the repairs to Bracer Phoenix. They'd already worked through all the diagnostics they could run on Guardian Bravo. The Arc Whip was good, hull integrity was good, Conn-Pod stability checked out okay... the only repairs Guardian Bravo needed were basically cosmetic, and could wait for another time. So while crews swarmed over the other three Jaegers, Guardian Bravo was moving slowly on a tracked platform out to the launch gantries on the far end of the tarmac. They had a path cleared, largely by bulldozing destroyed Scramblers and Jumphawks out of the way. Then outside crews had covered the missile craters in the tarmac with armor plates taken from Valor Omega and Titan Redeemer. It was ugly, but it worked well enough to get Guardian Bravo into place on a gantry. The crew waiting there locked her into place and cranes lifted the twin thruster pods up. Once they were swung into place near Guardian Bravo's back, the whole gantry lit up with the flare of welding torches and rang with the sound of impact wrenches.

Gottlieb watched the final maneuvers, clutching a data pad and a sheaf of papers with his original notes on the potential energy of Kaiju blood. He had hit a snag in the process because he couldn't get the fuel equation to balance. If they'd had the time to design a second component to add to the fuel mixture and create a hypergolic combination that would self-ignite, everything would have worked brilliantly. But as it was, they had to use the raw Kaiju blood, and its properties were not fully understood—at least not where potential energy was concerned. All the simulations he had run with raw Kaiju blood and a single ignition component came out slightly wrong. They either led to insufficient thermal energy release, or caused a runaway reaction that could not be controlled in the combustion chamber. In short, despite Gottlieb's best efforts so far, the Jaegers either wouldn't get off the ground or would explode at liftoff. He was starting to panic under the pressure.

Shao Liwen was also working on the fuel equation, and Gottlieb decided to run back inside and see how her work was going. If they couldn't crack the problem together, there was no way on Earth to stop the Kaiju from entering Mount Fuji... except for multiple nuclear strikes.

# 28

## KAIJU CONVERGE ON JAPAN
### INTERNATIONAL NEWS AGENCY STAFF
### REPORTS

Three Kaiju have survived the eruption of numerous Breaches around the Pacific Rim and appear to be converging on Japan, according to information released by the Pan Pacific Defense Corps.

The three Kaiju, first seen along the east coast of the Asian mainland, appear to be taking different routes that will intersect at some point in Japan, though the PPDC cautioned that their future movements could not be projected with any certainty.

A source within the PPDC, requesting anonymity because they were not authorized to speak about the details of the Breaches' appearance and collapse, said an unknown number of other Kaiju died while crossing Breaches that closed suddenly when the Drone Jaegers were simultaneously deactivated. The PPDC and Shao Industries have declined

continued...

to address questions about this event, but it is known that at least nine other dead Kaiju are present in the shallow waters near various Pacific population centers. PPDC facilities near those areas are offering help with environmental remediation as they prepare to remove the partial Kaiju carcasses. With rumors flying that the rogue Jaeger Obsidian Fury and the hacked Drones were all using Kaiju biotechnology, control over the samples of the creatures' tissue becomes even more important for future security...

Shao was calling his name, and Hermann snapped back to the present. He had wandered back into the Shatterdome and now he looked up to see Shao coming toward him, falling into step so he could see her new calculations as they walked on. "See," she said. "The raw fuel will undergo a chain reaction in the presence of any pure lanthanides, but there is possibly a way to use smaller amounts of the raw fuel in a primary combustion chamber and then inject the full supply into a secondary combustion chamber where the—"

"Yes!" Hermann said. "Yes. We must get to the lab and run these simulations immediately." Reaching out to a nearby Shao Industries technician, he started to explain what he needed. Shao took over, instructing the tech in careful Mandarin exactly what modifications the gantry crews needed to make to the thruster pods. She sent him on his way and joined Hermann for the short walk to his lab, where they would find out if it had any chance of working.

Her idea was sound. To stop the Kaiju blood from undergoing a chain reaction and consuming the entire supply at once—in other words, from going off like a bomb—they had to use extremely small amounts of the catalyzing lanthanide to ignite small amounts of the Kaiju blood. But then they had to feed that ignited Kaiju blood into a second combustion chamber where it would mix with an unburnt supply fed in through a second line. If they modulated that mixture correctly, they would have an amount of thermal release sufficient to fly a Jaeger but not overload the engines.

Outside on the launch pad, the gantry crews were already installing the second feeder lines and adding the secondary combustion chamber. They had to refit the exhaust nozzles and rewrite the operating software as well, and they could not complete that second task until Gottlieb and Liwen could provide a stable fuel-mix equation. They were close, but still not there. Liwen was moving numbers around on a holo display while Gottlieb worked the same numbers on the screen at his main terminal. At this point, it was a process of elimination. There was a value that would succeed. They just had to run the sequence over and over again until they found it. Part of that process could be automated, but part of it had to come from the intuition of scientists working in the lab.

"Gottlieb," Shao said. He looked over and saw she had found a solution.

He rushed over to the terminal next to hers, checking her numbers and running them again several times to make sure there was no error. The equation checked out. They had a primary combustion ratio.

Hermann felt a spike of sorrow as he realized he could not share this discovery with Newt. It was the kind of work they had done together once, and now Hermann was forced to do it again because Newt had fallen under the sway of the Precursors. Where was he now? What was he doing? Was he able to watch the Kaiju make their slow progress toward mainland Japan, and ultimately the slumbering caldera of Mount Fuji? Hermann hoped there was a way to cure Newt, if PPDC forces did not kill him when he was found. A sane Newton Geiszler would appreciate what he and Shao had done. He was one of the few people on Earth who could... which of course was what made him such a dangerous adversary as a tool of the Precursors. But if he could be cured...

"Gottlieb," Shao said. "Do you confirm my result?"

He nodded. "I do. Superb. This is going to work."


Outside it was morning. Four Jaegers stood at their launch gantries, with four new sets of thruster pods attached to their backs. Separate smaller impulse thrusters were also attached to their lower legs. Gipsy Avenger already had these, and J-Tech crews had added them to the other Jaegers to increase maneuverability. At dawn, Bracer Phoenix had paused on her journey out to the gantry so tech crews could do a test deployment of the Morning Star Hand grafted on from Titan Redeemer. With everyone in the Shatterdome watching, a remote operation team ran the Morning Star Hand system, raising Bracer's right arm.

The target was one of the fallen Drones, dragged out of the Shatterdome and now lying near the oceanside lifts. Jake and Lambert were back in the ready room, putting on their drivesuits and running pre-deployment checks on their Drift helmets. Over their commlinks, they heard the tech crews arguing about something in Mandarin. Then one of them ordered Bracer Phoenix to fire.

Jake and Lambert looked up at the video screen in the ready room, which was set to a feed from the tarmac. The Morning Star Hand exploded from Bracer Phoenix's arm, crossing the hundred yards of tarmac in less than a second. The impact on the torso of the fallen Drone sounded like a bomb going off. Pieces of the Drone's armor spun away over the water and the target itself was blasted off the ground, landing with a splash that slopped waves up to the edge of the tarmac. The water churned around the sinking Drone as Bracer Phoenix snapped the Morning Star Head back into place. Waiting Jumphawks, among the few that had survived the attack, dropped cables down to retrieve the Drone. As they pulled it up out of the water, they could see the enormous dent in the side of its armor. Both of them were imagining what that would do to a Cat-4 or Cat-5 Kaiju, gauging whether it would be enough.

Jake glanced over at Lambert. "Guess it works," Lambert said.

There wasn't much to add. Bracer wasn't their ride, anyway. They finished getting ready and headed for the Shatterdome.

Hours after they'd started work on the Jaegers, Jules caught up with Jake and Lambert in the Shatterdome to update them. They were in their drivesuits, headed for the launch pads and the long ride up the gantries to Gipsy Avenger's Conn-Pod hatch. Destroyed vehicles and discarded Jaeger parts and armor formed mounds of debris around the cleared areas of the Shatterdome deck. If Gottlieb's crazy plan was going to work, they would all find out soon. The last time they'd talked to him, he was full of enthusiasm, but they couldn't follow the technical details of what he was saying, so they just nodded and let him run out of steam. But the upshot, at least as far as they could tell, was that Gottlieb and Shao Liwen working together had solved the critical problem with using Kaiju blood as fuel. So Jake was cautiously optimistic that the thruster pods wouldn't incinerate them all as soon as someone gave the ignition command.

"Saber Athena, Guardian Bravo, and Bracer Phoenix are good to go," Jules said. Jake and Lambert had already signed off Gipsy Avenger.

"Not a lot to work with," Jake said. He was wishing they had Titan Redeemer still, but there wasn't time to get her back up and running—especially not since they'd cannibalized several hundred of her parts, including her main weapon system, to speed up repairs to the other Jaegers.

"Liwen's team kit-bashed some Fury tech into Gipsy that might help," Jules added.

Jake was about to ask what, but Lambert didn't seem to care. They'd find out sooner or later anyway.

"Prep everything we've got for deployment," Lambert said. PPDC policy called for full deployment of an individual Shatterdome's complement of Jaegers only in extraordinary circumstances. During the war several Shatterdomes had suffered attacks while defenseless, so the policy made sense, but if ever there had been an extraordinary circumstance, this was it. No point in holding reserves back now.

A moment passed between Jules and Lambert. Jake stayed out of it, deliberately looking the other way. There was nobody to see him off and wish him well. Hadn't been in a long time. He was used to it, and he would fight the good fight anyway. "Don't get yourself killed, okay?" Jules said, and kissed Lambert on the cheek.

Then she turned to Jake, surprising him. "You either," she said, and kissed him too.

Jake and Lambert watched her go. "Well, that's confusing," Jake said. Here he'd been telling himself how nobody cared, and then Jules had to go and confuse everything.

With a frown, Lambert said, "Let's stay on point. We only have four Jaegers. Against two Category Fours and a Fiver."

Feeling optimistic in the wake of Jules' kiss, Jake said, "Better than just Gipsy."

"Still need pilots," Nate said, not willing to concede the point.

Jake started walking again, skirting pieces of Titan Redeemer's discarded armor plating. This was the one part of the plan he wasn't worried about. "We have them."

The cadets stood in a tight group, wearing their cadet drivesuits and holding their helmets. All of them were there but Meilin and Tahima, who had been too severely wounded in the Drone attack to serve. Jake and Lambert walked up to them and nodded. Jake hoped the gesture was reassuring. He could have used a little reassurance himself. Out in the world, the Kaiju-worshipping cults were rejoicing. They knew Kaiju had returned, and they had also gotten wind about exactly how the Drone program had been corrupted. The sites of the fallen Drones were crowded with Kaiju worshippers, touching the Drones and ritually scarring themselves with the Kaiju blood that still seeped from the tissue within. The PPDC and local law enforcement were too overwhelmed trying to cope with the damage to stop them.

Cities around the world were burning from the Drone attacks, and a fresh wave of fear was causing unrest even in places that hadn't been directly attacked. The Kaiju were back. Ten years since the closing of the first Breach was enough time for people to begin to believe that it would never happen again. Thus the calls to scale back the PPDC, devote its resources elsewhere, lower expenses by putting Jaegers under Drone remote control. Mako had fought hard on the PPDC's behalf, arguing that the costs of being caught unprepared were unimaginably worse than the costs of keeping up the PPDC. Who could say the Precursors would never open another Breach? How could they ever know? And how would they look the people of the world in the eye if the PPDC was shut down and a new Breach opened and there was nothing to defend them with?

Jake was choked with emotion as he considered how she hadn't lived to see just how right she was... and then rage crackled through him. Whether he was under Precursor control or not, Newt Geiszler had built the Jaeger that killed Mako because she was about to reveal his plan. Jake still didn't know how she'd found out, and PPDC intel services were digging into her records to see what they could learn on that front, but the details weren't important in the end. She had known, and Newt had killed her for it. Or the Precursor inside Newt's mind. At that moment Jake wasn't sure he cared about the distinction.

He stood before the cadets, aware of their eyes on him, their expectations of him. He wasn't his father. He wasn't going to come up with a great line like "Today we are canceling the apocalypse." But he could come at things from a different angle, an angle he understood because he'd lived it.

"If my dad were here, he'd probably give a big speech, make you all feel invincible," Jake began. "But I'm not my father. I'm not… I'm not a hero like he was. Like Raleigh Becket and Mako Mori. But they didn't start out that way, either. They started as *cadets*, just like you. We remember them as giants because they stood tall. Because they stood together. It doesn't matter how many tries it took to get here. Or who your parents are. Or where you came from. Or who believed in you and who didn't. You're part of a family now."

He glanced over at Lambert and saw his partner acknowledging Jake's callback to Lambert's speech to the cadets a couple of days before. "This is our time. This is our chance to make a difference."

The cadets were standing straight and tall now, their young faces set in expressions of resolve. Jake looked from one to the next, making eye contact with each one. He was asking a lot of them, and they wouldn't know if they were up to the challenge until they were inside a Conn-Pod with a raging Jaeger on the HUD. There was no training for the flicker of terror any human being felt on seeing that.

After he'd had a brief moment with each of them, he nodded. "Mount up and let's get it done."

# 29

## WORLDWIDE PANIC
### EVACUATIONS ACROSS PACIFIC RIM AS
### KAIJU PASS THROUGH MULTIPLE BREACHES
#### PPDC CONFIRMS THREE KAIJU

Humanity's worst nightmare came true yesterday, as multiple
Breaches opened up across the Pacific Basin, resulting in the
appearance of three Kaiju and the destruction of many of the
Pan Pacific Defense Corps' Shatterdome bunkers.

The Kaiju did not immediately make landfall after appearing
separately in the East China Sea, the Sea of Japan, and the
Sea of Okhotsk. Their current pathways appear to be taking
them toward Japan, but all coastal populations are being
urged to evacuate.

The PPDC refused to confirm reports that the Breaches were
created by Drone Jaegers. Multiple eyewitness accounts
claim to have seen Drone Jaegers coordinating the Breach
creations, but Shao Industries spokespeople have vigorously

continued...

denied this, saying Shao Industries and the PPDC are continuing to work in partnership to fight all Kaiju threats.

The catastrophic failure of the Drone program, which resulted in rogue Drones destroying several Jaegers and causing incalculable damage in Pacific Rim cities from South America to Russia, is stimulating calls for investigation of Shao Industries and its founder, Shao Liwen. She was understood to be at the Moyulan Shatterdome near Shanghai and was unavailable for comment.

More on this developing story as it becomes available.

On the gantries, Ranger teams exited the elevators and ducked through their Conn-Pod hatches. Techs making last-minute adjustments still scurried up and down the scaffolding, mostly around the thruster pods. Everything else they'd done was working with existing systems that had been tested over a period of years. The thrusters not only hadn't been tested, they hadn't even been through a design process. They were cobbled together from Jumphawk fuel tanks, repurposed V-Dragon thrusters, and fuel lines adapted from plasma feeders. The software controlling them was a series of patched-together code blocks borrowed from other systems. The math checked out, and the materials had been tested under other circumstances, but the history of rocketry was a story of unexpected failures that only had obvious causes after engineers spent months picking through the pieces. Neither the PPDC nor the human race as a whole could afford that today.

Among the crews, a strange fatalism prevailed. They had to trust Gottlieb and Shao, so they did. There was no point worrying about what would happen if the thruster pods didn't work, because that wouldn't change the ultimate outcome for any of them. They could either die in an explosion on the tarmac, or die of starvation after the Precursors re-engineered Earth's climate. This was a time to take chances.

Amara, Jinhai, and Vik got settled in Bracer Phoenix's Conn-Pod. The three Drift cradles were arranged with two in the front and one in the back, attached to a rail that dropped down to the railgun turret. That was Vik's chair. Amara and Jinhai had the two front ones, responsible for moving Bracer and handling the other weapons systems—including the newly installed Morning Star Hand. They had all used it in simulations, but on Titan Redeemer's left arm. Jake and Lambert had warned them it would feel different in Bracer Phoenix. They accepted this warning the same way they accepted the possibility that the thruster pods wouldn't work. In other words, they shrugged it off, because they either had to make it work or they would die.

Each of them stood in the holographic rectangles marking the points where their boots would lock into the maglev field.

"Initiating neural handshake," Amara said.

They felt the psychic swirl of the Drift reaching through them and binding them together. Amara felt cool and resolved, Jinhai a little giddy, Vik excited at the prospect of combat. Jinhai grinned at the readout on his display as the floor dropped away and they hung in the maglev field. "Neural handshake strong and steady," he said. They could all feel it. They were a team. Jinhai and Vik had spent more than a year training for this. Amara was new to it, but her hard work with Sarah had paid off. *Almond Joy*, she thought, and she felt the other two react to the joke.

"So," Vik said. "How's it feel to be in a *real* Jaeger?" The joke was playful, not hostile like it would have been just a few days before.

"Bigger's... not bad," Amara allowed. She had a wide grin on her face just from the rush of the Drift, and the realization that she was in the Conn-Pod of Bracer Phoenix. It wasn't long at all since she'd been climbing out of Scrapper, figuring she was on her way to jail.

Now she was on her way to saving the world instead.

Renata and Ryoichi relaxed into their Drift, feeling the connection like an extension of the rapport they already had from countless hours of sparring and drilling together. Saber Athena felt like an extension of themselves, a perfect match to what they were already good at. "Strong and steady," Renata said, eyeballing the readout of their neural handshake.

"Just like me," Ryoichi said.

They reached out and tapped fists, careful to keep Saber Athena motionless in the launch gantry. Weapons systems checked out, the readings from the thruster pods were all green.

"A Kaiju is going to be all like, 'Not in the face!' Just like you, Ryo," Renata said. "But I'm gonna pop it in the face anyway."

"I knew my suffering would pay off," Ryoichi cracked back. They were both nervous, but they also couldn't wait to get rolling. Riding the Drift and experiencing the power of Saber Athena, they felt like they were born for this moment.

Suresh felt his pulse hammering as the neural handshake kicked in, but Ilya steadied him as he always did. Ilya took a deep breath, relaxing into the Drift. Suresh calmed too. Guardian Bravo felt solid and steady around them. Their neural handshake wavered for a moment, then settled into a strong equilibrium. They ran weapons checks. The Arc Whip had twin monitors: one for the plasma feed that energized its electrical discharge and the other for the integrity of the graphene strand of the whip itself. Both read out perfectly. The Drone assault hadn't touched them. A missile had hit the cradle near the left shoulder intake turbine, knocking it slightly off center, but Shao Industries tech crews had gotten it shipshape. All in all, Guardian Bravo was ready for duty. Suresh and Ilya didn't talk much as they got ready. Ilya didn't have much to say, and Suresh knew he had a tendency to start rattling on if he didn't keep his mouth shut when he was nervous. So they kept it low-key, checking everything out and waiting for their final launch orders.

*Man, I can't believe I'm doing this,* Suresh thought.

Ilya was right there. *Be cool, Suresh. You and me, we'll handle it.*

Jake and Lambert leaned into the Drift, just like the old days, running the checks on Gipsy Avenger and taking brief note of the changes the techs had made since the second encounter with Obsidian Fury. Jake felt none of the nerves from the first fight in Sydney. Then, he hadn't been inside a Jaeger for ten years. Now, with two combat deployments in the last ten days, he felt like he'd never been away. Lambert, whose training and conditioning ran back uninterrupted to when he was fourteen, rode the Drift like it was second nature.

They'd gotten a last status report on the location of the Kaiju before entering the Conn-Pod. Just as Jake's fingertip extrapolations had suggested, Raijin, Shrikethorn, and Hakuja had converged off the east coast of Kyushu, the southernmost of Japan's four main islands. From there they were covering the last four hundred miles or so together, apparently aiming to come ashore in Tokyo. That wasn't a direct approach to Mount Fuji, which had Gottlieb confused. He had developed a theory that they could not detect the location of Fuji while they were underwater, and so were guided by what seemed to be a Kaiju instinct to approach the largest city they could find. Whatever the cause, the Kaiju were holding steady on their course. Submarines from the Chinese, Russian, and American navies had attacked them with every torpedo they had, with little effect. The Kaiju either ignored the subs or destroyed them if they got too close. They were due to enter the Uraga Channel and then Tokyo Bay within the next hour or so.

This was grim news, because it meant the Jaegers wouldn't be there in time to stop the Kaiju from attacking Tokyo. Already the city was being evacuated ahead of the expected attack. Those who could were getting out of the city, heading north because the PPDC had briefed Japanese authorities on the Kaiju's expected path. But evacuating a city of twenty million took days if not weeks, and those who could not leave in time were filling Tokyo's hundreds of Kaiju shelters. The shelters had a decent track record from the Kaiju War. A big Kaiju intent on getting into one could do it, but the shelters were strong enough to withstand buildings collapsing on top of them, and provisioned with enough supplies to feed people trapped inside until rescuers could dig them out. In this case, if Gipsy Avenger and the other Jaegers didn't stop the three Kaiju, it wouldn't really matter whether the shelters survived or not.

Making an effort to look on the bright side, Jake realized that if the three Kaiju had made a beeline for Mount Fuji via Suruga Bay, a hundred miles to the west, the Jaegers wouldn't have been able to intercept them in time.

As it was, they were cutting it very close.

Within the next two hours, Gipsy Avenger would be toe to toe with the Kaiju, and that battle would only end with one of them dead. That was what mattered.

"All Jaegers," Lambert said over the commlink. "Sound off. Go/no-go for launch."

"Guardian Bravo, go," Ilya said.

Renata, almost simultaneously: "Saber Athena go."

"Bracer Phoenix," Amara said. "Let's go already."

"Copy that." Jake took one last look at the thruster pod readings, making sure there were no fuel leaks or pressure warnings. He didn't see any. "Command, we are go for launch."

\* \* \*

In the War Room, Gottlieb surveyed the main holo screen, watching the data readouts from the four Jaegers. Everything looked good as far as he could tell, but the proof would come when the thruster pods ignited. Jules Reyes hurried in from the Jaeger bay, scooting past War Room techs at support terminals. She stopped next to Gottlieb, spawning a holo screen at a terminal of her own to monitor the internal effect of the thrusters on the Jaeger's systems and hull integrity. She glanced over at Gottlieb, who acknowledged her and leaned into the comm. "Roger, Gipsy Avenger. Ignition in ten seconds. Nine... eight..."

Inside each Conn-Pod, Rangers and cadets alike stared a little harder at their HUD readouts, apprehensive but eager, willing everything to work. Suresh hummed a little song to himself. Amara clenched and unclenched one fist until she noticed Bracer Phoenix was doing the same. She forced herself to remain calm. Ryoichi counted down under his breath along with Gottlieb, wondering if his life was going to end on the word *ignition*. Renata laughed, and in the Drift he heard her thinking, *No way—you have to live long enough to beat me sparring at least once.*

"...two... one..."

Jake tensed. This was it.

"Ignition!"

**THE JOURNAL OF EXPERIMENTAL BIOTECHNOLOGY**
Volume 27 Issue 1, forthcoming

# NOTES ON THE REACTIVE AND COMBUSTIVE PROPERTIES OF KAIJU BLOOD IN CATALYSIS WITH LANTHANIDE ELEMENTS

Gottlieb, H., K-Science Division, Pan Pacific Defense Corps

## ABSTRACT

Kaiju blood is widely understood to have corrosive properties when in physical contact with terrestrial organic material, as well as most known metallic and plastic compounds. Further investigation has revealed a related property: large amounts of potential thermal energy. Initial experiments conclude that Kaiju blood reacts with excess thermal energy in the presence of lanthanide elements. Potential research pathways appear fruitful in the areas of propulsion and navigation, if significant obstacles related to the blood's chemical instability can be overcome. These obstacles include: the narrow window of controllable combustion and resultant danger of explosion or combustion failure; the difficulty of containing Kaiju blood in a vessel that will not corrode during storage and use; the difficulties in synthesizing Kaiju blood, a necessary step if the technological applications of these results are ever to achieve widespread practical use.

Further investigations are ongoing.

With a boom that echoed out across Qingchuan Bay, the four thruster pods ignited. Smoke and blue-tinged flames blasted out across the tarmac, wreathing the gantries in smoke. Slowly, each Jaeger began to rise on a pillar of fire. Gottlieb held his breath. The thruster pods had passed their first test by not exploding at ignition. But could they generate enough thrust? The mathematics said they could, but the mathematics had never been tested against these materials in this situation. That was the second test: whether the machines could withstand the liftoff. Jaegers were designed to absorb tremendous amounts of force via direct impact, but vibrational energies were different. Gottlieb had kept quiet about this, but he was haunted by the possibility that the thruster pods would work and the Conn-Pods would shake themselves to pieces due to the Jaegers' lack of aerodynamic design.

Video feeds from inside the Conn-Pods heightened his fears. They shook so violently that the pilots' vital signs registered spikes in pulses and breathing rates. He heard warning alarms blaring from inside Guardian Bravo's Conn-Pod. Suresh couldn't help himself. "That's not a good sound!"

Inside Gipsy Avenger's Conn-Pod, Jake and Lambert shared a nervous glance. Jake looked up at the top of the Conn-Pod, violently shaking even though the maglev field held him and Lambert fairly steady. "Come on, girl," he breathed. "Hold together…"

The Jaegers reached an altitude of fifty feet… then a hundred… then five hundred… and gradually their momentum took over and the shaking diminished. All four together arced across the sky to the east, trailing plumes of smoke and the sound of receding thunder. Gottlieb watched them, then looked back at the monitors. The pods were holding together. The Jaegers were holding together.

All alarms had switched themselves off as self-analytic subroutines determined there was no systemic damage.

Cheers echoed through the War Room. Gottlieb slumped into his chair, utterly drained. With a weak grin in Jules' direction, he said, "Knew it would work."

According to Gottlieb's projections, the Jaegers would cover the distance from the Moyulan Shatterdome to Tokyo Bay in about ninety minutes. Half an hour in, he asked them for a status update. "From here it appears the thruster pods are working as designed," he said. "Please advise if you are seeing anything different."

"We're flying," Lambert said. "That's the important thing."

"Vibrations are way down since liftoff. Everything is smooth," Jake added. "Guardian Bravo, Bracer Phoenix, Saber Athena, let Dr. Gottlieb know if you've got any problems."

"Is there going to be an inflight meal?" Amara joked.

Vik chimed in from Bracer Phoenix, stopping Amara before she joked again. "We are flying stable and steady. All systems appear normal."

"Here too," Ryoichi said from Saber Athena.

The Jaegers, holding formation, passed over the coast of Kyushu. Ahead of them stretched the mountainous mainland of Japan, green and streaked with clouds. Soon they would get a visual on Mount Fuji, but they wouldn't be stopping there. As expected, the Kaiju were coming ashore in Tokyo Bay.

"Ranger Lambert." It was Ilya on the comm. "No problems on Guardian Bravo. Should some of us divert and set up a defensive position at Mount Fuji?"

Lambert considered this, but not for long. "Negative. We've got three Kaiju in Tokyo. The sooner we can get there and engage them, the more lives we're going to save."

"I don't understand why they didn't go ashore in Suruga Bay," Gottlieb was complaining. Irrational behavior bothered him almost as much as the fact of the Kaiju trying to end the world.

"Thought you had a theory about that," Jake reminded him.

"Yes. But I have no way to test it, so it remains an unsatisfying conjecture," Gottlieb said.

"We'll make sure to ask Geiszler when we track him down," Lambert said. "Any news on that front?"

"No," Gottlieb answered. "That worries me. Newton enjoys gloating, as you know, and the presence of the Precursors in his mind exacerbates that character flaw. The longer he goes without showing himself, the more I begin to fear he has another... what is the expression? Trick up his sleeve."

"I hope you're wrong about that, Doc," Lambert said. "We're not playing with a full deck as it is."

"I don't—ah, I—yes. Full deck." Gottlieb forced a polite chuckle. "I too hope I am wrong. We shall see."

# 3 1

## KAIJU MAKE LANDFALL IN JAPAN
**City Largely Evacuated; Preparation Hailed**

The three Kaiju that appeared through multiple Breaches less than twenty-four hours ago made a rendezvous at the eastern end of the Tsugaru Strait and turned south together toward Tokyo. Kaiju have never been observed to work together in this way before, so scientists in the Pan Pacific Defense Corps and elsewhere have been at a loss to explain the behavior.

Anticipating a Kaiju incursion, every sizable city in Japan has been evacuated. Those who could not get inland have found space in the island nation's numerous Kaiju shelters, said to be able to withstand a pressure of ten thousand tons and offer accommodations to nearly five million people just in the greater Tokyo-Osaka area alone.

Information from the site of the Kaiju landfall is scarce, though it is known they have destroyed parts of the Rainbow Bridge and numerous other structures at the edge of Tokyo Bay. Jaegers from the Moyulan Shatterdome, the nearest PPDC facility with active Jaegers after the devastating Drone failure, are said to be deploying soon, but observers in the area report none have arrived so far.

It is reported that the Kaiju have inflicted widespread damage on the city center and are moving to the southwest, but due to the mandatory evacuations, reliable information from the area is difficult to find.

Where the Kaiju intend to go—or whether they have any intent at all— remains to be seen.

Raijin, Hakuja, and Shrikethorn rampaged through Shibuya. Behind them, a path of destruction a half-mile wide stretched back to the famed Rainbow Bridge, its curling approach ramp collapsed into the bay where they had come ashore. A thousand fires burned in the crushed remains of buildings. Near the Kaiju, those who had not yet gotten to a shelter fled in desperate throngs through the streets; in the wake of their passage, rescue operations were already beginning.

Raijin paused and reared up on its hind legs. It roared, drawing the attention of Hakuja and Shrikethorn. All three Kaiju swung around and saw the white-capped peak of Mount Fuji looming in the distance to the west. They changed course and plowed forward, destroying whatever was in their path.

"Did you see that?" Gottlieb said over the comm. "They are communicating. Raijin spotted Mount Fuji and relayed that information to the others. This is extraordinary."

"Extraordinary, got it." Jake was looking down as Gipsy Avenger streaked toward the Kaiju. They were nearly close enough, and closing in fast.

He took the brief moment they had to get a visual sense of the three Kaiju and how they moved. The images Gottlieb had captured from their individual Breach passages were sketchy, and didn't show much about how they moved. Now Jake soaked up every detail he could, knowing any one bit of information could mean the difference between victory and the end of the world. This was part of Ranger training, to study Kaiju and draw terrestrial equivalents as a way of anticipating how an individual monster might fight. It was an inexact science, but Jake knew of cases from the Kaiju War where it had saved Ranger lives.

Raijin was the biggest of the three, and Jake thought Gottlieb was right that it was intentionally leading the other two. At a glance Jake pegged it to be a hundred meters tall or so, but that was hard to guess with any precision because of the bony plates on its head and the way it leaned forward as it ran. It was bipedal, with heavy bony structures at its hips and a long tail that balanced the weight of its head. Its paws, each with two fingers and a hooked shorter thumb, were tipped with claws that glowed blue even in the bright sunlight. Whenever they touched something else, some kind of destructive energy flared. But its head was the unusual thing about it. Heavy armor plates tipped with spikes ringed its face and jaws, but the spikes faced inward. Between the plates, its brain glowed an angry red over an interior bony structure including fanged jaws big enough to swallow a school bus. There were rows of bright blue eyes on both the outside armor plates and the central face, under the infernal glow shining through the top of its head.

Just behind it, Shrikethorn was nearly as tall, but more massive and with two tails curling up over its back. The tip of each tail bristled with long spikes, and heavier spines grew from its arms and neck. The front of its head was a flat, bony projection similar to a hammerhead shark's, with a row of eyes at each end. When it opened its mouth, blue light glowed from inside, the same color as Raijin's eyes. That thought gave Jake an insight: All of Shrikethorn's spikes faced forward, on the front edge of its bony head. That might be useful to know. He filed it away for the fight to come. He also noticed that some of the spikes from its tail were embedded in nearby buildings. Jake couldn't tell if this had happened while it dragged its tail along the front of a building, or if Shrikethorn could somehow fire the spikes. He had a feeling he might learn for certain sooner rather than later.

Unlike the other two, Hakuja was comparatively low to the ground, with squat heavy legs and thick segmented armor plates running down its back from the back of its head to the base of its tail. The tail was armored too, and shorter than either Raijin's or Shrikethorn's. Its head was flat, with flaring bony protrusions on either side and pointed jaws. Three small eyes on either side of its snout burned a deep orange. Two spikes jutted up from the tip of the lower jaw, and when it roared Jake saw its tongue was bifurcated. Its claws had a different design than the other two as well, with three clawed fingers evenly spaced instead of the shorter opposable digit Jake saw on Raijin and Shrikethorn. The claws were long and hooked, and also thick. They put Jake in mind of a badger or a bear.

He absorbed all that in the seconds between Gottlieb's observation and the chime from their HUD that they were nearing contact.

"Go," Lambert said.

He jabbed the HUD and Gipsy Avenger's thruster pod cut out, dropping the Jaeger into a controlled feet-first fall directly toward Raijin. The Kaiju never looked up before Gipsy slammed down on it, smashing it into the ground. Before it could get up, Gipsy collared it and flipped it judo-style into a nearby building. The counterforce, and the leftover momentum from their dive, kept Gipsy Avenger skidding down the street for several blocks, plowing up asphalt and cars until she ground to a stop.

Jake and Lambert stood up straight again and raised Gipsy Avenger's right hand, smacking her left fist into it. This was their acknowledgment of tradition. Raleigh Becket had done this, first with his brother Yancy and then with Mako Mori. To Jake it was a salute to all their sacrifices, but particularly his sister's. He was fighting for the survival of the human race, but fighting to avenge his sister too. Somewhere maybe she was watching. Maybe his father was too.

"Gipsy to Command," Lambert said. "Targets acquired."

"Um, Roger that, Gipsy," Gottlieb answered. He was still uncertain about combat radio protocols. They heard him doing something in the War Room, and a moment later he said, "Everyone in the area is secured in underground shelters. You're cleared to engage."

That was one good thing, Jake thought. Their correct guess about where the Kaiju were headed meant they'd had time to get civilians out of the way. Diverting to save civilian populations caught in a battle had often put Jaegers in a vulnerable position in the past.

"Solid copy," he confirmed. "Going hot."

Guardian Bravo and Saber Athena landed behind Gipsy Avenger and jettisoned their thruster pods. A moment later Bracer Phoenix joined them, moving too fast to stay upright. She skidded through a plaza, crushing trees and benches, before getting her balance back. Jake heard Amara over the comm, trying to play it cool as always. "I meant to do that."

"Bracer Phoenix, on me. We'll take Raijin," Jake ordered. "Saber Athena, Guardian Bravo, you take the other two." Saber Athena was on Hakuja's side, and Jake thought it made sense to pit her superior speed against the slowest of the Kaiju.

"Copy that," he heard Suresh respond. Then, almost like he was convincing himself, Suresh added, "We were born to save the world."

"On my mark," Lambert said. The Kaiju roared out a challenge. "Three... two... one... mark."

The four Jaegers charged down the empty avenue toward the Kaiju. Saber Athena surged ahead, whipping her plasma swords out from their back-mounted sheaths and striking Hakuja faster than the Kaiju could defend.

The plasma blades scored deep gouges in Hakuja's armor. Hakuja lunged at Saber Athena, but the Jaeger was much too fast, spinning into a reverse kick that flung the Kaiju back to crash against a glass office building. Hakuja staggered, trying to recover.

Gipsy, at her own full speed, stormed past Hakuja and put everything she had into an overhand right, aiming straight at Raijin's face. Around the jaws, Jake and Lambert thought the skull tissue looked vulnerable. But in mid-swing, the armored plates around Raijin's head snapped closed and the Kaiju tensed for the impact. The punch landed, with everything Gipsy Avenger had. Jake and Lambert felt the shock all through the Jaeger's frame. But Raijin didn't go down. From the point of impact, blue lines of energy radiated out along the plates, crackling down Raijin's arms into its claws. They flared the same color of blue—and Raijin struck back.

The glowing claws raked across Gipsy's shoulder and torso. Gipsy shuddered from the blow, and the next thing Jake and Lambert knew, they were catapulted through the air. Bracer Phoenix ducked and Gipsy Avenger sailed past, smashing into the side of a building. Bracer Phoenix stood again and advanced, firing a barrage of missiles from her shoulder mounts. Explosions bloomed across the Kaiju's body as Bracer closed to within striking distance.

At first Raijin flinched away from the missiles, but as the explosions died away it spun back to its full height, backhanding Bracer Phoenix before the three cadets inside could get close enough to grapple. Knocked off her feet, Bracer destroyed a small building and sprawled in the rubble over on the next street. The battlefield footing was already treacherous, with mounds of rubble shifting under the combatants' feet.

Like Bracer Phoenix, Guardian Bravo had launched a

missile salvo to give her cover for a close approach. The first volley hit the target and she fired again, charging closer to Shrikethorn… and then skidding to an emergency stop as Bracer Phoenix crashed down in front of her. She barely stopped in time, dragging a fist on the street and setting off a car alarm near Bracer Phoenix's head.

Gipsy Avenger was just then getting back to her feet after the stunning force of Raijin's blow. Jake couldn't figure out how it had delivered so much power just with its claws, and through the Drift he could tell Lambert was just as confused. Then Gottlieb solved the problem, thanks to the data feeds from the battlefield back to the War Room. "Gipsy! Raijin's faceplates are absorbing your hits and throwing the energy back at you!"

That was a problem. If you couldn't punch an enemy in the face, your options for winning were compromised. Down the street, Raijin was coming after them again, its bony plates open so it could see the way ahead.

Jake had an idea. "Let's see it absorb *this*," he said, and touched the command to activate the Gravity Sling.

Gipsy Avenger's right hand reconfigured into the lens array and she reached out, catching a nearby building and dragging it down on top of Raijin. Fifty stories of concrete and steel crashed down on the Kaiju, knocking it flat and momentarily obscuring it in a cloud of dust.

But Raijin shook it off and kept coming.

Gipsy hit the Kaiju with another building. And another. And another, over and over, toppling entire blocks of office towers to thunder down on Raijin. "Let's see how many buildings this thing can take," Jake said grimly, reaching for another. Sooner or later it had to go down.

As Gipsy reached for another building, Saber Athena was tracking Hakuja, and found the armored Kaiju tensing to spring on Gipsy Avenger from behind. "Oh no you don't," Renata said, leaning into a sprint. She and Ryoichi timed the last steps to hit Hakuja with a flying knee, smashing into the side of its head just below the row of eyes. The other side of its head crushed several floors of the building it had been using as cover for its planned ambush of Gipsy Avenger, who was slinging down more buildings on Raijin. The Cat-5 was moving more slowly now, but it was still coming. Gipsy backed away before it, drawing it on.

Hakuja pivoted round to attack Saber Athena, hooking its claws into the Jaeger's armor. Saber Athena drove punch after punch into Hakuja's bony head, pummeling the Kaiju down. Renata and Ryoichi were so focused on their target that they didn't notice Saber Athena's HUD showing Shrikethorn coming around the corner two blocks behind them. Shrikethorn roared and its twin tails snapped up over its head. Dozens of armored spikes launched from the tails. Most of them crashed through the buildings still standing near Saber Athena and Hakuja, but several punched into Saber Athena's armor, burying themselves deep. Renata and Ryoichi cried out at the holographic impression of pain, momentarily losing their focus on Hakuja.

The Kaiju was quick to seize the opportunity. It leaped up on Saber Athena, gripping with its front paws and raking with the rear. Its immense mass drove Saber Athena back and she fell, demolishing the front of a Kaiju Museum erected near the spot where Onibaba had once fallen. The Ranger who put it down was Stacker Pentecost. Somewhere around here was the alley where Mako, terrified and wearing one shoe, had survived the battle and seen her adoptive father for the first time.

*Too many echoes*, Jake thought. *We've done this too many times. It has to end.*

Saber Athena was deadly on her feet, but grappling on the ground, Hakuja had the advantage. The Kaiju snapped and tore at Saber Athena's armor as Renata and Ryoichi fought to fend it off. They were keeping it from Saber Athena's head, but if they couldn't get up, they wouldn't be able to hold on forever. And things were about to get worse, because Shrikethorn was loping toward them, aiming to finish Saber Athena off. "Shrikethorn inbound!" Ryoichi shouted.

Renata activated their comm. "Hey, guys! We could use a little help over here!"

Bracer Phoenix had suffered a system brownout when Raijin nailed them with the stored kinetic energy of Gipsy Avenger's punch. They were just now back online and on their feet. "Copy that!" Amara answered. "Vik! Take out Shrikethorn!"

"On it!" Vik touched a screen and the recessed floor under her Drift cradle opened. She dropped down, fifteen stories in a flash, still linked to her partners, slamming to a halt in the firing emplacement behind the quad-mounted railguns built into Bracer Phoenix's midsection. They were built on a track that gave them a three-hundred-sixty-degree field of fire, and Vik had them powered up and locked in on Shrikethorn before the spiky Kaiju could get its claws into Saber Athena.

The barrage of railgun shells tore into Shrikethorn, blasting away pieces of its armor and splattering the street with Kaiju blood. Shrikethorn reared back and sprang away from Saber Athena to come after Bracer Phoenix, who held steady, forcing Shrikethorn to come straight through the railgun fire.

Guardian Bravo had also heard Renata's distress call. Suresh and Ilya were coming in hot, skirting the valley of collapsed buildings where Gipsy Avenger still battled

Raijin. "Saber Athena! Guardian Bravo coming to assist!"

"Activating Arc Whip," Ilya said calmly.

Power surged inside Guardian Bravo's Conn-Pod, brightening all the displays as the Arc Whip came online. Guardian Bravo slung the whip out to one side, flicking it out to its full length and leaping forward. They came down just behind Hakuja, slashing the whip down across the Kaiju's back. The unbreakable graphene strand cracked the armored plates on Hakuja's back and delivered a staggering punch of energy besides. Hakuja spasmed, letting go of Saber Athena. As the Kaiju turned to face Guardian Bravo, Ilya and Suresh were already spinning through a full turn, sweeping the whip around to snap into Hakuja's midsection. The force of the blow lifted the Kaiju off its feet and smashed it straight through a building back into the main avenue where Gipsy Avenger was still dropping buildings on Raijin.

Hakuja bellowed in wounded fury, the sound shaking down rubble from partially destroyed buildings. Then it bent and dug into the ground. Seconds later, it was gone.

"Yeah, that's right! You better run!" Suresh crowed, seeing the Kaiju flee. He looked over at Ilya, all of his normal diffidence swept away by the euphoria of the battle. "These things ain't that tough!"

Behind them, Bracer Phoenix was still holding Shrikethorn at bay with her railgun. Before them, Gipsy Avenger snapped the Gravity Sling again, and another skyscraper fell, crushing Raijin to the ground once more. The street heaved under Gipsy Avenger and the Jaeger lost her balance momentarily. Inside, the Conn-Pod HUD showed Jake the locations of all Jaegers and Kaiju in the field. He saw Hakuja on the move, passing directly beneath them... and headed toward Bracer Phoenix.

"Bracer, check your six!" he called, amazed that

a creature that size could move so fast underground. "Hostile inbound!"

Vik was on it. "Copy that!" she answered, watching her own HUD inside the railgun turret. She spotted the approaching Kaiju bogey and kicked the turret into a one-eighty, swiveling it around just as Hakuja burst up through the street behind them in an eruption of concrete, earth, and water spraying from broken pipes. Vik was already firing as she saw the Kaiju, blasting it point-blank in the face with all four barrels. "Yeah!" she shouted, seeing Hakuja stunned by the ambush. "Get some!"

Guardian Bravo was closing in on Shrikethorn from one direction, flicking the Arc Whip out to full extension, as Saber Athena dug herself out of the Kaiju Museum and attacked Shrikethorn from the other direction. Bracer Phoenix kept pounding Hakuja, keeping the bloodied Kaiju from getting all the way out of the tunnel it had dug under the street. Gipsy Avenger brought one more building down on Raijin, reaching over a block to sling the biggest skyscraper yet. The cumulative beating, and the greater mass of this last building, finally stopped Raijin. The huge Kaiju struggled to free itself from the mass of girders and concrete, shrieking in anger and frustration. Finally it was a static target, and Gipsy Avenger took advantage with a barrage of plasma missiles.

Jake almost didn't dare to believe it, but he thought they might have the Kaiju on the ropes.

# 3 2

## EDITORIAL: OKAY FINE

### I WAS WRONG.

How much more do I need to say? A week ago I believed that the Drone Jaegers were the future, that we didn't need the PPDC, that we should just turn the whole thing over to the Genius in White, Shao Liwen, and let her handle Jaegers from here on out.

Well, that first Drone deployment showed me the error of my ways, didn't it?

And then new Breaches opened up, and now the word from Tokyo is there are four Jaegers—human-powered Jaegers, with a total of nine Rangers, and may God* bless every one of 'em—putting the boot to the Kaiju. Where are the Drones? In pieces, because they got corrupted. Either by a software flaw or some kind of Kaiju thing, depends on which rumors you believe, but you know what? It doesn't matter. Real people are out fighting this battle for us. They're in machines, but they

continued...

aren't machines. We need to remember that. We need to put ourselves on the line for each other and not sit back and wait for machines to do it for us.

Go get 'em, Rangers. I'll never say a bad word about the PPDC again.

**Note**: NOT the God of the Kaiju nuts, who seem to think God is some kind of Cthulhu.

From a machine shop deep in the bowels of the Shatterdome, Shao Liwen was watching the feed from Tokyo. She was filthy, stained with sweat and grease from the machines she was working on. After the Jaegers had launched, she had realized there was possibly one more thing she could do to help. But judging from what she saw on the screen, maybe they didn't need any more of her help. "They're winning," she said, trying not to sound too surprised.

"That's what we do," Gottlieb said from the War Room. Then after a pause he added, "Most of the time."

He was watching the same holofeed Shao had down in the machine shop. Hakuja was badly wounded, Shrikethorn and Raijin hurting but still dangerous. The fight wasn't over yet. But all four Jaegers were still in good shape. Only Saber Athena had suffered any damage to speak of.

And even though the battle between Jaeger and Kaiju had already moved miles toward the outskirts of the Tokyo megacity, Mount Fuji was still miles away.

For the first time since he had understood the Precursors' plan, Gottlieb was feeling confident—at least mostly confident—that they were going to win.

The holo screen over his terminal, showing operational data on all four Jaegers as well as assessments of the Kaiju's status, flickered and went out. A moment later it came back on, but now the data visualization was replaced by a head-and-shoulders shot of Newt Geiszler, looking into what must have been a data pad camera. Behind him, part of a Shao V-Dragon was visible on what must have been a rooftop, against the backdrop of the Tokyo skyline. In the middle distance, Gottlieb could see the smoke rising from the site of the battle, and hear the roars of the Kaiju over the thunder of railguns and missiles. Far away, partially masked by the smoke, was the magnificent peak of Mount Fuji.

"Newton," Geiszler said, his tone accusatory and worried and angry all at once.

"Hey, buddy," Newt said. "*Moshi moshi*. So you finally figured out your little rockets. Good for you, Hermann." He put a little mocking twist on Gottlieb's name.

"That's not all we've figured out," Hermann said.

Jules had seen Newt appear and left her terminal to stand next to Hermann. "We know what you're trying to do."

"It's not him," Gottlieb objected. "It's those things in his head."

Newt shrugged. "Everybody has things in their head. Mine are just a lot more fun."

"I've been in your mind, too, Newton," Gottlieb reminded him. He had to appeal to the connection between them, the history they had shared, the awful danger of the Kaiju Drift they had survived together. That was the only way they might be able to bring him back. "You're stronger than they know. You can fight them. You can stop them from doing this."

Just as it had the last time, this appeal seemed to give Newt—the real Newt—a momentary burst of strength. He twitched, trying to break free of the Precursor control. "I... I couldn't stop Drifting with the Kaiju brain. I tried, but she made me feel so... alive. They're in my mind. They're controlling me. I'm sorry, Hermann—"

"You can fight them!" Gottlieb cried. "You can stop them from doing this."

For a moment Newt froze, and when he could move again, Gottlieb could tell the moment had passed. The Precursors were in control again. "Nice try," Newt sneered. "You don't even know what *this* is. How all the pieces fit together. Want me to show you? Want to see what else I was whipping up in Siberia? Yes? No? How about *yes*."

He raised one finger in a flourish and stabbed it down

onto his data pad, holding eye contact through the camera the whole time. "This is gonna be so cool," he said. "I mean, not for you guys. For you it's gonna suck. Sorry. But not really."

The screen went blank.

A PPDC combat operations tech near Gottlieb straightened and tensed as her screen lit up with multiple new bogeys. "We got movement! Multiple hostiles! Three kilometers, southeast!" She swiped the tactical view over to the main holo screen at the center of the War Room. A cluster of red dots had sprung to life near the group of Jaegers.

Gottlieb immediately got on the comm. "Command to Strike Team. Are you reading this?"

He heard Jake first. "Where'd they come from?"

Gottlieb didn't have a read on the location—or, for that matter, what all the bogeys were. Before he could say anything, he heard Shao over the internal Shatterdome comm from down in the machine shop.

"That's one of my automated factories," she said.

Gottlieb remembered Newt telling her that he had commandeered production at her automated facilities. He had managed to build an entire Jaeger with nobody noticing. These bogeys weren't that big, but there were… He tried to count them and lost track. They were too close together. What could they be?

"Newt," Lambert growled. He tapped at the HUD. "Triangulating his signal…" Now that they had the Kaiju on the ropes, he was already thinking forward to when they could put the traitorous scientist in handcuffs. Or in the ground. That would be fine with him, too.

When the HUD had stored Geiszler's location, Lambert returned to the main tactical HUD view. "Hostiles are one kilometer and closing."

*Dammit*, Jake thought. They were minutes from

putting the Kaiju down for good. Bracer's railgun shells had shattered Hakuja's armor, the combined attack of Guardian Bravo and Saber Athena had Shrikethorn down, and Raijin was still trapped under the last building Gipsy Avenger had dropped on it.

But they had to meet this new threat, at least for long enough to figure out what it was. "All Jaegers, disengage from Kaiju and brace for contact!" he called over the comm.

The four Jaegers stepped back from the battered Kaiju and turned just as the new threat appeared.

Swarming around the corner from the direction of Shao's factory came a tidal wave of tentacled cyborg monstrosities the size of small trucks. They flooded the street and surged up and over the collapsed remains of all the buildings Gipsy Avenger had thrown down with the Gravity Sling. They looked like Kaiju, with fanged mouths and multiple glowing eyes surrounded by a fan of cranial spikes. Ridges of bone-like protrusions ran down their backs, flattening into smaller spikes that stuck out laterally from their tails. But at the same time they were obviously mechanical, with metallic alloys formed to resemble the organic features of a true Kaiju. They moved in leaps and bounds, springing and scuttling by the hundred toward the waiting Jaegers. The chittering, buzzing noises they made merged into a sonic assault like a million cicadas, maddening in its intensity even though the Jaegers' sensors did all they could to filter and deaden the cacophony.

Jake watched the HUD as it tried to target them and failed. There were too many, moving too fast. One of them, or even a dozen, probably couldn't have done much damage to a Jaeger before the Jaeger got a grip on them and just crushed them in her fists—but this many? How could they fight this many?

"Any ideas, Gottlieb?" he asked.

Gottlieb was silent. Everyone in the War Room was stunned. This wasn't a threat Jaegers were designed to address. Down in the machine shop, Shao Liwen looked on in horror, realizing just how completely she had been deceived. Newt Geiszler had turned her genius against her. He had made Shao Industries into the engine of humanity's end.

Bracer Phoenix opened up with the railgun, raking the swarm without making an appreciable difference in its numbers. They didn't even try to avoid the barrage. "Hold your fire, Bracer," Jake ordered. With more confidence than he felt, he explained. "We're going to need that railgun loaded when we take care of these little ones and get back to the real fight."

But this was the real fight, at least right now. The swarm poured toward them, the sound growing even louder, and the Jaegers braced for it.

From the rooftop, Newt watched. The Ripper swarm was a thing of beauty. He had made them all by himself. Well, okay, he'd had a little help in the form of design suggestions from the Precursors, but his hands had typed the code. It made him proud to look at them. The Jaeger pilots must have been completely terrified. Newt wanted to let them stay in that head space for as long as possible, but it was time for the real show to begin. *All good things must come to an end*, he told himself. *Like the human race.*

He touched a blinking button on his data pad.

When the robots were within a hundred yards of the Jaegers, they dropped into fighting crouches... and then their heads turned as the swarm abruptly changed course.

Instead of stampeding into the waiting Jaegers, they veered off to the side, around the block… toward the wounded Kaiju, lying near each other between the pit Hakuja had dug and the toppled tower pinning Raijin.

The swarm poured over the Kaiju, and within seconds the Kaiju had disappeared under the hundreds—maybe thousands—of silvery bodies. They roared in agony, rearing up and then falling back into the churning mass. "What are they doing?" Ilya wondered aloud. "Are they on our side?"

Amara echoed the question. The Jaegers stood back and watched, completely mystified by what they were seeing and hearing.

"Dude," Suresh said. "That is so nasty."

In the War Room, Gottlieb and Jules stood together as the three big Kaiju bogeys were blotted out by the horde of smaller red dots. The surveillance display started to behave erratically. One of the big bogeys seemed to blink out, but a moment later it was back as several smaller ones—but not as small as the individual members of the swarm. Then it was one single bogey again. Larger than before. The others began to coalesce as well, a galaxy of tiny red dots adding themselves to the three large ones, reconfiguring them…

Gottlieb had a terrible realization. "I don't think so," he said slowly, answering Ilya's question.

On the street, Jake watched the activity in and around the pit subside. Smoke and dust rose into the air. It looked like the army of smaller Kaiju robots had completely consumed the larger Kaiju. No sign of them remained.

But on the HUD, there was one immense bogey.

They felt the ground beneath them shake and saw a motion in the pit. Something began to rise.

At first they thought it was one of the Kaiju, with the

smaller creatures hanging on it the way remoras hung on a shark. Then it kept rising and the watching pilots saw that its head was no longer just Raijin's head, or Hakuja's, or Shrikethorn's. It was bigger than any of them. Bigger, Jake realized with a sinking feeling in the pit of his stomach, than all three of them put together. It kept rising, standing up out of the pit, and Jake realized that Newt Geiszler had saved the best part of his plan for last.

He had waited until the Kaiju were already wounded, perhaps dying, and then pulled off the ultimate Dr. Frankenstein trick, remaking all three Kaiju into one gargantuan monster. Its head was as big as any of the Jaegers, and when it reached its full height it was as tall as any of the buildings remaining in that part of Tokyo. The smaller robotic creatures were gone, folded into its mass. Some of them were still visible as attachments to its tail and the edges of its armored carapace. Others were completely gone, chewed to pieces and remade.

Stunned, they watched it emerge from the pit, pieces of itself still knitting themselves into place. The last to come together was its jaw, still pointed like Raijin's but bearing two-hundred-foot spikes like Shrikethorn's. The blue glow of Kaiju energy emanated from its throat and glittered in thousands of points on its back and limbs, where the smaller bots had stitched themselves together into a flexible plated exoskeleton.

As its shadow fell over the Jaegers, Lambert said, "Well, he's pretty big."

On the rooftop, Newt felt a surge of pride. Until he'd seen it happen, he hadn't been one hundred percent sure the plan would work. But now he knew he never should have doubted himself. He'd run the numbers, he'd reworked the design a hundred times over ten years. The Rippers had been created for one purpose, and they had served that purpose perfectly.

He wondered what Hermann was thinking now. Who was the real genius? This was K-Science, baby, the real deal. The greatest accomplishment of a human mind... and the last. Newt knew he was destroying the human race, and even knew he should feel guilty about it. But the Precursors had shut him off from that part of himself. All he could feel was exaltation at his creation, and at the power he had brought into this world.

Across the devastated battlefield, Mega-Kaiju roared. The ripple of sound shattered windows for miles and lifted destroyed cars from the few remaining clear areas on the streets. It stepped up out of the pit and lumbered toward the Jaegers, gathering speed. As it went, its tail twitched, each flick destroying anything in its path.

"This is the way the world ends," Newt said with cold satisfaction. "Not with a whimper. But with a bang. A very, very big bang."

In Gipsy Avenger's Conn-Pod, Jake gave the only order he could. "All Jaegers, advance and fire everything you've got!"

Gipsy led the way, barraging the Mega-Kaiju with rockets and using the Gravity Sling to batter it with rubble. The other three Jaegers advanced in a flanking formation, unloading with plasma cannons and particle beams. Missiles exploded harmlessly or deflected off the plating, which absorbed the energies of the cannons as well. The Mega-Kaiju rocked back on its haunches and pounded a fist into the ground with a tectonic boom. The shockwave rolled down the devastated street, throwing all four Jaegers into the air. In four Conn-Pods, alarms sounded and pilots flailed for balance as they found themselves suddenly weightless. The Jaegers mimicked the motion, their gyroscopic equilibrium destabilized by the shock and their Conn-Pods' maglev fields malfunctioning in the absence of directional gravity. All of them landed in an awkward heap, except for Guardian Bravo, who managed to keep her feet.

Seeing the other three Jaegers needed a moment to recover, Suresh and Ilya took the lead. Guardian Bravo charged forward, readying the Arc Whip and peppering the Mega-Kaiju with cannonfire. "Guardian, wait!" Jake shouted over the comm. They had to stick together, fight as one, or against a monster this big they wouldn't have a chance.

"We got this!" Ilya shouted back.

He locked in on the Mega-Kaiju's head, looking for a target. "Go for the eyes," Suresh suggested.

Ilya swiveled the targeting reticle over the immensity of the Mega-Kaiju's head. "Which ones?" He counted more than a dozen.

"All of 'em!" Suresh saw the Mega-Kaiju rearing back for another earthquake punch, but this time they anticipated the move. By the time the Mega-Kaiju's fists were slamming into the ground, Guardian Bravo was airborne, kicking off a building parkour-style and slashing the Arc Whip toward the Mega-Kaiju's eyes. Suresh raised his voice in a battle cry as the whip snapped toward its target.

But Guardian Bravo was not the only combatant who was learning to anticipate the enemy's next move. The Mega-Kaiju got one hand up and caught the Arc Whip, as energy crackled around its fist. Guardian Bravo was still in the air, but now the Mega-Kaiju was in control. It swung the Jaeger around like a rag doll, smashing her back and forth across the street into buildings. When there were no more standing within its reach, the Mega-Kaiju flung Guardian Bravo away, using the Arc Whip for extra momentum. The damaged Jaeger pinwheeled away across the city, smashing off a distant office tower and plowing into the lower floors of another. The second building collapsed on Guardian Bravo as she came to rest.

All four Jaegers were down. Newt Geiszler watched in delight. "Yes!" he shouted, raising his arms in triumph. "That's what I'm talking about!" His creation had put them down in seconds, and now it thundered forward, toward the outskirts of the city and the ultimate target beyond. It was a beautiful day, Newt thought. Clear skies, the white peak of Mount Fuji vivid against the blue sky.

But this would be the last blue sky Planet Earth ever saw.

# 33

JAKE AND LAMBERT STRUGGLED TO STABILIZE Gipsy Avenger, which had taken more damage from the shockwave and the secondary impact than in the whole fight with the three Kaiju. Sparks showered in the Conn-Pod as overloaded circuitry shorted out. There was a plasma leak somewhere near Gipsy's power core, not critical yet but nothing they could ignore either. Lambert swiped and punched commands as fast as he could, patching systems and rerouting the links between the Conn-Pod and Gipsy Avenger's weapons control systems. They were going to be all right, but they were a long way from one hundred percent.

Jake was more worried about Ilya and Suresh. "Guardian Bravo, sit-rep!" he barked over the comm. "You guys okay?"

There was nothing but static on the comm.

"Ilya," Jake said, more urgently. "Suresh. Report."

Ilya heard Jake's voice and started to come to his senses. He could feel blood dripping off the side of his head. Some of it was getting in his eyes. He blinked and fumbled to activate the comm. "Guardian's down. I'm pinned in the Conn-Pod. Suresh…"

He was looking around the Conn-Pod for Suresh, trying to wipe the blood out of his eyes and get them refocused from the crash landing. Pain lanced through his hands as he touched his own face, and he looked down to see that some of his fingers were broken. Lowering his head, he also saw Suresh, and the crumpled wreckage of the Conn-Pod around him. Girders from the building that had collapsed on them were punched through Guardian Bravo's cranial armor, and...

He tried to breathe, keep control, react like a Ranger would. "Suresh... Suresh didn't make it, sir."

Jake and Lambert heard this and it hit them hard. The death of any Ranger was a tragedy, but the battle-tested veterans knew what they were getting into. The kids, though... they had never counted on a Kaiju war. They had trusted the PPDC and their senior Rangers to train them, guide them, protect them. But the war had found Suresh instead.

"Copy, Guardian," Jake said slowly.

"We'll send help soon as we can." Lambert had Gipsy Avenger's balance problems back under control. The Jaeger pushed herself up and stood.

"Bracer Phoenix, report," Jake said.

Amara's voice was loud and clear. "We're a little banged up, but still in the fight."

"Us too," Renata chimed in from Saber Athena. She sounded more optimistic than she was. Ryoichi was preoccupied responding to system warnings and actually getting them vertical again. Saber Athena should have been able to land upright after that shock. The fact that she had fallen said she'd taken more damage from Hakuja than either Renata or Ryoichi had expected.

She realized she hadn't given her call sign. "Saber, I mean. Saber Athena, sir."

Jake let out a long breath. Okay. They still had three Jaegers. Things could be a lot worse. He started punching in coordinates from the holo map of the area around Mount Fuji. "Bracer, Saber, prepare to intercept at the following coordinates."

"Haul ass and don't be late," Lambert added. Once a cadet trainer, always a cadet trainer.

"Copy," Amara said. "Bracer Phoenix, hauling ass."

Gipsy Avenger took off, building speed as she chased the Mega-Kaiju toward the lower slopes of Mount Fuji. Bracer Phoenix and Saber Athena were close behind. Trapped in the damaged Conn-Pod of Guardian Bravo, Ilya could not stand the idea of piloting the only Jaeger that couldn't make it to the final confrontation. He struggled to shoulder the neural load of Guardian Bravo himself, forcing the Jaeger to break free of the debris trapping her. "Sir," he said, voice high and tight. "I'm going to try to pilot Guardian myself."

"Negative," Lambert responded. "Stand down, Cadet."

They had all heard the stories about what happened when a single pilot tried to take on the entire neural load of a Jaeger. Some Rangers could handle it for a little while, but the long-term physiological and neural consequences could be crippling. Lambert wasn't going to bend on this. He already felt personally responsible for losing Suresh today, and the fight wasn't over yet. He wasn't going to put another cadet in danger, especially when Guardian Bravo would be operating at diminished combat capacity with only one pilot to handle its operations.

"I can help, sir—" Ilya protested.

Lambert cut him off. "Ilya, *stand down*. That's an order."

"We know how bad you want back in the fight," Jake added. "But even a seasoned vet can't pilot a Jaeger without help."

As the words left his mouth, a whole new train of thought fell together in Jake's mind. Jaegers were built for two-Ranger piloting teams because the neural load of piloting a Jaeger was too much for one brain. That knowledge locked together in his mind with a memory of Gottlieb talking about the Kaiju brain they had recovered from Obsidian Fury. Not a central brain, but a secondary organ, a cluster of nerves and synapses like you might ordinarily find at the base of a Kaiju's spine.

Ahead of them, he saw the Mega-Kaiju heading for the base of Mount Fuji, and he had an idea. "Gipsy to Command. Do you have a tactical scan of the hostile?"

In the War Room, a technician by the name of McKinney answered his query right away. "Assessing data from their sensors." She pulled up everything they had from various remote scans and got it together on a single screen.

Jules watched the image begin to resolve. She leaned into the comm to update Jake. "We have it, Gipsy, but it's still compiling."

"No time," Jake said. "Can you locate the brains?"

Gottlieb was working the scan now, taking over from McKinney. He zoomed in on a detail of the Mega-Kaiju's head. Multiple layers of bony spikes and crests protected its brain, all under the final outside layer of the cyborg mechs that had woven themselves into a seemingly impervious exoskeleton. "Hostile's central brain mass is heavily armored," Gottlieb informed them. He waited a brief moment for the associated scanning programs to bring back a result about kinetic damping values and energy ablation, other defensive variables. None of the numbers looked good. "Your weapons won't be able to penetrate."

Lambert was following the conversation while he kept

Gipsy hot on the Mega-Kaiju's trail. He also had the benefit of being in Jake's mind, thanks to the Drift, so he saw where Jake was going. "What about a secondary brain? This sonofabitch have one of those?"

Still working the holo screen as it compiled data from different local and satellite sources, Gottlieb swiped away a number of layers to get to the basic anatomical breakdown of the Mega-Kaiju as they understood it. The image on the screen was astonishing. Three Kaiju, stitched together into one. The skeletal structures of all three were still visible on the screen, along with the brutal modifications made by the army of smaller robots from Shao's factory. Under other circumstances, Gottlieb would have spent hours or days marveling at the incredible research, intuition, and manufacturing skill that went into creating something like this—but today all he wanted was to kill it.

Three areas lit up on the screen, designating three points near the Mega-Kaiju's hindquarters, at the base of its three tails. "Hostile has *three* secondary brains," he reported. "One for each component Kaiju." Jules captured the tactical scan and swiped it over to the Shared Intel Battlefield Server, available to all Jaegers in the field.

"Sending intel."

Jake and Lambert watched as the anatomy scan consolidated on Gipsy Avenger's HUD. "Intel received." They were still chasing the Mega-Kaiju, and Jake wasn't sure they were going to get there in time. But if they did, they were going to need to put it down fast.

"Taking out the secondary brains won't kill it," Lambert said.

"Maybe not," Jake agreed. "But it'll sure as hell slow it down." He called out to the other two Jaeger crews. "Saber Athena, Bracer Phoenix. Check your HUDs for updated target package."

There was a brief pause as Renata and Amara accessed the new information. "Package confirmed for Saber Athena," Renata reported. Amara echoed a few seconds later.

"Follow our lead," Jake said. "And stay frosty." They had no idea what might be coming next.

Lambert did have an idea about some steps they could take to be extra prepared, though. "Might be a good time to fire up some of those Obsidian Fury weapons Liwen grabbed us," he said.

Jake grinned. "Read my mind, partner." He didn't know what all those systems might be yet, since, as Jules had said, crews had kit-bashed them in as they worked, but he did know about one, and he was looking forward to using it.

They were gaining on the Mega-Kaiju. As they got close enough to attack, Gipsy Avenger snapped its arms out straight and Obsidian Fury's twin plasma chainsaws slid out of their forearm housings and locked into place. Still running, Gipsy leaped forward, kicking up off a building as Guardian Bravo had to gain enough altitude. The Jaeger soared in a high arc over the Mega-Kaiju's tails and slashed the plasma saws across its back as it came down. The saws tore through the extra layer of plating formed by Newt's creatures. Pieces of them cascaded down the Mega-Kaiju's back. Gipsy Avenger landed and ducked the sweep of the Mega-Kaiju's tails as it rounded on them to strike back.

Saber Athena, right behind Gipsy Avenger, came flying in with another aerial attack, aiming for the spot weakened by the plasma saws. The Mega-Kaiju raised a claw to smash Saber Athena down into the ground, but a volley of missiles from Bracer Phoenix distracted it. It lumbered around to face Bracer just as Amara and Jinhai threw the Morning Star Hand. Its spikes snapped out as it flew straight and true into the Mega-Kaiju's face, rocking its head back and snapping off one of its mandible tusks.

Thinking the Mega-Kaiju was stunned, Bracer Phoenix tried to jump onto its back, where the secondary brains were housed low along its spine. But the Mega-Kaiju reacted quickly, spinning around to swat Bracer Phoenix out of the air. The Jaeger landed hard in a block of low buildings, crushing them. Saber Athena tried to dance in and open the wound on its back wider. The Mega-Kaiju anticipated this attack too, swiping a claw around as Saber Athena lunged forward, extending its sword.

The Mega-Kaiju's claws tore through Saber Athena's legs, ripping them off just below the hip joints. Saber Athena hit the ground and the Mega-Kaiju loomed over her, roaring in triumph. Grimacing with the agony of biofeedback, Renata and Ryoichi tried to crawl away, dragging Saber Athena along by her arms. The shriek of alarms in the Conn-Pod drowned out the Mega-Kaiju's roars. Jake saw the creature raising its double tail over its head. He shouted a warning, but even if Renata and Ryoichi had heard it, there was no way for them to avoid Mega-Kaiju's attack. The twin tails snapped forward and down like a scorpion's, impaling Saber Athena and stabbing deep into the ground. The crippled Jaeger spasmed as her power core flared from the damage inflicted by the tail spikes. Renata and Ryoichi cried out, feeling their Jaeger die around them.

Jerking its tail back, the Mega-Kaiju lifted Saber Athena off the ground and flung her aside. "Renata! Ryoichi!" Lambert called. "Status!"

There was no answer. Saber Athena, legless and shattered, crashed to the ground and lay still.

Gipsy Avenger now had an opening, but at terrible cost. Jake and Lambert knew they couldn't waste this chance. Keeping an eye on the HUD tactical scan of the secondary brains' locations, they sprung forward onto the Mega-Kaiju's back, driving both plasma saws deep into the plating over the base of its spine, straight into a secondary brain. The Mega-Kaiju screeched in agony, and one of its legs went limp. The dead weight put incredible strain on the network of stitching that held the parts of the Mega-Kaiju together. They began to split apart, tearing themselves to pieces.

On the HUD, one of the three secondary brains winked out. "One down, two to go," Jake said. He and Lambert dragged one of the plasma saws free in a fountain of mech parts and Kaiju blood. The Mega-Kaiju thrashed, snapping off the other saw and launching Gipsy Avenger away. Jake and Lambert tried to brace themselves as they smashed through an elevated train track, scattering the stopped cars, and landed hard in an open space beyond the track.

With the Mega-Kaiju facing back toward Gipsy Avenger, Bracer Phoenix had a clear shot at the gaping wound in its back. Vik dropped into the railgun turret again and unleashed a furious barrage. Railgun shells chewed apart the plating around the wound, but she couldn't keep the gun on so small a target while the Mega-Kaiju was still moving. Bracer tried to circle for a better angle, but the Mega-Kaiju turned to keep its back out of the field of fire. "I can't punch through!" she shouted.

Jinhai looked around for some way to keep the Mega-Kaiju still. On top of a nearby building, he spotted a tall steel spire. "Target that spire! I'm gonna try something!"

Vik didn't ask any questions. She swung the turret around and opened fire. The first burst of shells tore the top off the building and sheared the spire loose. Bracer Phoenix ran to catch it, leaping high into the air. Amara watched the spire start to spin. They had to time this perfectly. She reached out and caught it, pivoting in her Drift cradle as she did, feeling Jinhai in perfect synchronicity with her move.

Bracer Phoenix spun in midair, turning the spire over and gripping it with both hands. The Mega-Kaiju dragged itself forward, one leg still dead.

As Bracer Phoenix fell through the arc of her jump, Amara drove both hands down, watching the holographic spire in her hands punch deep into the Mega-Kaiju's back toward the two remaining secondary brains. The tip of the spire stabbed straight through one. It darkened and winked out. The Mega-Kaiju bellowed again, and more of its body sagged. Amara heard cheering over the comm, from back in the War Room, and she realized she was cheering too.

A moment later, Bracer Phoenix was rocked as the Mega-Kaiju lashed around and seized the Jaeger in its monstrous jaws. It shook the Jaeger like a dog killing a rat. Inside the Conn-Pod, the Mega-Kaiju's fangs punched in close to the three cadets. The Conn-Pod began to crumple. "All pilots, eject! Eject!" Jinhai hit the ejection button and his Drift cradle slammed up into his ejection pod. Right behind him came Amara. Vik was the last to reach her pod, rocketing back up on the maglev track from the railgun turret down in Bracer Phoenix's waist.

The three pods blasted free of Bracer Phoenix's head just as the Mega-Kaiju bit down and crushed the Jaeger's upper half. They crashed down in the wreckage and rubble near where Saber Athena had fallen. The Mega-Kaiju chewed on the wreckage of Bracer Phoenix and then tossed it away.

Now Gipsy Avenger was the only Jaeger left, and the Mega-Kaiju was still alive. But as Jake and Lambert circled it, looking for a way to get at that third brain, they saw the scale of the damage they'd already done. The Mega-Kaiju was bleeding from a hundred wounds, and huge gouges showed in its outer armor of Newt-monsters. It dragged one leg but still kept going, doggedly heading for Mount Fuji. Some of the smaller creatures lost their grip and fell off, dying as they hit the ground or were crushed under the Mega-Kaiju's immense claws.

*Now it's one on one,* Jake thought. *Gipsy Avenger and the biggest Kaiju the world has ever seen. Fate of the world at stake.*

Gipsy Avenger dug herself out of the rubble on the other side of the destroyed elevated train track. On the HUD, they got another look at the Mega-Kaiju's wounds, hoping to find an exploitable weak spot. But Gipsy Avenger had taken some damage, too. Losing the plasma saw had damaged that arm, and the general pounding had generated a long list of damage alerts. Their weapons systems were rebooting and parts of their sensor package were damaged.

But they were still alive, and Jake knew they could finish the Mega-Kaiju off even if they had to do it with just Gipsy Avenger's fists.

"Jake…" Lambert worked the holo screens, furiously trying to get Gipsy's weapons back online.

"Yeah, I know," Jake said through gritted teeth. They couldn't let the Mega-Kaiju get much more of a head start, or they would never catch it. They leaned forward and Gipsy Avenger leaped from the far side of the tracks, landing on the Mega-Kaiju's back again. It overbalanced and tumbled to the ground. Gipsy blasted away at it with her plasma cannon as Lambert got it working again, but the Mega-Kaiju kept going, dragging Gipsy Avenger across the ground. A blast from the plasma cannon struck one of the wounds in the Mega-Kaiju's back and it arched in agonized fury, lashing out with its tail. The tail gouged a hole in the back wall of Gipsy Avenger's Conn-Pod and tore into Nate's Drift cradle. Nate grunted in pain as it shredded one side of his drivesuit and cracked his helmet. Then it was gone. In the Drift Jake could feel Nate's shock and agony from the deep wound in his side.

"Nate! C'mon, stay with me, brother—" He could see Lambert struggling, and feel it in the Drift. Nate's eyes fluttered closed and Jake felt his presence disappear from the Drift.

"Warning," an AI voice said. "Neural handshake lost."

Jake suddenly felt the whole neural load of piloting Gipsy Avenger. He staggered, and the Jaeger did, too. The Mega-Kaiju dug its claws into Gipsy's armor. Jake tried to fight back, but he couldn't break the Mega-Kaiju's grip. He heard blood roaring in his ears and his mind started to fragment. Old memories that he had shared in the Drift came back, superimposing themselves on the present moment. He heard his father's voice, the click of Sonny's gun; when he looked out through Gipsy Avenger's shattered face shield he saw Mako, over and over, slipping away on the other side of a window, just beyond his grasp. When she fell away he saw her younger, grinning, her face beaded with sweat and her hands wrapped around the staff she'd just used to flip Jake onto his back. He felt Gipsy Avenger moving around him. The maglev field flickered and caught him again. He blinked, trying to remember where he ended and Gipsy Avenger began. *You'll never be a pilot*, his father said. Rage flooded through him, snapping him back into focus. Through the cognitive haze of trying to handle Gipsy Avenger on his own, he saw the world tip sideways as the Mega-Kaiju threw Gipsy out of its way. Gipsy Avenger hit the ground hard enough that Jake blacked out for a moment. The next thing he saw was the Mega-Kaiju loping away through the outer reaches of Tokyo, heading for Mount Fuji and the end of the world.

# 34

## JAEGERWATCH:
## DID YOU SEE THAT!?!?!!?!?!?

If you do not have the drone feed that I have, bro and sis and cuz, I pity you, because the things I am seeing from Tokyo defy the imagination. I am seeing four Jaegers take on three Kaiju... then the three Kaiju get run over by an insane horde of tiny little robot monster things that, what, like chew them all up and turn them all into one giant MEGA-KAIJU and it's like nothing I've ever seen.

I have to remind myself people are dead, and I'm posting this online from a safe place like a thousand miles from the nearest place where a Kaiju ever appeared.

But that giant Kaiju was something. Is it still there? The drone feed from Tokyo cut out and I haven't been able to find another one. Most of the city's evacuated, and whoever that brave soul was who stuck around long enough to fly a drone out into the middle of a fight between Jaegers and Kaiju, I salute you.

continued...

Give me more.

But don't forget that these are real people out there. I try not to forget that. It's easy when you only see them on a screen, but they're real. You only ever think of them because they're inside giant machines, but they're real.

And they save the world for us. I'm going to try to remember that more. You too, okay?

"Yes!" Newt cheered. "Get up from *that*, you pile of junk!"

All of the Jaegers were down. The Ripper experiment had paid off perfectly, forcing the Jaegers into close combat where they were vulnerable to the Mega-Kaiju's superior physical force. Now the Mega-Kaiju was passing close by the rooftop where Newt had watched the whole battle unfold. He fell silent as the looming bulk of the Kaiju drew close. The rooftop was about level with its head. The Mega-Kaiju looked over toward him, a deep rumble coming from its throat. Newt watched it observing him, and he had the fleeting thought that it would be one world-class irony if it killed him on its way to end the human race.

The Kaiju's head swung closer, and it paused on its way. It was close enough that Newt could see the damage inflicted by the Jaegers: burns, open slashes through its limbs, layers of its dermal armor sheared away. Blood ran down its flanks and dripped from its tail, leaving a trail of sizzling spots on the street. The monstrous muzzle was close enough to touch, its twenty-foot teeth towering over Newt as it inhaled his scent. It lingered for another moment, then turned away and resumed its steady progress toward Mount Fuji.

Newt blew out a long sigh. Then he chuckled. There had never been anything to worry about. And he hadn't really been worried after all. "Bye!" he called after it.

In the Moyulan War Room, Gottlieb thought furiously. If their last Jaeger was out of commission, their only possible option was Shao Liwen's little basement project. "Liwen!" he called into the comm. "Is there anything you can do to help?"

"I need more time!" she snapped.

"We don't have any." The Mega-Kaiju was picking up

speed as it skirted the foothills around Mount Tanzawa and emerged into the wide plain surrounding Mount Fuji. "If hostile reaches Mount Fuji—"

Jake Pentecost's voice crackled over the comm. "Gipsy to Command! Lambert's down."

Gottlieb eyeballed calculations he'd been running since the three Kaiju appeared and he was able to get good data on them. The results were not good. He told Pentecost even though there wasn't anything Pentecost could do about it. "Command to Gipsy. If my calculations are right, the amount of blood in that Cat-Five is just enough to ignite the Ring of Fire."

Jake registered this. Lambert was out, and Gipsy Avenger was the only Jaeger left even able to stand. "Understood," he said. "Not gonna let that happen."

He was going to stop the Mega-Kaiju. Or die trying. Better to go out via a stroke than sit there watching as the Mega-Kaiju climbed Fuji-san and ended the world.

"Jake, you can't operate Gipsy without a copilot—" Gottlieb insisted.

But unless Gottlieb had another idea, that was exactly what Jake planned to do. He still felt the Drift, and could still link with Gipsy Avenger's systems. He tried to stand. Gipsy got part of the way up and a blinding pain shot through Jake's head, right behind his eyes. His nose was bleeding. *We Pentecosts, we always seem to get nosebleeds*, he thought. *But only when we're about to do something heroic.*

Another voice cut through over the comm. "Gipsy Avenger, this is Amara Namani! Stand by for assist!"

On the HUD, Jake saw Amara's signal, moving fast along the rooftop of a nearby building. It was partially destroyed, its interior exposed and bits of concrete cascading in small slides down its exterior walls. She was running hard toward Gipsy Avenger.

Jake had just gotten Gipsy up on one knee. He wasn't sure he could get her any farther.

Amara kept coming, at a dead sprint. Jake understood what she was about to attempt... and understood it wouldn't work. "Amara, don't! You won't make it!"

"I'm gonna," she panted.

"Don't!"

"Gonna!"

With that last word, she jumped, kicking out over the void between her and Gipsy Avenger. She was never going to make it. She started to fall, not even halfway across the gap.

Jake surged forward, feeling the blood pour more freely from his nose as he leaned out and extended Gipsy Avenger's hand, fingers spread. In that moment, he saw Mako again, felt the sorrow of her death and his admiration that even knowing she was going to die, she had made sure he would be able to finish the work she had started. His overtaxed mind slipped back to the Drift with Amara, to another time when she had jumped across a gap and no one had been there to save her. But this time, she did not plunge down into dark water, and no Kaiju annihilated the loved ones she was trying to reach.

Gipsy Avenger caught Amara just before she would have crashed down into the rubble of concrete and rebar in front of the building.

Jake barely kept his balance, raising her up so she could scramble in through the hole in Gipsy Avenger's face shield. Barely keeping it together through the agony in his head and the unpredictable shifts in his mind under the neural load, he tried to glare at her. "Told you," he said.

"Since when do I listen?" she shot back. But in her eyes he could see how shocked she was to see the state of Gipsy

Avenger's Conn-Pod. Not to mention that Jake was in rough shape, and Lambert much worse off than Jake.

"Amara," Lambert said, barely clinging to consciousness. "You're up."

Amara rushed over to the maglev platform and initialized Lambert's ejection sequence. She took his Drift helmet and stepped back. "What are you doing?" Jake asked.

"Getting out of the way," Lambert said. He grimaced as he tried to move out of Amara's way. "Thank God you're crazy enough to kick that thing's ass."

Then he looked over at Jake and they locked eyes. "You got this, brother. Show 'em what you can do."

Behind that, Jake heard Lambert telling him that he could have been great.

Well, now he would have to be.

Jake gave Nate a nod. Amara hit the final command in the ejection sequence. Nate's Drift cradle opened and he was raised up into the escape pod. There was a soft popping sound, and a whoosh. "Escape pod ejected," Gipsy Avenger's AI said.

Amara was already locking herself into Lambert's empty Drift cradle. "You ready for this, smallie?" Jake asked.

"One way to find out," she said, looking straight ahead and getting her helmet settled.

Jake reset the Drift initialization and let Gottlieb know. "Stand by, Command. Initiating neural handshake."

Gipsy Avenger was still on one knee amid the debris, looking as beaten as the devastated city around her. Jake felt the Drift fade out. His mind relaxed, clearing of the crazy superimpositions he'd felt while trying to handle Gipsy Avenger on his own. He looked over at Amara as the reboot brought them both into the Drift together, through the welter of images and impressions and on into a strong and steady neural handshake.

As one, they stood, and Gipsy Avenger stood, rocking her left fist into her right palm. They started to march forward—and Gipsy's right leg buckled. Alarms blared in the Conn-Pod. A hologram of the leg appeared on the tactical HUD, showing extensive damage in the battle with the Mega-Kaiju. She crashed back down to one knee. Amara frantically punched commands.

"Right leg's down!"

Gipsy Avenger's AI voice calmly described the nature of the problem. "Warning: cascading failure. Multiple systems."

"Reboot!" Jake yelled.

Amara worked her holo screen furiously. "I'm trying!"

"Command to Gipsy. Hostile is two kilometers out and closing fast on the summit of Mount Fuji!" Gottlieb warned.

Satellite and virtual overlays showed the Mega-Kaiju plowing steadily through the forested terrain of Mount Fuji's slopes leading up to the treeline. Above the Kaiju, the steep snow-covered shoulders of the mountain were all too close. "We need to intercept!" Jake said.

"How? We can't even stand up." Out of sheer stubbornness, Amara tried to get Gipsy to her feet again, but it wasn't going to happen.

Jake had an idea. It was crazy and virtually certain to fail, but it was better than nothing. "Maybe we don't have to." He started punching commands into the holo terminal. Amara, understanding through the Drift what he was thinking, looked at him like he had lost his mind.

"That's a really bad idea," she said. No snark, no insults, just a simple declaration. That alone told Jake how scared she was by what he was contemplating. But he figured she could sense that he was just as scared, and fear couldn't be allowed to stop them now.

"Gottlieb," he said. "Is there enough fuel left in any of your thrusters to get us into the atmosphere?"

"The atmosphere?" Gottlieb echoed. They heard him mumbling to himself as he ran some quick equations. "Possibly, but there won't be enough to slow your re-entry."

"Not going to slow down. We'll come in hot and drop Gipsy right on top of that thing."

Jake heard Amara's thought before she said it out loud. "We'll use my escape pod, smallie," he reassured her.

"Jake," Gottlieb came back. "There's only one thruster pod with enough fuel remaining to reach the troposphere. Sending location."

When the location popped up on the tactical HUD, Jake sagged in the Drift cradle. It was too far away, back near the site of their initial engagement with the Kaiju. "It's too far away," Amara said. The grim realization set in. "We're not gonna make it."

# 35

A NEW VOICE CAME OVER THE COMM. "GIPSY Avenger." It was Shao Liwen. "Systems are online!"

Jake had no idea what she was talking about.

"Sending help!" she added.

*What kind of help?* Jake wondered. They had no Jaegers left.

"I've located the thruster pod," Liwen explained. "Stand by!"

The cargo doors of a modified heavy-lift Shao V-Dragon opened as it banked over the apocalyptic ruin of Tokyo. Out into the void rolled Scrapper, dropping through the air and opening up just as it crashed through the roof of a damaged restaurant and landed heavily, collapsing the floor. Quickly it looked around and headed out into the street, closing in on the location of the thruster pod where it had been jettisoned at the beginning of the fight. The air was thick with hanging dust and the smoke from a thousand fires burning in the wreckage. Scrapper moved unerringly through it, climbing piles of rubble and kicking aside small obstacles.

In the Moyulan Shatterdome machine shop, Shao Liwen stood in a redesigned set of Conn-Pod rings, retrofitted from the remote Drone control suites so she could operate Scrapper from afar. She trotted forward and bent over, picking up a holographic thruster pod. Then she turned around and ran into the Drift cradle, propelling Scrapper through the ruins on a path that led toward the looming, stranded bulk of Gipsy Avenger in the distance. Newt Geiszler had used her factories, her inventions, her expertise, to execute his plan. What happened in her company's name was her responsibility, and Shao was going to do everything in her power to atone for that failure. She'd had the idea to mobilize Scrapper early in the day, and had kept at it even after it seemed like the field Jaegers weren't going to need any help. Now she was glad she hadn't quit, because Scrapper was no longer just an afterthought. Now the little homemade Jaeger—with some improvements Shao had made—was mission critical.

"Scrapper!" Amara beamed as she saw her creation appear from the smoke on Gipsy Avenger's HUD.

She got a direct visual through Gipsy's broken face shield, and her smile got even wider. Shao Liwen had worked on Scrapper! Shao Liwen! She'd always been one of Amara's idols, and to think that Shao had deemed Scrapper worthy of her attention...

Amara got a grip on her pride. "Okay, we got a rocket," she said. But she was also running calculations about their thrust and potential altitude, and her face got grim. "Thrust is too strong. We won't be able to hold onto it."

"I upgraded Scrapper's weapons!" Shao answered. "I can weld it to your hand."

"Nice," Amara said. She could appreciate a good field hack, and Shao was still the best.

Scrapper approached and dropped the thruster pod.

Gipsy Avenger bent low to pick it up. Jake oriented it so Gipsy could hold it out at an angle with the exhaust nozzle pointed behind them. Scrapper climbed up onto Gipsy's arm as plasma blasters with Shao Industries logos unfolded from its shoulders. The blasters fired, melting the thruster pod's clamp assembly onto Gipsy Avenger's hand. While Shao worked, Amara watched, admiring Shao Liwen all over again. "We'll only get one shot at this," she said.

Jake was also watching, and itching to get going. The Mega-Kaiju was too close to the summit. They didn't have time to make sure everything was perfect. "Then we better make it count."

The words were just leaving his mouth when the heat from Scrapper's blasters ignited the thruster pod.

Gipsy Avenger wasn't braced for the sudden thrust. She surged forward, blasting horizontally along the ground, scraping up a wave of cars and pavement, careening off buildings. "Ignition! We have ignition!" Shao exulted back in the machine shop, but Jake and Amara were completely out of control.

Outside, Scrapper's foot hung up on one of Gipsy Avenger's stabilizer fins. "I'm stuck!" Shao said as she struggled to get Scrapper free.

"Stay there!" Jake answered. "You're an extra ton we can drop on that thing!"

Slowly Jake and Amara got control over the thruster pod, aiming it so the exhaust was pointed at a shallow angle toward the ground. Gipsy Avenger angled upward, shooting into the sky. They wrestled against the power of the thrust, pushing the angle a little steeper and shooting higher into the sky. They burst through a layer of high clouds over the city. Every alarm in the Conn-Pod seemed to be going off, as the vibrations from the thrust and the atmospheric friction tore pieces away from the heavily damaged Jaeger. "Hull integrity under strain. Approaching hazardous altitude," the AI warned. "Temperatures dropping rapidly."

"Yeah, we get it," Amara snapped.

Another warning blared in front of them. The thruster pod, shaking in the makeshift housing of Gipsy Avenger's fist, was threatening to disintegrate. "She's coming apart!" Amara shouted.

Jake watched their altitude. Gottlieb had already done the math for their downward trajectory. If they could just make a few more miles... "Almost there!" he called back.

Without their drivesuits' life-support systems, they would long since have passed out from lack of oxygen. And even those would soon run low; they were only designed for emergency use, and among the other systems damaged in the fight with Raijin and the Mega-Kaiju were the linkages to Gipsy Avenger's full life-support systems. Jake was suddenly grateful this had not occurred to him before, or he would have been terrified that his suit had a leak that would kill him up here where there was no air. Through the Drift he could tell Amara had no such misgivings; her mind was alive with the thrill of the moment, and as Jake felt that, some of the thrill and wonder transferred to him.

The sky was black around them, and full of stars. Below, they could see the vast urban sprawl of the Tokyo-Osaka megaplex laid out, and to the east the green and white cone of Mount Fuji. It was a beautiful sight, and looking down at it Jake felt a fierce love for all of Planet Earth and its people. He would do anything for them, up to and including sacrificing his life if need be. There was no sound, and for a long moment there was no gravity as Gipsy Avenger reached the apex of her trajectory. Jake had a fleeting memory of a similar weightless moment in Scrapper, right after he'd met Amara. Then they were pounded back into their cradles as Gipsy Avenger turned over and began to fall. "We're locked on target," Amara said, tracking their path on the HUD.

"Get out of there!" Gottlieb called over the comm. "Eject."

On the HUD, another alarm flashed. They were no longer locked on the target zone at the edge of Mount Fuji's crater. "We're drifting off course."

There had been so many alarms going off that Jake didn't notice the target warning right away, but now it had all of his attention. The projection of their return trajectory was going to miss Mount Fuji by miles. That first burn, straight ahead instead of up at an angle, had altered the distance they had traveled when they finally did get oriented in the right direction. Now they had to find a way to course-correct or Gipsy Avenger was just going to put a big crater in a town square somewhere north of Fuji... while the Mega-Kaiju took its final swan dive into the caldera. Amara was already thinking hard about a solution, considering and discarding possibilities faster than Jake could grasp them.

"Use the plasma cannon!" she announced, and started pecking commands out on her holo terminal. The tactical HUD showed the correction, and the correct angle of the plasma burn. Eight seconds would do the trick.

There was only one problem. The cannon wasn't built for continuous fire because it had a tendency to overheat and melt down its housing... and Gipsy Avenger's arm. But it was long past time to worry about that.

Amara brought up the source code of the plasma cannon's fire control software. Jake marveled at this. He wouldn't have had any idea where to find that code, let alone access it—yet here was fifteen-year-old Amara, hacking a Jaeger she'd never been in before while it fell out of the sky towards its certain destruction and her probable death.

If she noticed his admiration, she didn't react. "Disengaging safety protocols," Jake said. He found the failsafe and disabled it. They nodded at each other and thrust their left hands straight down. Gipsy Avenger's left arm deployed its plasma cannon. They shifted their posture slightly to match the simulation in the tactical HUD, and then they fired the cannon.

Normally it fired single bursts, with a minimum interval of a half-second, but Amara's quick hack had removed that limitation. Instead of bolts of plasma energy, the cannon poured out a continuous stream. The countdown on the HUD was at 7... 6...

Gipsy Avenger shuddered, plummeting down at near-terminal velocity as the plasma cannon shifted their trajectory to aim them back at the Mega-Kaiju. Gipsy's arm began to glow as the plasma cannon overloaded. Pieces of overheated armor broke off and spun away behind them. New alarms shrieked in the Conn-Pod, and the system AI repeated a warning: "Warning. Exceeding structural limits. Exceeding structural limits."

None of this would do any good if Gipsy Avenger shivered to pieces on her way back down, Jake thought. But they didn't have any other solution. Amara was counting down the burn, matching the numbers on the HUD. "Four seconds... three... two..."

The plasma cannon burned out. Weakened by the heat and the incredible stresses of the flight, pieces of Gipsy's forearm shattered and fell away. Eyeballing their path, it looked like they were headed straight for the rim of Mount Fuji's caldera. On the HUD, the Mega-Kaiju was squarely in the middle of the targeting reticle. Amara confirmed this on the holo display of their downward trajectory, recalculating their path based on the adjustment from the plasma cannon. "Target locked!"

"Jake! Amara!" Gottlieb was watching their path and velocity from the War Room, and he saw they didn't have much time. "You need to eject!"

They hit the thicker part of the upper atmosphere and Gipsy Avenger started to glow from the friction of re-entry. The rest of Gipsy's face shield burned away in a swirl of superheated plasma, along with more pieces of her destroyed left arm.

It was time to bail out. "Disconnect!" Jake could barely scream over the raging wind and the sounds of Gipsy Avenger threatening to break apart as they plunged toward Earth. Amara reached for the buckles holding her into her Drift cradle, then froze. What if the wind howling in the Conn-Pod sucked her out through the gaping hole in the front of Gipsy's head?

Jake reached out a hand, leaning across toward her. "It's okay! I got you!"

She swallowed, tensed… and touched the command that unlocked her from the Drift cradle. It opened and disconnected from her drivesuit. The wind rocked her, nearly pulling her loose before she got a grip on the frame of the cradle. Slowly she worked her way toward Jake, but she couldn't get close enough to him without letting go. Realizing this, Amara watched Jake, gauging the distance. She would have to jump. Again. Jake saw the terror in her eyes, and knew it went all the way back to when she was a child on the pier at Santa Monica. Her life must have seemed like a long series of jumps with no guarantees that anyone would be there to catch her on the other side.

He held his hand out, beckoning. They had to launch the escape pod or it would still be moving too fast for them to survive its impact with the surface. The altitude counter on the HUD counted down with sickening speed.

Amara crouched and jumped. The wind dragged her toward the hole in the front of Gipsy's head and she stretched out toward Jake, desperate and terrified. He lunged forward in his own cradle, feeling the straps dig into his shoulders... and he caught her hand as her legs swung around toward the hole. Straining with the effort, he pulled her close. As soon as she got within arm's reach, she clung to him, trembling with the terror of a brush with death.

Jake grinned, keeping one arm wrapped around her and punching in the escape pod initialization sequence with the other. "Gipsy to Command," he announced. "We are getting the hell out of here."

A bright red warning bar appeared on the HUD. The escape pod wasn't responding. "Warning," Gipsy Avenger's AI said. "Escape pod inoperable. Warning..."

Jake looked at the holo indicator counting down the kilometers to impact. It was moving way too fast for them to come up with another plan. His glance shifted to Amara, and he saw she was coming to the same conclusion.

"I'm sorry, smallie," he said. It was all he could think of.

She mustered a brave smile. "For what? We got to save the world." After a beat she added, "Your dad would be proud."

Jake nodded, grateful for the sentiment. Would his dad be proud, now that Jake Pentecost was about to continue the family tradition of sacrificing his life in a last-ditch effort to save the world? He had fought hard today. They'd put two Kaiju down, and were about to take out a third. Maybe Jake was never going to be a great Ranger, but on this day he'd done everything he could.

A loud crackling noise from behind them interrupted the moment. Jake looked over his shoulder, thinking he would see the back of Gipsy Avenger's head starting to break apart from the re-entry stress. But instead he saw a plasma beam cutting through Gipsy's armor at the rear of the Conn-Pod. There was already a hole there from the Mega-Kaiju's tail, and the beam enlarged it. Then a familiar metallic hand pushed through the gap and tore away another section of Gipsy's head, revealing Scrapper clinging to the outside.

"Gipsy Avenger." Shao Liwen's voice rang out over the comm. "You guys need a lift?"

# 36

ON THE BACK OF GIPSY AVENGER'S HEAD, Scrapper clung tight, rocking in the powerful turbulence of their fall toward Earth. Shao hadn't been able to communicate while they were coming through the electromagnetic disturbances of the upper atmosphere, and then she couldn't move Scrapper when they were in the re-entry phase or the stresses would have torn the little Jaeger free. Only now could she act, and she had Scrapper's plasma torches cutting a ragged hole through the back of Gipsy Avenger's head. Sweat burned in her eyes and dripped from her chin as she finished the work and reached out. Scrapper tore loose the piece of armor she had cut and let it tumble away. Then Scrapper rubbed a hand around the inside of the hole, trying to cool the edges. Shao leaned Scrapper in close and opened her torso Conn-Pod hatch. Scrapper's feet were braced on a metal ridge at the base of Gipsy Avenger's skull, and her hands now dug into the battered armor on either side of the hole, pressing Scrapper as close as it could get.

"Twenty kilometers to impact!" Gottlieb warned over the comm. "Get out of there!"

Inside the Conn-Pod, Jake and Amara judged the situation. They had to get out of the Drift cradle and across the Conn-Pod, through the hole, and into the damping alcoves inside Scrapper's Conn-Pod—all with hellacious wind ripping through the Conn-Pod from front to back now that there were two holes in Gipsy Avenger's head. Scrapper was close to the back hole, but there was still plenty of room for them to miss the transfer and go flying off into the sky.

But that was the plan they had, so that was the plan they were going to execute. Jake started the sequence of commands to disengage the Drift cradle from his drivesuit.

He touched the final command and the Drift cradle unfolded and disconnected. The raging wind in the Conn-Pod immediately flung Jake and Amara across toward the hole leading to Scrapper's Conn-Pod. They hit hard against the wall on either side of the hole and slid down, bloodied and stunned. Neither of them had had time to get their hands up before hitting the wall.

Gottlieb's voice was high and tense in the comm. "Impact in ten seconds!"

Jake shoved Amara ahead. "Go! Go!"

They scrambled up and dove through the hole, Amara first and Jake right behind her. The cramped Conn-Pod inside Scrapper's torso didn't have the updated maglev field or a next-generation Drift cradle, but it did have two alcoves with motion-damping hydraulics. Amara and Jake squeezed into these and braced themselves. Jake couldn't do math fast enough to figure whether the alcoves would be enough protection when they hit... but then again, if they didn't do the job, he wouldn't be around to worry about it. In these last ten seconds, he felt calm. Not fatalist, because he knew they had done everything they could and he no longer held the cynical illusion that nothing he did would ever be good enough. But calm. He had done his job. He had lived up to the standard set by the Rangers who came before him… including his father. That was enough to give him peace.

"Hang on," he said.

"I am hanging on!"

"Hang tighter!"


In the skies over Mount Fuji, Gipsy Avenger streaked down, trailing smoke and shedding pieces of herself. Below, the Mega-Kaiju bounded up the last stretch of the snow-covered slope leading to the vast crater at the mountain's summit. It tipped its head back and roared, the sound echoing out across the sky. When it leaped in and dug through the layers of stone covering the vent below the crater, it would annihilate itself in the upwelling magma and begin the end of the world.

As the echoes of its roar died away, the Mega-Kaiju heard another sound. A screaming in the sky. It looked up.

In the last second before the end of Gipsy Avenger's long fall back to Earth, Scrapper flung its arms out and jumped. Gipsy Avenger plummeted away below and Scrapper curled into a ball, falling at an angle away from her.

The explosion of Gipsy Avenger's impact whited out sensors in the Shatterdome War Room and registered on seismometers all over the planet. The fireball rolled down the slopes of Mount Fuji as the snowpack flashed into steam. Clouds gathered over the peak, condensing around the heat of the blast as it rose in a column of fire and dust thousands of feet into the sky. The shock wave caused landslides all across the mountain's upper slopes, and caved in the steep interior of the crater just over the rim from where the Mega-Kaiju, moments ago, was crouched to spring. A casual observer might have thought the mountain was erupting for the first time since 1707, and in the War Room, Gottlieb understood the visual irony—since such an eruption was exactly what they had just sacrificed their last Jaeger to prevent.

The question was: Had it worked?

And had Jake and Amara survived? There was no signal from Scrapper. Electromagnetic noise from the explosion of Gipsy Avenger and the sudden lightning storm made it impossible to know what was going on. The blast of fire began to fade. Winds swirled around the peak, twisting the column of smoke into a vortex that gradually dispersed as it eddied higher away from the site of the impact. "Jake," Gottlieb said, "Amara. Status, please."

The sudden condensation of clouds around the peak brought snow that began to fall over the upper slopes as the site of Gipsy Avenger's detonation cleared. Jake and Amara kicked at Scrapper's Conn-Pod hatch. It was damaged from the blast. Scrapper had held its ball form until the blast wave hit, but the shock had shorted out most of the little Jaeger's systems. It opened up, arms and legs going limp, as it crashed down through the stunted trees at Mount Fuji's treeline and came to a halt in an open space, with snow and earth plowed up around it.

They got out and saw the snow... but they also saw the Mega-Kaiju, above them, still struggling to get to the rim of the crater.

Part of it, anyway. Everything below the middle of the Mega-Kaiju's torso was gone, smeared and scattered for hundreds of yards down the slope. Its blood sizzled in the wet earth. Still it tried, digging into the stones near the summit and pulling its mangled body up. It tried to rise, and sagged back down, agonized roars subsiding to groans. One last effort dragged it to the very edge of the long fall into the crater, its claws hooked over the edge… and then it collapsed. Its eyes dimmed and it was silent.

Watching, Jake and Amara realized that against all probability, they had won. Cheers rang over the comm from the War Room as the Mega-Kaiju's locator bogey blinked out. They heard other voices joining in, the exultant cadets grouped together on a rooftop near where their Jaegers had fallen.

And on another rooftop, Newt Geiszler stood seething. "All right. Okay. Sure. Plan *B,* then. Always a Plan B."

He turned toward the Shao V-Dragon, its engines still warm on the far end of the roof—and walked straight into Nate Lambert's fist. The crack of the punch was followed a second later by the meatier thud of Newt hitting the ground.

"That's about enough of that," Lambert said to the unconscious Newt. He grimaced at the effort of throwing the punch. It felt like he'd torn something loose in his side, but by God, it was worth it.

The minute he'd managed to get out of the escape pod, he'd checked his drivesuit data feed to make sure he still had Newt's location. He did. It had taken him a while to get to the building, and then he'd had to climb thirty flights of stairs because the power in the building was out, but when he'd come out on the rooftop and found Newt Geiszler standing there watching the remnants of the explosion that had put the final nail in the coffin of his plan… well, that had been a moment to savor.

The only thing better was knocking that sonofabitch on his ass. "Command," he said into the comm, "this is Lambert. Be advised, I just caught us a Newt."

In the War Room, Jules closed her eyes as relief flooded through her. Then she heard Jake's voice.

"Copy that, Nate. Good to hear you're still with us."

"You too, brother. Knew you could do it."

On the mountain, Jake looked over at Amara, who was removing her helmet and turning her face up to the snow. "I had a lot of help," he said.

"Nice work, Ranger Namani," Nate said.

Amara closed her eyes, basking in the compliment— Nate Lambert had called her a Ranger! She fluttered her eyelashes as she felt snowflakes land on them. Then she looked over at Jake, amazed. "I've never seen snow before."

"Yeah," Jake said with a grin. "Almost makes you forget the giant dead monster over there." He looked upslope at the remains of the Mega-Kaiju, and thought of the other Kaiju, as well as all the multitudes of Kaiju mechs scattered between here and there. He was also thinking of Newt Geiszler and how easy it was to twist genius to evil purposes. Was Newt a bad person? Jake didn't know. Maybe it was true the Precursors got into his head. Maybe the potential power of harnessing and engineering Kaiju biotechnology was just too much for him to resist. In the end, it didn't matter. Lambert had tied off that loose end. His mood got more serious as he considered just how close they had all come to dying—and considered too that Suresh hadn't made it, and neither had all the Rangers originally assigned to the Jaegers that lay destroyed back in Tokyo.

Neither had Mako.

"I feel like you're about to make another one of your big dumb speeches," Amara said.

"Dumb?" he shot back. "That speech was inspirational. It literally saved the world."

"Whatever you say, sensei."

"What did I tell you about calling me that?" Jake scooped up a snowball and pegged it in her direction. She shrieked with delight as it hit her, and threw one back.

*All right, then.* He bent and scooped up another, then

paused. "Wait," he said, as her words finally registered. "Did everyone really think it was dumb?"

Amara just laughed and threw another snowball. Jake did too. This time they both connected.

# ABOUT THE AUTHOR

**ALEX IRVINE'S** novel *A Scattering of Jades* won the Crawford Award for Best New Writer. He also won awards for Best New Novel from *Locus* magazine and the International Horror Guild and was a finalist for the Campbell Award for Best New Writer. He is an acclaimed writer of novelizations including *Transformers Exodus*, *Iron Man: Virus*, and *Pacific Rim*, which won the Scribe Award for Best Adapted Novel.

# PACIFIC RIM™
## UPRISING

### ASCENSION
#### THE OFFICIAL MOVIE PREQUEL

**FROM DIRECTOR STEVEN S. DEKNIGHT
NOVEL BY GREG KEYES**

It's been ten years since humanity's war with the monstrous Kaiju ended and the Breach at the bottom of the Pacific Ocean was sealed. The Pan Pacific Defense Corps remains vigilant in anticipation of the Kaiju's return, expanding and advancing their fleet of massive mechs known as Jaegers and accepting the best and the brightest candidates into the Jaeger Academy Training Program to forge the next generation of heroes. Training is competitive and positions are few. Ou-Yang Jinhai and Viktoriya Malikova grew up in the ashes of the Kaiju War and followed different paths to join the latest batch of cadets at the Moyulan Shatterdome, the most prestigious PPDC training location in the world. Yet not long after their arrival, tragedy strikes as a deadly act of sabotage casts suspicion on the new cadets. Together they must work to clear their name and discover the truth as dark forces conspire against them and new threats surface from both sides of the Breach...

**LEGENDARY.COM**

**TITAN**BOOKS.COM

# PACIFIC RIM
# EXTINCTION
#### THE MINIATURES GAME

## CHOOSE
## YOUR SIDE

It is 2035, 10 years after the events of Pacific Rim, and the war is over. By piloting towering robotic warriors known as Jaegers, humanity defeated the terrifying monster threat of the Kaijus. Beneath the Pacific Ocean, the monster gateway known as 'The Breach' has been closed, and with it the threat of Kaiju invasion is over. As the world struggles to rebuild in the aftermath of the Kaiju war, the Jaeger-piloting heroes of the PPDC (Pan Pacific Defense Corps.) remain vigilant.

## WWW.RIVERHORSE.EU